De

of

I hope you enjoy the book.

mers!

Fondly,

Karen

Murder Most Civil

by

Karen Frisch

Karen Frisch

Mainly Murder Press, LLC

PO Box 290586
Wethersfield, CT 06109-0586
www.mainlymurderpress.com

Mainly Murder Press

Copy Editor: Jennafer Sprankle
Executive Editor: Judith K. Ivie
Cover Designer: Patricia L. Foltz

Mainly Murder Press
www.mainlymurderpress.com

Copyright © 2010 by Karen Frisch Dennen

ISBN 978-0-9825899-4-6

Published in the United States of America

2010

Mainly Murder Press
PO Box 290586
Wethersfield, CT 06109-0586

To Mark

my knight whose armor shines brightest
for restoring my optimism and faith
when they were at an ebb.
Love always.

One

Boston, September 1860

"You say he might have been murdered? Here on Beacon Hill?"

Hearing the alarm in her housekeeper's voice, Henrietta Newell Cobb paused on the foyer staircase. Monday was not her day to receive callers, but her own errand seemed less urgent suddenly than that of her caller. While a friend awaited her, and her pug had spotted the leash in her hand, neither had anywhere else to go. Her unexpected guest sounded in need of the police.

Fudge trotted at her heels as she removed her gloves and followed Mrs. Biddle's voice to the receiving room doorway. There she studied her caller with a mix of apprehension and intrigue.

"Madam, this is Mrs. Myrth McLaren." Her housekeeper hesitated. "She says her visit has to do with Professor Newell."

While Mrs. Biddle's discretion kept her from stating the obvious, the wife of the controversial antislavery activist was not what Henrietta had expected. Myrth McLaren was a woman of only medium height, taller still than Henrietta, though as she turned to face Henrietta her bruised and swollen left eye suggested she had not come with happy news. Henrietta had seen enough instances of wife-beating from her work at the shelter to recognize the signs of a recent assault. Her brother Freddy must have referred the woman to her.

"Mrs. McLaren, please have a seat." Addressing her guest sympathetically, she indicated a velvet chair. She did not ask who had inflicted the bruise. Many women would not tell. "Let us take care of that injury with a warm, soothing poultice."

"The injury will heal. That's not why I've come."

Although the cut of Myrth McLaren's dress lagged behind the current fashion, it flattered her too well to invite criticism. The crinoline whispered as she turned, the bodice detailed with the pleats and tucks made popular by the newly invented sewing machine. Henrietta judged her to be twenty years younger than herself, making her about forty. The woman's elegance surprised her. While Angus McLaren was an abolitionist of some renown, Henrietta understood him to belong to the working middle class.

"Thank you for seeing me on short notice, Mrs. Cobb," Myrth resumed after Mrs. Biddle left. "I take it you've heard of me."

"I'm familiar with your husband by reputation."

Her confused blush puzzled Henrietta. "I hoped Freddy had mentioned me. What I'm about to tell you may come as a shock. I haven't much time. Even now he might still be at my house."

Henrietta wondered how her brother found time to cultivate her acquaintance. A member of Boston's prestigious Compass Club, a group adamantly opposed to slavery, Freddy was ordinarily more consumed with the beakers and flasks on his laboratory shelves at Harvard than with social matters. Henrietta watched her dog make his way to Mrs. McLaren, sniffing her skirts and retreating to his spot by the hearth when she didn't respond.

"I'd no idea Freddy had become so politically active," she admitted. "I'm glad he sent you. I'm sure the shelter has room."

"My connection with Freddy has nothing to do with charity," Myrth said. "I came because I fear my husband's been murdered."

Until now Henrietta had assumed McLaren inflicted his wife's bruises. It hadn't occurred to her that he, too, was injured. The agony in Myrth's voice suggested she regarded him with deep affection.

"Tell me what happened," Henrietta said gently.

Myrth hesitated before she rose and began pacing. The September sunlight from the window fell on perfectly parted hair, giving it the same chestnut hue as the chrysanthemums in the corner vase. The motion gave the room a faint floral scent.

"I was to meet Freddy at three. I barely escaped with my life. I would ask you not to judge him harshly," Myrth added in a plaintive tone. "He is innocent of any wrongdoing."

"Wrongdoing?" Henrietta repeated, turning to follow her movements. "From whom did you escape?"

Myrth's mouth quivered as tears spilled down her cheeks. "I can only hope Angus isn't lying dead in our home at this moment."

In a city braced for war, Henrietta knew, men were not above murdering for principles. Angus McLaren had taken an unpopular stand on an issue that divided Bostonians. The killing might be politically motivated. Myrth's next request contradicted her own.

"Don't summon the police, I beg you. This doesn't involve politics. I was the intended victim." Myrth dropped into a chair, choking on her words. "Freddy and I have enjoyed each other's company for four months now. We share the deepest of feelings."

Henrietta felt herself flush to the roots of her dove gray hair. Her defenses rose at the implications and motives of this elegant stranger who had called with such an improbable story.

"I would remind you," she said, "my brother is married to a woman of considerable eminence. Not only is Corinthia about to be installed as president of Harvard's Ladies Benefactors Society, but her father, Williston Brayman Atwood, is an abolitionist like your husband. You might have heard of him and of her also."

Henrietta pronounced each word with deliberate irony to mimic Myrth's own introduction. She didn't often feel compelled to defend her sister-in-law, yet she could not allow this intruder to threaten her brother's family with insinuations.

Myrth flushed slightly. "None of that changes our feelings."

It shook Henrietta to the core to see Freddy involved with this woman. Until now she'd hoped her own romantic scandals were the last of the family's embarrassments. She felt the chill of public disgrace blow through the room as the angel Gabriel proclaimed the death of yet another Newell reputation. "Where is he now?"

"I wish I knew." Myrth's closed eyes flew open as if fearing her assailant stood waiting to strike. "It's imperative you not tell the police, Mrs. Cobb. Freddy's welfare is at stake."

Henrietta's concern mixed with irritation. "Are you saying he's confronted a murderer at your house?"

"Freddy was late. He probably arrived after it happened."

Henrietta felt an absurd sense of relief, glad for once her brother had a habit of tardiness. It might have saved his life.

"But you fled the scene." A new thought struck Henrietta. "Did you see the killer? You witnessed enough to suspect murder."

"It's pointless to accuse at present. I have proof of a sort that I'll reveal in time. There are others I must protect now."

"My brother, for instance," Henrietta said indignantly. "The police have helped others in your situation. Why not go to them?"

"They'll think I killed him." A sob escaped her. "If I came forward now I'd be murdered before I reached the station house."

Myrth rose and resumed pacing. The only person who'd want to kill her, Henrietta mused, was the murderer, someone Myrth must have seen. Could she be trusted? She might have committed the crime of which she spoke, but if so, why would she come here?

Frustration overcame Henrietta. "You got here safely."

Myrth paused as if realizing how irrational her claim sounded. The little composure she'd had shattered.

"It was worth the risk to help Freddy. I intend to trap the killer. Please don't tell anyone I've been here." Her eyes moist, Myrth gripped her arm so tightly Henrietta winced. "Thank you for taking the time to see me. I'll return when I am able."

Myrth McLaren turned abruptly and swept from the room before Henrietta could utter a word. The story was so implausible she wasn't sure whether to feel outraged or grateful. She had no idea what to make of such a disclosure. If her visitor were to be believed, Freddy was implicated not only in murder but in romance as well.

This was the first she had heard of that. Their ambivalent relationship kept her brother from speaking of little other than his scientific pursuits. He was so protective of even the most impersonal topics that merely considering his private life seemed too intimate. The idea of an illicit romance was unimaginable.

Was the woman a lunatic? Henrietta realized suddenly she might have let a murderer escape. She rushed to the foyer, where the open door permitted a shaft of cool air to enter. Before her, Louisburg Square's cobblestone street lay silent, as empty as the green it encircled, the autumn sun glinting on the wrought iron fence.

Henrietta closed the door slowly. If only Neville hadn't left for Europe last week. Her son would approach the dilemma with calm and reason that would lead to a logical solution. His absence left her feeling bereft. A sense of loss threatened, yet she could not begrudge him the chance to go abroad. She was thankful Neville had been younger than Alec when the Mexican War broke out, leaving her one son.

To whom could she turn? Her sister Fanny was at a charity meeting. She could hardly discuss the incident with her sister-in-law. Corinthia frequently complained Freddy had no interest in women's affairs. *No interest indeed,* Henrietta mused. There was Celia Chase. In the two months Celia had been her companion she had proven discreet and trustworthy. Henrietta would wait until Celia finished her errand.

Dazed, she returned to the receiving room. Sensing her tension, her parrot fluffed his azure and yellow feathers and began to sing in a nasal whine. Visitors never failed to comment on the pets that included an alligator in a tank on a side table and a parrot whose singing reflected his sailing heritage before he became her pet. Mrs. McLaren was too upset to notice either.

"Give me some time to blow the man down," Captain Kidd sang.

"Time is precisely what I don't have," Henrietta muttered.

"Such a nice lady," her housekeeper reflected when Henrietta summoned her to the foyer. "It's a good thing she knew of your reputation for charity."

"She knew no more of my reputation than I knew of hers."

"I assumed she knew you'd protect her," Mrs. Biddle said, surprised.

"That's what she expects, though I'm not sure what it is I'm to protect her from." Henrietta drew on a glove. "Please have my carriage brought round. I'll send word where Celia can find me."

Henrietta wondered what role slavery played in the drama. Angus McLaren's outspokenness had made him so many enemies that the newspapers never suffered a shortage of controversy. Was Freddy among them? He normally spent Monday afternoons at the medical school, but if Myrth's story were true he wouldn't be there.

Henrietta could either call at the station house or at Freddy's home where Corinthia waited. Neither appealed to her.

First, she decided, she would pay a brief call on a friend who kept a list of abolitionists' addresses.

The McLarens, she learned, lived on Beacon Hill's north slope. Although the ride was only two blocks from her home, the class division became evident almost at once. The charm of sun-dappled lanes off Joy Street gave way to stark streets flanked by boardinghouses as the carriage turned into May. Henrietta watched a nanny pushing a perambulator past a cigar shop, a girl of about six at her side. Their placid pace gave her hope that Myrth's fears were unfounded. She wondered what she would say if Freddy weren't there. How would she explain her presence to the police?

The carriage rolled to a stop at the entrance to Sentry Hill Place, a narrow courtway of brick rowhouses. Henrietta dismissed her driver and proceeded to the far end of the alley, her heels echoing on cobblestone. As she entered the front hall and mounted the stairs to the second floor, she noted shabby wallpaper lining a curved stairwell, its wood scarred, the carpeting threadbare. With his high standards Freddy must find the place repulsive.

Her heart lurched when she heard muffled voices near the landing. From the doorway she saw her brother's profile with his white side-whiskers and beard, his piercing eyes subdued. Though he was barely of medium height, the breadth of his midsection emphasized his presence. A wilted bouquet hung from his hand.

He hadn't seen her. Wordlessly, she entered the flat where a porcelain vase lay in fragments. An enormous fern sprawled on its side, soil spilling onto a faded rug beside a patch of blood. In the center was a man's footprint. In a far doorway two policemen conversed with a stout woman in an apron who appeared to be the landlady. Henrietta took advantage of their preoccupation to draw Freddy aside. He reached for her shakily, his countenance pale.

"Etta! What are you doing here?" he asked in a low voice.

"I had a visit from your friend," she told him.

She caught her breath as her glance fell upon the fireplace. The body of a man in shirtsleeves and trousers was sprawled face down by the fire. Blood dribbled into his beard from slashes on his cheek. She wondered if feminine fingernails had inflicted such gashes. A marble bust, its base stained with blood, rested beside the body, a silent observer to whatever tragedy had occurred here. Horror swept over her. Angus McLaren had been a large man. Even in death he seemed tall. As she stared, perhaps because she did, a policeman covered the body discreetly with a blanket.

"Myrth called at your house?" Freddy clutched her hand when the policeman turned away. "Then she is safe."

"She claims she was the killer's target," Henrietta said. "She had a bruised eye and wants me to pretend I never saw her."

"You must do as she says."

His voice was a staccato whisper. The last time she had seen him in a state of such intensity he had been a child, insisting he had not pushed his friend into Boston

Common's frog pond. She had no time to consider his request before a policeman approached them.

"Lieutenant Tripp," Freddy introduced them, "may I present my sister, Henrietta Newell Cobb."

The lieutenant smiled and bowed to her. "You came to your brother's aid quite promptly, Mrs. Cobb."

Suspicious of the implication, she glanced at Freddy. His expression was blank, as if the gravity of his plight eluded him.

"As it happened, I was paying a charity visit down the street," she said, pleased with her inspiration.

"Then you attend Tremont Temple," Tripp returned.

His assumption that she belonged to the congregation told her he knew as well as she that most local residents were working class black families who needed no charity. In addition to being tall and impeccably groomed, the lieutenant was sharp. She knew she must be equally as sharp. If he asked her friend's name, she would be trapped in a lie, one the landlady might be able to refute.

"Were you also calling on Mrs. McLaren?" Tripp continued.

To that she had no reply. Freddy rushed to her aid.

"Mrs. McLaren had invited both of us to tea." Her brother lied so skillfully Henrietta regarded him with new esteem.

"After your sister paid her charity call," Tripp finished.

"That's correct." Freddy spoke as genuinely as if it were.

Henrietta felt mortified. His explanation made it seem as if she, too, was acquainted with the McLarens. At worst, the police might suspect she knew of the affair, if indeed they knew. She doubted Tripp believed her. He motioned to a velvet settee against the wall where they sat out of view of the body beneath the blanket.

"I must ask you again, Professor, exactly what happened," he said. "I understand it's awkward, but Mrs. Baker discovered you in a compromising position. You see the difficulty."

"Yes, I see," Freddy snapped. "I really can't tell you more than I already have, but I'll repeat myself for Etta's sake. Mrs. McLaren summoned me here. She was most anxious I arrive no later than three. I knocked several times before the door swung inward. It must have been unlatched. I called out but received no reply."

"What did you see in the apartment?" the lieutenant asked.

Her brother indicated the room with an impatient sweep of his hand, his voice unsteady. "The flat as you see it. The porcelain in fragments, blood on the rug. I wondered what the devil had happened. I stumbled over a candle stand and saw McLaren stretched out before the fire. I recognized him as her husband."

Freddy paled as he described the grisly discovery. While Tripp made a notation in his book, Henrietta let her gaze wander about the room. Two oval tintypes, formal portraits of Myrth and her husband, hung above a piano on the far wall. Angus McLaren's expression was purposeful, his pale eyes intense. To his right Myrth appeared dignified and serious. *She had looked more relaxed when they met,* Henrietta thought, *than in this stiff portrait.*

Brushing a hand across his brow, Freddy closed his eyes briefly. "I reached down to help McLaren but realized the effort was futile. Then Mrs. Baker appeared in the doorway. From the look on her face, I realized she had mistaken me for the killer."

It was worse than Henrietta had feared. She surmised the landlady heard Freddy stumble and came upstairs to find him bending over her tenant, the body still warm. From the flowers he was holding when Henrietta arrived, he obviously planned to visit McLaren's wife. She was surprised the police hadn't arrested him already. She glanced at the landlady, her round white face like a dinner plate, composed now but so blank it gave no clue whether she would offer sympathy or blame. While she kept her distance at the far end of the parlor, Henrietta sensed she heard every word.

The lieutenant turned to her. "Mrs. Baker, what did you do when you found Professor Newell kneeling beside Mr. McLaren?"

Her plaster face grew anxious. "It's hard to recall, I was so undone by the sight. I think I asked how it happened."

"Did you visit here often, Professor?" Tripp asked quietly.

Freddy frowned. "Several times I escorted Mrs. McLaren home after walks. A fortnight ago I hung that painting for her."

Henrietta glanced at the fireplace, startled by the portrait that faced her. It depicted a chestnut horse emerging from a forest with a young Myrth astride, unclothed but for the russet hair that concealed her frame as it flowed imperceptibly into the horse's mane. The similar coloring and exaggerated length made it difficult to separate the two, giving the painting a mythological quality. Supple arms and a long expanse of leg along one flank were painted with delicate strokes in warm pink and beige tones.

It was the vivid emotions that captivated Henrietta. Myrth was a woman of exceptional beauty, her high cheekbones and expressive eyes immodestly sensual, determination defining the mouth, defiance the nose. In contrast to the cold tintype, this portrait dominated the room. Its essence was decidedly untamed, yet it contained a realism that prevented its subject from being idealized. Henrietta sensed it reflected her character.

A young patrolman stepped forward, following Freddy's gaze. "Never thought I'd get to see the famous Godiva painting."

"Mr. Baker doesn't approve of it," Mrs. Baker said. "I doubt he'll want her here either, but she's gone, and the rent's paid."

"You'll need to leave the flat as it is in case she returns, although I think we've seen the last of her." Tripp turned to study the canvas. "What was Mr. McLaren's opinion of the work?"

"He didn't fully appreciate its realism," Freddy said dryly.

"Rest his soul, he didn't like it," said Mrs. Baker. "With these old walls it's hard not to know what goes on."

As anxious as the police to hear what the landlady had to say, Henrietta refrained from pointing out that such old walls tended to retain sound rather than reveal it.

"How were relations between them?" Lieutenant Tripp asked.

"Weren't what I'd call happy. They had no children. She had bruises, poor thing. Said she bumped her cheek on the bedpost, but I knew better. She was a lady at one time with servants. She wasn't about to be bossed by the likes of him." Mrs. Baker eyed the fireplace keenly. "That's probably how he got those scrapes."

"When did you last hear them argue?" Tripp asked.

"Shortly before three. He never came home from work early except today. I read about thefts in the area and thought I might lock the downstairs door." She shot Freddy an accusing look. "Mrs. McLaren said she expected a caller, so I left it open."

Henrietta guessed the police surmised that Freddy arrived at three, witnessed the couple arguing, and retaliated with murder. Yet it was obvious even to Mrs. Baker that the incriminating scratches on Angus's face had been made by a woman.

"Had you seen the professor before?" Lieutenant Tripp asked.

"I'd seen them together, but I didn't think nothing of it." Mrs. Baker bristled. "What Mrs. McLaren did was her business."

"It's her safety that concerns me, Lieutenant," Freddy said tersely. "She wasn't here when I came at three as she requested."

"If you see her, Professor, please tell her we're concerned as well." Tripp's tone indicated he expected the two would meet.

Sarcasm sharpened Freddy's tone. "Certainly you don't think she overpowered a man nearly half again her size."

Tripp studied the portrait. "Judging from the angle at which McLaren was struck, I'm confident a woman using both hands could heave a bust of that weight with force enough to kill a man."

Having met Mrs. McLaren, Henrietta had no doubt the canvas's seductive subject was capable of heaving her own bust at Freddy with effective results. In a moment of fury a woman of average height would have no difficulty striking a man in the temple. Myrth claimed her husband was the victim, but she had been the target. Angus had enemies. Did she as well? Henrietta was certain Freddy hadn't murdered him. Myrth could have fled with a lover who murdered her husband, leaving Freddy to shoulder the blame.

Tripp's next remark filled Henrietta with alarm. "I suggest, Professor, that you remain in town during our investigation."

"I've no intention of leaving." Freddy's tone was indignant.

"I regret having to inform you," Tripp added gravely, "that at this time you are our main suspect--"

Henrietta felt much worse as Tripp turned to her. "--and you, Mrs. Cobb, a possible accomplice."

Two

Henrietta watched as two officers examined an empty spot on the mantel lined with a pair of candlesticks, a bowl of wax fruit, and a vase. She recognized the gaunt features of Caesar sculpted into the bloodied marble bust on the floor. If the police hadn't been present, she would have tested its weight. Without lifting the bust she found it difficult to judge. The killer was either angrier than McLaren or cleverer. She doubted Freddy was either.

She surveyed the flat, seeing the situation as the police must. They had no reason to believe anyone else was present as Myrth claimed. At this moment Myrth appeared very guilty, at least to Henrietta, with Freddy a very convenient suspect.

"It isn't fair that she should come home to an empty house," he argued with Mrs. Baker. "The police have requested your help."

"I'll comply out of respect for Mr. McLaren," Mrs. Baker said, "but I expect relatives to take the furnishings afterward."

They might as well, thought Henrietta, *for married women have no rights to their own property.*

"I've no idea what'll become of the picture. Mr. Baker wants it disposed of. It's all such a sad state of affairs." Mrs. Baker colored. "Begging your pardon, Professor, I meant no offense."

"None taken," Freddy assured her. "I'd be happy to relieve you of it. I have the bill of sale, as I purchased it for her."

Henrietta wished Freddy had been a bit more circumspect in sharing such information. If only he had the eloquence of Mr. Emerson. Her brother was far too blunt for his own good.

While the police focused their attention on the bedroom, she seized the chance to learn more about the McLarens. A pair of columns divided the parlor from the dining room. The furniture was stylish but not new, a flaw Myrth had attempted to disguise with cushions and a linen tablecloth. Earthenware dishes lined a sideboard while needlepoint roses brightened the walls. Two sets of plainly curtained French doors led off the dining room. To the right appeared to be a tiny bedroom, to the left a small kitchen.

Henrietta winced as she bumped her knee on the open door of a sewing chest. The torn yellowed corner of an envelope and bits of flowers lay on the floor beside it. Noting the unusual shape, she picked up a piece. Though pressed long ago, the funnel-shaped purplish petals retained an unpleasant odor. Freshly picked, they would make a flattering arrangement, if one kept some distance.

Laying the flowers down, she saw that Mrs. Baker had joined the police while her brother studied the portrait of Myrth. Suddenly weary, she rubbed her eyes and joined him.

"I don't imagine the police require you to stay any longer." The kindness in his voice turned conspiratorial. "Can you meet me this evening? I want to hear about your visit. I've arranged to keep the portrait. Perhaps you might take it in your carriage."

"Don't be preposterous, Freddy. It links you to this woman." Despite his concern Henrietta found it hard to hide her impatience. "Try to show some sensitivity for Cora's feelings."

"Very well, I'll put it in my study behind the door. Myrth felt rather melancholy of late and wished she had never posed for it. I was glad to save her further embarrassment by buying it."

"Think of the embarrassment it will cause Cora, Freddy. We all make mistakes. Mrs. McLaren was wise in recognizing hers."

His gaze remained fastened on the portrait. "It must be twenty years old, though I can't decipher the artist's name from that scrawl. I wonder if Sam Ingraham would know who painted it."

On hearing the name Henrietta brushed the emotional wounds from her mind. "That was a long time ago. I doubt he would remember."

"The picture might be all I have left of her. I hope by taking it home I'm able to help her put her past to rest."

"Forget the past. It's your future we must contend with right now. It's all any of us have." *And some don't even have that.* She pulled on her gloves with unnecessary force.

Freddy frowned at her. "Are you feeling ill? Your eyes look strange. The pupils are dilated."

"I'm tired." She did feel warm and a bit parched. She gave the flat a final glance. "I think you've done all you can here."

"I can never do enough for Myrth," he said quietly. His own eyes looked old and tired. "I love her, you see. I hope that in time, Etta, you'll be understanding rather than judgmental."

She did not know what to make of such forthright sentiment. Expressing feelings of any depth was so unlike her brother it embarrassed her. Yet his remark had struck a chord. Given their past, his words seemed ironic.

"Not to make less of the situation than it warrants," Freddy continued in a controlled tone, "but this is temporary. Once the police find the killer, I'll no longer be a suspect."

Henrietta fastened her cloak, trying to keep her patience. "Locating a murderer isn't as simple as finding a lost money clip," she reminded him. "Proving murder is even more difficult."

Minutes later, seated in her carriage across from Celia Chase, Henrietta related the scene in the McLarens' flat and the details of Myrth's confession, an encounter so distant it seemed unreal now. Her companion listened without interrupting, staring in disbelief at times. When she finished Celia smiled with irony.

"You are so full of benevolence," Celia announced, "the last thing I'd suspect you of is murder."

"At the moment the police don't share your view." Henrietta fought to check her frustration. "I'm sure they think Freddy went to meet Myrth while her husband was at work, Angus surprised them, and Freddy reacted with violence. It makes sense except Freddy finds even the most minor domestic dispute distasteful. Of all people for Mrs. McLaren to turn to, I seem the least likely."

"I'd consider her trust a compliment." Celia's face held surprise. "She might not inspire your trust, but she had to be desperate to jeopardize her safety by calling on you to confess."

"But I've never met the woman."

"Either your brother had flattering things to say about you, or Mrs. McLaren has heard of your reputation."

Considering their differences, Henrietta thought the latter more likely. "Freddy did seem surprised to hear of her black eye, giving credence to his claim that she was gone when he arrived."

"In some curious way it does seem possible, even plausible."

There was that accent again, Henrietta mused, *reminiscent of Maine.* The late afternoon sun in the carriage window set fire to Celia's copper hair, swept into a bun at the nape of her neck. While she knew little more about Celia's background than about Myrth's, in the time she had known her, she had come to trust her.

"The timing couldn't be worse with tensions high and civil war predicted. The difficulty lies in Angus's political views." Henrietta was relieved to be in her carriage again even if she must share it with the offensive painting. "Why would Freddy want such a thing? It isn't as if he has a place to hang it."

Celia stared at the portrait as if assessing the personality. "Mrs. McLaren certainly is a striking woman."

"But did she strike her husband? Neither I nor the police have any way to find her."

Celia put forth a reassuring thought. "They must suspect her as well as your brother if the landlady heard the couple arguing. If she's running from the police, she'll already be in hiding."

"She certainly can't go home. What will she do?"

The question was rhetorical. Henrietta reflected on women at the shelter who had lived on the streets. In her work with the Women's Collective, she had often tried to persuade women to abandon their lifestyle for more dignified work. Even when they were offered other employment, the money on the street was better.

Yet Myrth possessed a quality Henrietta had seen on meeting Celia. While Celia's situation was different, she remembered Freddy's words of admonition when she told him she had invited a stranger to lodge with her. She ignored his objections, seeing Celia's faded dignity and elegance, qualities he perhaps saw in Myrth. Just as with Celia, she was convinced Myrth had been born into better circumstances.

She was also sure Myrth was neither as trustworthy nor as innocent. Considering her self-control in the face of murder, Myrth wasn't likely to fall into the wayward ways of street life. *An unusual name,* Henrietta mused, *and evidently an unusual woman.*

"Perhaps Professor Newell will tell you more when you see him this evening," Celia offered.

"I'm not sure I want to hear, but I hardly have a choice."

Henrietta toyed with her glove, too distracted to focus until she realized Myrth's claim that politics was not involved might be a lie. Boston was the center of abolitionist activity, but Angus McLaren had taken a controversial stand. As slavery spread west Northern commercial concerns clashed with Southern agricultural interests, while plantation owners chose to preserve their heritage at the cost of a unified nation. The combination led to strong emotions. *Not unlike Freddy's,* she reflected.

She had begun to feel she knew as little about her brother as she did about Celia. Three people were not who they seemed to be—not Celia Chase, if that was her real name, Myrth McLaren, or even her own brother. At this point Celia seemed the most trustworthy.

"At best," Henrietta acknowledged, "I've lied to protect Freddy. At worst, the police will view me as an accomplice."

"Only if they find out Myrth visited you," Celia countered.

"I suppose I'll have to make sure that doesn't happen," Henrietta muttered. It troubled her to find herself opposing the law. Too late, she realized she had put her own fate at risk to protect a stranger at Freddy's request, and neither the police nor Corinthia was likely to view her decision favorably.

In the gaslight of Freddy's study that evening, Henrietta tried to be objective as she scrutinized her brother. Outwardly he appeared the same, his lined face placid, white hair thinning. Yet his behavior was so uncharacteristic, she might as well be talking to a stranger. If not for the canvas leaning against the wall, she could have convinced herself Myrth's visit had never occurred, and Freddy was not the prime suspect in a murder.

She related the details of Myrth's visit as he demanded, then waited for him to reciprocate. When he did not she studied the painting critically, comparing Myrth's luscious features to her own. Henrietta's face was too ordinary to be remarkable except for the set of her mouth, with lips that thinned when she was angry, a look her father had been able to read instantly. She wondered what he would think of Freddy's situation.

"I'm not sure I'd recognize Myrth if she were suitably attired." Her sarcasm failed to penetrate his mood. "You know, Freddy, women do sometimes take advantage of their beauty in order to survive, but to fall in love with a painting is absurd."

"That's unkind, Etta, not like you." Freddy sat behind a mahogany desk that divided them. "She had no advantage whatsoever in this. At least that scoundrel McLaren got what he deserved."

"The police don't see it that way." Henrietta sought for the words that would reach him. "I wish you had confided in me."

"It isn't precisely dinner conversation. What a ghastly day." He pulled a Turkish Oriental from an inlaid cigarette box but let it linger in his palm. "I hope the killer's caught soon."

"Frankly, I think we know who killed Mr. McLaren."

Freddy gazed at her with a naïvetè that appalled her. "Who?"

"Has it occurred to you it might have been Mrs. McLaren?"

"Don't be ludicrous, Myrth isn't guilty. I don't know why she hasn't contacted me. I'm worried sick about her." The wrinkles on his brow seemed to have multiplied in a few hours. While his concern was sincere, Henrietta was troubled by his inability to comprehend that the danger he faced outweighed his childhood prank of pushing a pal into Boston Common's frog pond.

"Try to see yourself as the police do, standing over a dead man whose wife you coveted. I know you didn't kill him, but can't you see how their perspective differs?" She spoke more gently when her entreaty met with silence. "Being secretive will get us nowhere. Myrth trusted me. How long have you known each other?"

"Four months," he admitted after a pause. "For modesty's sake we limited our encounters to public places at first."

At least they had shown some sense. Henrietta attempted to lighten the conversation. "Here I was thinking you'd hardly strayed beyond the mildew of your medical library. Obviously, you've strayed more than I realized."

Freddy shot her a dark look. His hands fumbled with the cigarette until he managed to light it.

"It's a lovely name, Myrth McLaren," she said seriously.

"No name suited a woman so. I've never known anyone more refined or endearing. She's from a wealthy Lenox family with whom she fell out of favor after marrying. An immigrant factory worker couldn't hope to fulfill her needs like a Harvard professor." His scathing tone changed as if he sensed a forthcoming rebuke. "This isn't a dalliance. I'd hoped you of all people, Etta, would understand. Our relations were platonic until recently."

Dismay swept over Henrietta at his admission. While she could appreciate the courage his confession required, his expectation of understanding from her seemed misplaced. She had never experienced feelings for anyone other than William during her own marriage, even when his affair with a younger woman and subsequent departure ten years ago forced her to make excuses to society. She wanted to spare Corinthia the same awkwardness.

While her sister-in-law was a highly regarded organist in her own right, her life with Freddy entwined around Boston society with an eye to marital prospects for their daughters. Cora's father had provided the endowed chair Freddy occupied at Harvard as well as his research funding—in reality, his entire livelihood. In the face of his indiscretion, Henrietta's protective nature surged to the fore.

"Have you told Cora? Never mind, I see you decided to test my reaction first." She resumed with a brittle smile as he looked askance at her. "I'd hoped our family's brush with scandal would end with William, but apparently that isn't to be. Still, your standing in the community might convince the police of your innocence. I'll vouch for your character."

"They would hardly consider you an impeccable character witness if they knew the company you keep," Freddy said wryly. "Your neighbors in Louisburg Square aren't fond of the fallen women you have as houseguests, even if it is for charitable reasons."

"If I were you I wouldn't be so quick to judge," she warned.

Freddy's laugh betrayed his discomfort as an urgent knock startled them both. Even before the doorknob turned and her sister-in-law filled the doorway, Henrietta knew it was Cora. Her footsteps were heavier than the pedals of the organ she had mastered as she had the entire household from servants to spouse. Despite her formidable manner, Corinthia Atwood Newell was blessed with features most would consider pleasant but for a long nose and eyes as keen as a hawk's. *With her outdated halo of brown curls, she might have been the most attractive in the family,* Henrietta thought, *if she smiled rather than scowled.* She joined them in the study, her gray eyes bright with unexpected news.

"I didn't know you were here, Etta." Her tone reflected her indignation at being excluded. She thrust a calling card at her husband. "Mr. Stafford is downstairs. He says you needn't concern yourself with jail just yet. What on earth is he talking about?"

"Let us adjourn to the receiving room," Freddy said, rising. "The study is too personal a place to convey unfortunate news."

"You owe me the courtesy of an explanation," Cora retorted.

"I don't wish to repeat the story twice," he said curtly. "I called on a friend to find her husband had been murdered."

"Murdered! What friend of ours is in mourning tonight?"

"It is not a mutual friend, Cora."

"I see."

Cora's face hardened, her silence demanding an explanation Freddy was not prepared to give. As she left the room in stony silence, Henrietta looked to her brother for a signal. She wasn't surprised when he gestured for her to accompany him downstairs. Perhaps he hoped to avoid a second slaying by revealing his affair with other family members present. She suspected Cora would release her anger later in private, and heaven help him then.

They descended the staircase to the foyer where Felicity and Prudence waited with their mother. Henrietta wondered how Freddy would explain himself to his daughters, struggling in their late teenage years with romantic notions of their own. Beside them, Fanny Newell Browning, Henrietta's younger sister, had not yet removed her cloak. With the lion's share of the Newell charm, Fan possessed a sweetness that masked her strength. If Freddy were to find forgiveness within the family, it would come from her first.

"Father, Mr. Stafford is being very official and won't tell us a thing," complained Prudence, the younger of the two.

"Wait in the drawing room," Corinthia commanded. "Your father will speak with you later. Fanny, come with us."

"Is this why you asked me here, Freddy?" Diplomatically Fan turned to her nieces when her brother didn't reply. "I suppose my Ladies for Liberty petition can wait. You girls both look well."

Felicity and Prudence were too intrigued to leave. Henrietta rewarded their curiosity with a smile she hoped they would find reassuring before she followed their parents into the receiving room. James Fenton Stafford, the family solicitor, waited by the window, his spectacles halfway down his nose, his dark attire matching his eyes and neatly clipped beard as if it were the continuation of a whole rather than merely complementary dress. Solemnly, he studied them over his glasses as Cora planted her massive frame in a gilt chair apart from her family. Henrietta and Fan strategically selected chairs near their brother.

Freddy extended his hand to Stafford. "Good of you to come, James. Don't spare me. How bad is it?"

Stafford's visage was grim. "You needn't worry about arrest for the moment. Jail would be truly insufferable, I fear."

"Would someone please tell me what happened?" Cora demanded.

Stafford glanced sharply at Freddy, assessing the situation. "It seems," he volunteered, "that while calling on the wife of the renowned abolitionist Angus McLaren today, Professor Newell was the first to learn of the man's untimely demise."

Incomprehension settled on Cora's face as she digested both bits of information, her mind focusing on the first. She looked at Freddy with suspicion. "Are we acquainted with the McLarens?"

Freddy flushed scarlet beneath his white whiskers and beard as the solicitor rushed to fill the silence.

"Given the current political climate, I imagine the visit had to do with raising funds for the Union. It seems Mr. McLaren came home unexpectedly early and met his killer. It's a great loss. He was well regarded at his job at Sam Ingraham's piano firm."

The mention of the familiar name for the second time today startled Henrietta. Pushing it from her mind, she kept her gaze on Corinthia instead.

"I didn't think much of McLaren," Freddy retorted. "He took every advantage of Myrth. She ought to have left him long ago."

"And what advantage did you take, Frederick?"

Slicing into the conversation, Cora's voice changed from suspicious to disdainful as she realized Freddy intended to meet Myrth alone. Was it confirmation Henrietta saw in her derisive stare? Maybe Cora had suspected an affair. Stafford's diplomacy was comforting, but Henrietta knew it would take more than tact to keep the police at bay as the solicitor turned to Freddy.

"Right now the antislavery contingent has lost one of its own, and they are clamoring for justice. In time people will forget your indiscretion, and your good name will be restored."

"What of Mrs. McLaren?" Freddy demanded. "What if the barbarian who murdered her husband has also harmed her?"

Fanny stiffened with shock, but it was the fervency in her brother's tone that surprised Henrietta.

Stafford shrugged. "There's no evidence of another caller."

"That's outrageous," Freddy protested. "Myrth did not kill her husband. She isn't the kind of woman who does such things."

"What kind of woman is she, Frederick?" Corinthia's face was white.

Freddy's countenance reddened in contrast. "She is a good woman, a decent woman who behaves in a becoming manner."

"And beautiful," added Stafford. "She was the subject of the Godiva painting that hung in the Compass Club until recently, when it was sold to an anonymous buyer."

"Why, that's Frederick's club," Cora exclaimed.

Henrietta spoke up before Cora could make the connection. "Our focus must be on helping Freddy, not on the widow."

"While the police consider her a suspect, Frederick had the motive and opportunity to kill McLaren," Stafford warned, turning to him. "It doesn't sit well that you planned to meet her alone."

Cora spoke in his defense for the first time. "It's entirely probable Mrs. McLaren arranged the murder with the intention of framing my husband. Isn't it apparent she lured him to her home?"

While Henrietta was certain Cora's reasoning was correct, her sister-in-law's unaccountable calm made her wonder if she was genuinely surprised by Freddy's revelation of infidelity. Henrietta could imagine nothing more humiliating for Freddy than to be found in such compromising circumstances. And for Cora, who already felt he spent an excessive amount of time away from home.

"It's logical, but the police suspect Frederick." Stafford leveled his gaze at Freddy. "You might be more prudent next time. It was rather incriminating to bring flowers."

Henrietta was acutely aware of Cora's anger and wondered why Freddy was not. Cora's expression made it clear that she was more perturbed by the relationship than by the suspicion of murder. Henrietta spoke up quickly.

"If Mrs. McLaren didn't kill her husband, is it possible she had an admirer who did?"

"How many do you think she had?" Freddy retorted. "I've no doubt Myrth will send an explanation. If this country can deliver mail between Missouri and California, by God, surely a note can find its destination in a city as civilized as Boston."

"I'll arrange for you to talk with the police and reaffirm your innocence." The solicitor laid a hand on Freddy's shoulder. "You have a sensible family, Frederick. Listen to them."

After Stafford had departed Fanny addressed Freddy quietly.

"Is Mrs. McLaren painted as the name Godiva implies?"

"The portrait is tasteful," he snapped. "The point is, no one of sense could believe she overpowered a man McLaren's size."

"Of course not," Fan murmured. "The police will certainly clear your name. They are very skilled at such things nowadays."

Henrietta smiled involuntarily. Dear Fan, always the optimist, had voiced Freddy's simplistic solution. From her perspective any situation could be mended with a desire to reform. In the pall of breached fidelity, Henrietta felt less hopeful. Cora rose from her chair, her large frame trembling with rage. She shot Fan a glance that would have frozen the sun had night not already fallen.

"How could it be worse, I'd like to know? My husband is about to be charged with murdering a man whose wife he fancies. I trust you'll understand if I don't share your confidence."

Henrietta doubted Freddy had considered the consequences of his actions until this moment. His wife's reckless words had turned his face a purplish hue, but he wisely did not interrupt. Cora's fury was palpable from across the room. Even in silence her heartbreak cut through her pride, exposing her vulnerability.

"I wonder if your flowers will be kept as evidence," Cora continued sarcastically. "If you choose to engage in promiscuity, Frederick, there's little I can do to prevent it. I considered you above cavorting with women like this Devil's strumpet."

"You do her a grave disservice by speaking so." He measured his words carefully. "Your insinuations are truly inappropriate."

"Perhaps," Fanny ventured, "rather than debate her virtue--"

"She has no virtue." Cora's voice shook. "It's bad enough he slept with her, but I will not have him accused of murder."

"That's why we must prove his innocence," Henrietta cut in. "Myrth isn't likely to return to help us, since it was probably her fingernails that left scratches on her husband's face."

Corinthia's head whirled. "How do you know this, Etta?"

Henrietta wished at once she hadn't spoken. Cora would not believe her any more than Lieutenant Tripp had. "I was visiting nearby. From the depth and spacing it's clear they were made by a woman."

"Remember Myrth was injured as well," Freddy defended her.

"She can fend for herself," Cora retorted, "as we must."

"You don't understand, Cora. I love her."

Cora flinched as if she had received a physical wound. For a moment no one spoke. Then her determination reasserted itself.

"Men your age do not fall in love, Frederick," she said coldly. "They have quiet affairs, that is all. What makes it worse is that Etta aided you in your indiscretion."

Henrietta's heart skipped a beat. Cora shot her an ominous glare.

"In two months I will be installed as president of Harvard's Benefactors Society. It's an honor that is dear to me, as my father and brothers graduated with distinction."

"As did I," Freddy snapped, facing her from a distance, "and my father before me. I'm aware of the heritage we must uphold."

"Yet your thoughtlessness has jeopardized our standing in society. I won't have my name disgraced, nor do I intend to allow you to ruin our daughters' reputations. Do you hear, Frederick?"

Henrietta thought it unlikely anyone within the entire peninsula of Boston and perhaps even the environs of Dorchester and Roxbury had not heard. She suspected both she and Fanny would willingly pledge their fortunes to ensure Corinthia's silence.

"I will give you all the support you need during this period of misfortune you've brought upon us." Cora drew herself up. "I'm also giving you an ultimatum. If you do not clear your name, you leave me no choice but to ask my father to withdraw your research funding."

It was, Henrietta suspected, a satisfying solution for Cora. Her standing in society would remain solid as long as her husband held his position. What mattered to Freddy was the research that Williston Atwood and his daughter had the ability to expropriate.

"As for you, Etta," she continued, "I find it unthinkable that you could condone such an act. I plan to ask my father to withhold funding for the school project so dear to your heart."

The heart so attached to the night school for children sank. Henrietta's committee to address the matter of educating the hundreds of young children in Boston who worked to support their families had just initiated a series of evening classes. She was its most loyal supporter and Atwood its biggest contributor. It seemed absurdly unfair that one impulsive decision should threaten such a cause. Would Atwood be so petty as to remove funding at Cora's request? The wives of other abolitionists might also withdraw support. Too late, she berated herself for her involvement.

"Surely a project like this need not suffer because of my actions," Henrietta protested. "Don't be unreasonable, Cora. We must support Freddy rather than release our anger haphazardly."

"Frederick's projects have kept him away from us for too long as it is." Corinthia's tone was bitter as she turned to him. "You don't know what it is to live in misery as I have."

Snatching up his greatcoat, Freddy turned toward the door.

"I have a feeling I'm about to find out," he muttered.

Three

In the faint glow of gas lamps, Henrietta made her way down Tremont Street a half-hour later, relieved to escape the tension at Freddy's. She waited in the shadow of King's Chapel, her church, its stone facade cold and massive in the moonlight, until a hansom cab passed, and she crossed to the foot of Beacon.

The police didn't know her brother as she did, but Freddy certainly didn't beat anyone to death with a bouquet. The only one who could prove his innocence was Myrth, who could remain hidden as long as she chose in a city the size of Boston. Henrietta dreaded the impact of publicity on Freddy if the newspapers reported his affair. No supporter of abolitionism, the *Post* would feel little regret announcing McLaren's murder in its morning edition. Nor would they hesitate to pounce on a scandal. Just when people were beginning to forget Professor Webster.

She wondered if Oliver Wendell Holmes, Freddy's colleague, would think he did away with McLaren as Professor Webster had with Dr. Parkman. Ten years before, John Webster had been hanged for the murder of philanthropist George Parkman. No one imagined a Harvard chemistry professor would be intimidated enough by Dr. Parkman to murder him simply to end his demands for a loan repayment. It caused such a sensation even Charles Dickens had visited the site while touring

America. Mental images of the laboratory furnace in which Webster had disposed of the body made Henrietta cringe. That was a scandal. She hoped Freddy wouldn't be the cause of another.

Whether he deserved it or not, his family would support him. Her siblings shared the same affection with their children that she did with Neville. She wondered how her relationship with Alec would have grown had he survived the war. Two years after Alec's death William left her. In time, she had traded her loss for a commitment to social justice and literacy projects. Yet nothing had eased a decade of loneliness. *Had things been different,* she mused, *my life might be as happy as Fan's.*

Even Freddy must feel lonely at times, as Myrth's presence proved. Henrietta didn't relish having to defend him. Contemplating Freddy's woes kept her from worrying about the night school. A permanent site offered stability, but there were books to buy, parents to convince, employers to pacify. She wondered if it was too lofty a goal to try to educate working children, mostly Irish, many with parents in jail.

She took a deep breath, refusing to allow herself to wonder what would happen if her actions cost the committee the chance to try.

"I feel like one of Mr. Poe's characters," Henrietta confessed over a pot of tea. "His plots fit my situation frightfully well."

Celia laughed. "In this case, though, we haven't found any purloined letter or tell-tale heart to lead to a solution."

They were seated in the receiving room where they could enjoy the exotic pets Henrietta had just finished feeding. She saw Celia's gaze rest on the Caiman as if she were weighing the danger.

"Ozymandias is striking, isn't he? I bought him from a friend visiting China. The locals called him Ji Yue, or Hungry Moon. One night a fisherman ventured into the Yangtze River. The others saw Ji Yue's jaws open in the moonlight and take part of the man's leg. They wanted to be rid of Ji Yue. My friend wanted his leather. He paid them handsomely to wrestle him from the river."

Celia sipped her tea. "I imagine you paid him handsomely to get Ji Yue as a pet. Hungry Moon suits him, but I like Ozymandias."

"What would Shelley think? 'Look on my works, ye mighty, and despair.' I wonder how many victims he claimed." Henrietta shook her head. "I don't want my brother to become a victim. It's too coincidental that Myrth summoned him in time to find her husband dead. It seems a convenient way to end her marriage."

"It's unlikely she would invent such a farfetched story," Celia countered, "then take the time to call on you."

"If only I could be sure her intentions are honorable."

How ironic, Henrietta mused, *that Freddy trusted Myrth but remained suspicious of Celia.* They'd met one night on Chestnut Street. Celia was breathless from running, her features delicate beneath the grime. In the flicker of gaslight she appeared to be no more than a girl when two streetwalkers mistook her for one of their own. Henrietta could have taken her to a shelter across town, but it was a long walk for someone so exhausted when her own home was around the corner.

In the days that followed Celia was unfailingly courteous, helping with the linen presses and china closets, her manners impeccable though her face mirrored anxiety. Henrietta suspected she was running not from the police but from a husband, with Chase indicating her situation rather than her name. They had shared meals and conversation for two months, nearly as long as Freddy had known Myrth. Henrietta never inquired about rooms at the shelter, preferring to think of her as a permanent guest.

From the outset Celia had shown interest in the night school, asking about the fledgling committee's plans. Suspecting Celia was better suited to moral reform than household chores, Henrietta suggested a change.

"Since this crisis forces me to set aside teaching, perhaps you might consider taking over for me temporarily," Henrietta proposed. "Have you any experience with children?"

Celia paled. "I have a great deal of experience with them."

Henrietta kept her suspicions on the matter to herself. "We plan to teach working children practical skills to prepare them for more than the factory. Mr. Atwood has been so supportive, we want to name the school after him. The ABC School—the Atwood Betterment Conservatory. All that remains is to find a location."

Her spirits lifted as Celia brightened with anticipation. "That's a challenge I'd be happy to accept," she replied.

"I'm glad that's settled," Henrietta said with relief. "It will give me time to visit Mrs. McLaren's landlady. I suspect there's a great deal more she could say, and I imagine she'll speak more frankly to me than to Freddy."

The chance that Mrs. Baker might recall seeing someone other than Freddy the day of the murder prompted

Henrietta to call on her the next day. As she opened the wrought iron gates to Sentry Hill Place, she wondered if Angus's death had nothing to do with abolitionism but was instead rooted in some personal matter. Before the lamp post in the center of the lane, she saw a darkened alley on the left where an intruder could hide. A street sweeper might miss someone in the shadows. Mrs. Baker was another matter.

Her knock was answered by Myrth's landlady, a dustmop in her hand, wisps of gray hair framing her circular face. Flushed with exertion, Mrs. Baker recognized her with a start. Her face tightened until Henrietta explained her reason for calling.

"I wondered if Mrs. McLaren had returned or if anything more was disturbed." While Myrth might return to retrieve items, Henrietta knew she was more likely to seek shelter elsewhere.

"No, she hasn't returned." Mrs. Baker grimaced. "Seems to me we've had enough disturbed lately. Mr. Baker's none too pleased."

"I hope our removing the portrait spared you some indignity. It's a shame it caused bad feelings between the couple."

"A terrible eyesore, that. Mr. Baker's relieved it's gone."

Henrietta wondered if Mrs. Baker wasn't more relieved than her husband to be rid of such a spellbinding distraction. "Did you by chance notice anyone about yesterday who didn't belong?"

Mrs. Baker frowned. "There was an Irish lad. Such a fresh thing I'd have had the police here even without a murder. Poor fellow must work in industry, for he'd lost part of a finger."

"The third finger of the right hand? In a plaid shirt and cap? With a shock of dark hair?" Henrietta wasn't surprised the young truant was involved. On her visits to Willie McCurdy's home, he had never worn anything else, probably because he had nothing.

"Aye, with eyes the color of smoke. Wore his cap at an angle to hide his face so he'd look older. Handsome tyke."

Henrietta felt elated. "Was it before or after the murder?"

"It was while I waited for the police. He probably lingered because of the confectioner's up on May," Mrs. Baker volunteered. "Too many kids. Guttersnipes, Mr. Baker says. You know him?"

"I hope so. I'll ask him about it."

More likely, Willie had gone to the tobacconist's, Henrietta suspected. Since he usually worked on Fridays, a talk with his boss might be in order. She hoped Willie might have seen the man who left his footprint in the parlor.

"What a sight. All that blood." Mrs. Baker's face returned to its dinner plate pallor as she confided with embarrassment, "Mr. Baker wants it cleaned up soon. Makes us feel low class."

"I share your humiliation," Henrietta said earnestly. "My brother did come to meet Mrs. McLaren, but I assure you he isn't guilty. I'm afraid the murderer remains free. Do you know of anyone who might want to harm her?"

"Not a soul." Mrs. Baker seemed startled by the concept.

"Perhaps Mr. McLaren made enemies with his strong opinions. I've a favor to ask, Mrs. Baker. I fear I left a glove upstairs."

After a pause, she invited Henrietta inside. "It upsets me to see the place, though it's cleaner. I didn't disturb a thing."

Except for the absence of the body, the apartment was just as Henrietta remembered. Mrs. Baker had obeyed police instructions, although Henrietta didn't remember ashes outside the fireplace grate where Angus scuffled with his killer. She had noticed the dying embers on her previous visit and thought it fortunate he hadn't been burned. Mrs. Baker saw the floor at the same time.

"The police must have left that soot," she exclaimed. "I don't think they'd mind if I clean it."

Hoping to view the flat privately, Henrietta watched as Mrs. Baker seized a dustpan. A knock downstairs lifted her hopes.

"That'll be Sadie, the little match girl," said Mrs. Baker. "She comes for tea and talk as much as to sell matches."

"I'll clean this while you chat," Henrietta offered.

"You're a kind soul. Join us when you've found your glove."

She left Henrietta to sweep up the remains. Amid the soot she noticed flecks of gold, evidence of Angus's final struggle. He must have damaged his wedding band as he fought for his life.

Setting aside the dustpan, she came eye to eye with the bust of Caesar, now back on the mantel. She fingered the murder weapon through her glove, so heavy it nearly slipped from her grasp. The lieutenant was correct. Even a woman of slight stature would have the strength to strike with enough force to kill.

Looking about, Henrietta entered the bedroom, dominated by a mahogany bed, armoire, and shaving stand. Only the bureau suggested a feminine touch, its lace scarf displaying a comb and brush set, buttonhook, and other trinkets. She inspected a cameo brooch and jet choker laid out beside a jewelry box. While they didn't appear to be of value, respectable women didn't leave jewelry lying about. Myrth left in a hurry.

Tempted by the intimate surroundings, Henrietta opened the top drawer. A generous supply of lace undergarments nestled inside, but it was the bills lying on top that surprised her. A woman who arranged to do away with her husband was in no position to leave money behind. Had it been a sudden act of violence, leaving Myrth so distraught she fled in panic? The theory cast the probability of her guilt into doubt, a possibility that dismayed Henrietta.

Leaving the bedroom, she explored the kitchen and found it adequate for its farm table, chairs, coal stove, and well-stocked pantry. She returned to the parlor, pausing by the sewing chest on which she had bumped her knee the day before. Four issues of *Harper's Bazaar* were scattered on top with a filigree chatelaine that held a tiny scent bottle, silk purse, and three keys. One was heavy and ornate, another delicate enough for a jewelry box, the last a house key. Myrth couldn't return to a locked flat without it, another indication she'd left quickly.

Near the keys sat a work box embellished with inlaid wood. Inside Henrietta found a tatting shuttle, colored thread, and sewing tools. She closed the box, noticing the purple flowers she laid on the chest yesterday. The petals reminded her of an exhibit of plants she had seen at Harvard. Poisonous plants. She placed them in her glove and slipped them into a pocket. She knew just the person to identify them and made a mental note to write him.

She tried the ornate key and found it fit the keyhole on the door. Myrth must have unlocked the sewing chest and forgotten to close it. Stooping to peek inside, Henrietta saw piles of fabric lining the shelves with autograph books tucked beneath. She flipped through one, reading decade-old greetings from minor stage celebrities before replacing the book on the shelf.

Reaching behind the linens, her fingers encountered a small stack of daguerreotypes, some without frames, others in leather cases lined with velvet. All were of actors from the past except two. One was a blurred photograph of a young man gripping the reins of a horse, the other a picture of an older woman in modest dress. Why did Myrth keep these locked away? More bits of violet flowers lay on the bottom shelf. Henrietta pocketed them with the rest.

She knew if she didn't go downstairs soon Mrs. Baker would come looking for her. Closing the sewing chest, she examined a desk with binders that held household accounts. A single sheet of paper protruded from a pigeon hole as if filed in haste. She felt only a brief pang of guilt removing it.

Her heart leaped as she recognized Angus's will. He had been frugal. For a foreman his estate had been considerable. The bulk of it went to Myrth while a sister inherited some furniture. The only other person cited was a Nicholas Trindell who would receive the bust of Caesar.

Odd that the murder weapon held sentimental value for Angus. Hearing footsteps approaching, Henrietta hastily replaced the will. Mrs. Baker eyed the floor with gratitude.

"What a nice job you've done. Did you find your glove?"

"I found what I needed, thank you." Henrietta glanced about, turning serious. "I find it odd that this incident happened so suddenly. Did the McLarens behave differently in recent days?"

"She was as charming as ever. He could be short-tempered." Mrs. Baker paused. "Now that you mention it, Mr. McLaren was that way more often than not lately. Seemed angry about something."

"Someone was angry enough to kill him. The police view his wife as a suspect. We can only surmise about her guilt."

The landlady blinked. "I'd surmise she didn't do it."

It was evident Myrth had won over Mrs. Baker as well. "Then you were fond of her despite the painting."

Her face softened. "She was a lovely lady, kind and refined. I hope nothing bad's come of her." She lowered her voice as she reached for the doorknob. "Just don't tell Mr. Baker I said so."

Henrietta arrived at King's Chapel later than usual Sunday morning, having decided at the last minute to bring Celia. While her family would react to Celia's presence with thin-lipped disapproval, Henrietta welcomed her companionship. The wind that whipped through the portico made her shiver, but she suspected it was warmer than the reception that awaited them indoors. As the bells chimed the quarter hour, she and Celia were preparing to go inside when they were hailed by Garrison and Edith Morse. She happily delayed entering the church to chat with friends.

"Marriage suits you both. Eight months already." Henrietta lowered her voice. "I'm glad someone has reason to be happy."

Henrietta's junior by fifteen years, Edith shared her commitment to education and allowed it to fill her days with purpose. Of Garrison's many charms Henrietta remained convinced it was his agreeable manner that had won her friend over. The only thing she could fault him for was his dislike of dogs.

He acknowledged her reference with a nod. "I was troubled to hear of Freddy's misfortune. Mr. Garrison might have been more generous, I think."

"Few newspapers are as diplomatic as the *Transcript*." The city's papers hadn't spared Freddy, assigning blame equally to him and Myrth. The *Liberator* especially made Henrietta cringe as William Lloyd Garrison faulted Freddy for allowing his lust to claim the life of a dedicated abolitionist. "I expect a chilly reception today."

Edith nodded. "There isn't always an excess of warmth in the congregation, I fear. Never mind, it will blow over soon enough."

"I just hope it won't affect our school funding." Briefly she explained the impending threat regarding Mr. Atwood. "If Cora goes through with her plan, it might ruin all we've worked for."

"I can't blame her. I'd be surprised if she hadn't heard the rumors. I see you haven't." Edith smiled as Henrietta stiffened. "Mr. Atwood will surely put social good above personal matters. At any rate Garrison had always found Mr. McLaren uncooperative."

The news startled Henrietta. "I didn't realize you'd met."

"Ask in the right places, and you'll hear how unreasonable he could be," Garrison warned. "As headmaster at the School of Industry, I had the job of placing rehabilitated boys at Ingraham Piano. McLaren consistently refused to give them a chance."

The revelation filled Henrietta with new hope. "I'd also like to learn more about his wife. I know she was a model once."

Garrison smiled, amused. "You've heard of the Godiva portrait. I know of it only by reputation. Once I'm officially a club member, I'll have the pleasure of viewing it firsthand."

If only he knew the painting had been purchased and by whom. She hoped Freddy didn't invite him into his study anytime soon. She studied the Morses as they chatted with Celia, surprised how deeply she envied Edith her happiness. Such joy was more than one dared hope for late in life. Edith spoke up abruptly.

"Here comes Bertha Ingraham without her husband as usual."

They watched as Sam Ingraham's wife and sons approached the church with stiff steps. Henrietta sat across from them but avoided Bertha, whose presence was an old injury that had never fully healed. Studying her critically, Henrietta decided that Bertha, with her fading hair and dour face, had aged gracelessly. Henrietta had always wondered what Sam saw in her.

"I'd love to know her opinion of McLaren. Her sons are ready to go to war at the first order." Edith paused. "She says she'll go to any length to prevent it. She's so defiant about going to war it will be anticlimactic for her if we don't."

"I doubt she'll be disappointed," Henrietta said dryly.

She returned Bertha's curt nod as her sons waited, allowing her to enter first. While her fears were justified, Henrietta wondered what steps she would take to keep them from enlisting.

The Morses moved away discreetly as Freddy's family arrived. Cora swept past Henrietta, head high, her face pinched as if she were prepared for a trying morning. Her daughters followed, their expressions as grim as if they were going to a hanging. Taking her cue from their silence, Celia slipped wordlessly to one side.

While no accusations were made, Henrietta observed, some acquaintances verbalized their support in a distant manner. Most ignored Freddy out of sympathy or embarrassment. She decided to save the details of her call on Mrs. Baker for later. A visit to the barber explained Freddy's reluctance to remove his hat until the last minute. Knowing how fastidious he was, she said nothing.

"It's the most damnable thing," he muttered. "These side-whiskers look as if they were trimmed with a hatchet. I can't get a decent cigarette anywhere on Beacon Hill. I'm not even at ease with my own servants. It's as if I've betrayed them. They want me to get the gallows." Looking old and vulnerable, he shook his head as if to cast off suspicion. "Women don't simply disappear. Someone must have seen Myrth. I intend to post handbills about town inquiring for her. This has been such a shock. I've no idea what to expect next."

"I hope not murder, though I can't blame Cora for thinking of it. Still, you've nothing to fear if you're innocent."

Henrietta tried to ignore the glare he gave her. "For God's sake, Etta, do you think for a second I'm not?"

"I'm merely trying to view you as others do. As for Myrth, the less said the better."

Freddy entered the sanctuary as if the portico of King's Chapel had been laid on his shoulders. She knew he needed no reminder of his familial responsibilities. Cora might have been more circumspect about the school, but Henrietta didn't blame her for issuing him an ultimatum. Cora had few options. Divorce would leave her ostracized and rob their daughters of any chance of a respectable marriage.

Although Celia's presence created a strain in the Newell pew box, Henrietta knew it would keep emotions at bay. Through lowered eyes she observed Freddy and Cora. While their shoulders touched, the tension in their faces betrayed a distance physical closeness could not bridge. Felicity's eyes were downcast in shame, her expression melancholy. As misnamed as her sister, Prudence let her gaze circle the congregation as if seeking forgiveness. With hours of misery looming, Henrietta decided Cora's gossiping wasn't as unbearable as she thought. The matter of whether Mrs. Everton owned too many ball gowns and the frivolous behavior of the Richmond daughters were topics more welcome than silence.

Her gaze scanned the sanctuary and fixed on Bertha Ingraham. Seated between her sons, Bertha wore the look of the prematurely widowed. Sam's seat had been vacant often of late, making Henrietta wonder if financial concerns or something else was affecting his attendance.

She faced forward as the organ strains rose, announcing Reverend Belcher's arrival in the pulpit. An attentive stillness enveloped the congregation as the minister requested prayers for the McLarens. Henrietta's neck prickled as stares fastened on her family. Freddy had broken the gentlemen's code of discretion by admitting his fondness for the foreman's wife. How many would avoid the family because of scandal? The indignity of having to endure public scrutiny would be murder in itself to Corinthia.

Fully convinced Myrth killed Angus, Henrietta wondered if she had invited Freddy to her apartment to bolster her resolve to confront her husband. Why risk his anger by displaying the portrait if she weren't on the verge of leaving? Myrth must have believed Freddy would abandon his wife for her, something Henrietta knew he would never do. He had too much to lose.

She listened with heightened interest as Reverend Belcher reminded the congregation to attend the upcoming antislavery lecture at Faneuil Hall regardless of their political beliefs. His unbiased discretion as he appealed to the divided hearts of the congregation impressed her. Abolitionism inflamed so many that most ministers were reluctant to condone or discourage it.

Bertha's head was bowed now but not in prayer. Sam's wife had listened attentively as the minister acknowledged McLaren's contribution. Now, to the astonishment of all, she rose to her feet, her iron gray dress rustling disapproval. Reverend Belcher paused, creating a silence that spread through the sanctuary as all faces turned toward the source of the disruption. The coughing stopped. No one so much as whispered.

With a look so disdainful words were unnecessary, Bertha took up her hat and veil and exited her pew box. With measured steps she walked to the back of the church and out the door, her head so high Henrietta was surprised she didn't strike it against the balcony on her way out. A silent scathing criticism lingered in her wake.

In the unexpected stillness Henrietta sensed a threat, heavy and immediate. She turned forward again with slow, awkward movements. Surely most faces would not reflect approval of Bertha's sentiments. No one had followed her example.

The faces that stared back were as cold and unyielding as the granite walls that surrounded them. Henrietta felt no forgiveness. Instead she felt blame, as harsh and dangerous as murder itself.

For the first time she understood how Freddy must feel. She felt alone and numb and very far from friends.

Four

Reviewing her correspondence several days later, Henrietta recognized Corinthia's penmanship in the pile with foreboding. Her apprehension vanished once she saw it was a dinner invitation. She was encouraged to see her sister-in-law carrying on with ordinary functions. If only her father would do the same and refuse to deny the school its funding as Cora wished.

She set the note aside. Myrth's flowers lay in a little cluster on her blotter, withered but still streaked with pinkish-purple. They were too old to have been from Freddy, she noted with relief. She found it hard to imagine poison in the delicate petals.

Rhythmic squeaking from a cage in the window drew her attention as her squirrel Flash turned his exercise wheel. The activity provided a diversion from watching the tree from which he'd fallen when she rescued him. He reminded her that the botanist who could identify the slender, trumpet-shaped flower was a pen stroke away. Who else beside Henry David Thoreau could determine the potency of the plant as a possible poison? Taking up pen and paper, she began to write:

Louisburg Square, Boston
September 12, 1860
Dear Mr. Thoreau,

I enjoyed seeing you in Concord while visiting Mr. Emerson's family. My invitation to you to speak at my literary salon some Saturday when you're in town remains open.

Today I write on another matter. I've enclosed what remains of an enchanting flower, hoping you can assign it a name. Though it was pressed long ago, the traces of pink might help identify it. I believe I saw it in a display of poisonous plants but hope I am mistaken.

Perhaps I shall host you at a dinner one day with a centerpiece of these delightful flowers.

Your humble servant and faithful reader,
Henrietta Newell Cobb

Horsecars and wagons competed for space with private carriages on Tremont Street the next morning. Beset with trepidation about her mission, Henrietta waited, letting them continue toward their destination. At least she was accompanied by Celia, who smiled encouragingly as if reading her thoughts.

"This visit might help you learn something of significance about Angus McLaren."

"Our reception is about as predictable as Freddy's future," Henrietta warned. "With him blinded by infatuation it's apparently up to me to clear our names."

King's Chapel lay before them as they crossed the street between a brewer's dray and a delivery van. Beyond the intersection of Tremont and School Henrietta saw the sign she sought: Ingraham and Sons Piano Manufactory. The tallest building on the block, it featured a mansard roof, the five-story facade graced with cast iron window lintels and floral scrollwork. McLaren had worked here, yet her reluctance to encounter Sam Ingraham made her hesitate.

She opened the front door to the tentative sounds of a piano slightly out of tune somewhere above. Celia paused to admire the first-floor warerooms that showcased the firm's instruments. The facility didn't use child labor, but since Sam permitted it on his other properties, Henrietta felt he should help the reformed adolescents from Garrison Morse's School of Industry.

Checking her annoyance as she approached a clerk, she asked if they might speak with McLaren's supervisor. He instructed a boy standing nearby to fetch Mr. Fordham.

"Terrible tragedy," the clerk mourned. "Mr. McLaren will be missed, and who knows what's become of his poor wife?"

What indeed, Henrietta wondered. She was glad he hadn't summoned Sam. Discovering who painted the Godiva portrait wasn't worth the awkward encounter that would ensue. Mr. Fordham arrived moments later, a compelling presence at a rugged six feet with abundant side-whiskers, his sleeves rolled up to the elbows beneath a work apron. The strength in his face was marred by a muscle that flicked angrily in his jaw and a revolting snort that soon made itself apparent. He nodded in greeting.

"Thomas Fordham, fourth floor supervisor," he said. "Don't know if I can help you or not. Depends what you're looking for."

"I'm investigating the murder of Mr. McLaren," Henrietta hedged. That much was true. Fordham's tone hinted he recognized the name from the newspaper, reinforcing her notion that caution was advisable. "I'm seeking information about his position here."

"I can show you where McLaren worked." He assessed their formal attire. "I don't suppose a little dust will hurt."

As Henrietta thanked him Fordham led them to a second floor room in which four rows of pianos stretched the length of the building. From this startling perspective she observed the neat lines of square pianos, each so compact it might be mistaken for a sideboard.

"McLaren managed the finishing room where the varnishing and tuning is done." Fordham indicated the instruments with a sweep of his hand. "Might I interest you in one? It's a Boston favorite."

Henrietta recognized the pianos being tuned from the homes of friends. Her drawing room contained the grand piano her mother had mastered and she had attempted with less than happy results.

"I'm afraid charity work doesn't allow me time to play," she admitted. "I'll be frank, Mr. Fordham. I hope to clear my brother of a connection to Mr. McLaren's death. Had he worked here long?"

A hardness in Fordham's manner told her he was a man to be reckoned with. "Fifteen years. He had sound judgment and mechanical talent. Earned the men's respect the hard way. He knew what oppression meant as many here do."

"Do you hire many Scots?"

"Most are German or Swedish. We use Irish for heavy labor."

And cheap, she thought. Drowning in poverty and discrimination, most Irish were openly hostile to antislavery. While they eked out a bleak existence, the wealthy with whom they crossed paths supported blacks who lived in comfortable, even affluent circumstances by comparison. The same Bostonians turned a blind eye to Irish immigrants. She wondered if an employee had feared

Angus's influence on working class voters. Had his controversial stand filled the workplace with such dissension someone resorted to murder?

Too farfetched, she decided. She doubted any Irishman had killed Angus. Political disagreements jeopardized desperately needed jobs. The Irish were so easily replaced their opinion didn't count.

"Had he fired anyone with a grudge against him?" she asked.

"Not that I recall. We hire reliable men, not slackers."

"Fifteen years is a long time. Did he ever hire runaway slaves before the Fugitive Slave Act was passed ten years ago?"

Fordham tested a piano key. "He hired some recently, but the boss let them go. He doesn't lure slaves from their owners."

Ownership of an individual was only one matter on which Henrietta and Sam disagreed. The South undoubtedly accounted for a sizable portion of business Sam and his brother wouldn't want to lose. Fordham's tone did not invite questions, an unfortunate turn since she had many. Smiling, Celia approached the row of pianos.

"May I try?" she inquired politely.

At his nod Celia seated herself at the bench, plaid skirts rustling. Her fingers skimmed the keyboard, the rippling melody enfolding the room through her skilled understanding as Henrietta listened in awe. Celia was full of surprises.

"Chopin, I believe," Henrietta ventured.

"One of his early nocturnes." Celia smiled at Fordham. "It's a fine instrument. No wonder it's a household favorite."

Fordham relented a bit. "It's among Boston's best."

"How did the Irish feel about McLaren's abolitionist views?" Henrietta resumed.

"The men are here to work, not to be converted." His tone was noncommittal as he snorted. "And most aren't Irish."

From his aloofness she couldn't tell if Fordham regretted the loss of Angus or resented her presence for another reason. She was about to continue when footsteps and whispers echoed in the stairwell as two women neared the second floor. One carried a spool of piano wire, the other several chipped ivory keys.

"Mary, Annie, come here a moment," Fordham instructed. "You, too, Harry and Joe."

At his command the women jumped to attention. Two of the men who had been polishing piano cases joined them.

"Mrs. Cobb's inquiring about Mr. McLaren. You worked for him for several years, correct?"

"There was no better boss," one woman said softly. "He was right kind. He expected hard work but appreciated it."

"He was the sort who'd go to war if it came to that," a man added. "Regular fellow, tough but above board."

"Is there any word of his lovely wife?" the woman asked.

Other workers began to congregate. From their hopeful faces it was clear they cared more for Myrth than for her husband.

"I'm afraid the police are investigating Mrs. McLaren as a suspect in her husband's murder," Henrietta admitted.

"If she done it he must've deserved it," one woman spoke up. "She was a saint, a real lady. Remembered us every Christmas."

Many concurred, some wiping away tears. As Fordham dismissed them Henrietta wished she could tell them Myrth was alive. She found their reaction unexpected and frustrating. Rather than suggesting a motive for murder, her visit had established the workers' fondness for the couple.

"Had you met Mrs. McLaren?" Henrietta asked Fordham.

"Many times. Upper class, like yourself. I hope she's safe."

Startled by the comparison, she held her tongue. After hearing their opinions she felt awkward asking the next question.

"Do you know anyone who might have intended her harm?"

"No one wished her anything but well, Mrs. Cobb." Fordham removed a pair of work gloves from his pocket. "It won't be easy turning out sixty pianos a week without Angus. He'll be hard to replace."

"How did the bosses feel about him hiring runaway slaves?"

He adjusted his gloves with unnecessary concentration, the muscle in his cheek twitching. "Better once they left. Hope I've been of help."

"What is it you supervise, Mr. Fordham?" Celia asked as the interview neared its end.

"Manage the reed and bellows room--and fill in here now." He smiled tersely. "Good luck, ladies. I hope you prove your brother is innocent, if indeed he is. I'll see you out."

If the foremen had equal standing, Henrietta mused, *Angus's death might mean a promotion for Fordham.* As he reached for the door it was opened from the other side, bringing her face to face with the man she might have married.

"Etta," Sam said easily. "What a pleasant surprise."

Relieved of his burden, Fordham withdrew in silence. Samuel Endicott Ingraham had aged well, his hair still thick, his smile charmingly crooked, with a confidence born of success. The blue eyes retained a readiness for conversation that filled her with trepidation. Her attraction to Sam had diminished after she married William but had never disappeared. He was one of few people to whom speaking required more courage than she possessed. She collected herself and introduced Celia, who discreetly turned her attention to the pianos.

"I'm sure you've heard of Freddy's misfortune." She kept her tone casual as if debating the merits of the latest melodrama.

"Even when one tries not to listen it's impossible not to hear." Sam smiled. "Is it McLaren that brings you here today?"

Whether he was genuinely interested or concerned merely for the sake of business, she seized the chance to learn more. "His wife, actually."

An emotion she couldn't interpret struggled on his face before vanishing. "His wife was charming. I can't see her as a suspect. I hope she's safe. Fetching name, Myrth."

"That barely begins to describe her. I've seen the portrait. It's fortunate her hair is long as it's her only covering."

A grin she hadn't seen in decades animated Sam's face. "I saw the Godiva in the club's game room. Discovering its identity was more of a shock than Angus's death."

Henrietta was glad he didn't know Freddy was the new owner. "What was your opinion of McLaren?"

"He was a valued worker. His death's a great loss."

Remembering Bertha's abrupt exit from church, she raised the next issue delicately. "I imagine his politics offended many."

"I run a factory, not a lyceum. Tom Fordham knew him better than I."

"He was very helpful. Thank you."

In reality neither Fordham nor Sam had been especially forthcoming. Abolitionism was such a source of tension her attempts to discuss it in depth had failed, and she was hesitant to pursue it. As Sam turned to address Celia it was clear the interview had ended.

He escorted them to the exit, the echo of their heels breaking the silence. Henrietta sensed Angus had been more of a threat to his employers than to his workers. If Southern states represented much of the firm's profits, his efforts to aid slaves might be reason enough for murder.

Wishing them a pleasant afternoon, Sam left them in the foyer. Celia waited while Henrietta fumbled with her gloves. She had tried to remain objective, yet in those few minutes with Sam half her life had vanished. The charity work and committees she chaired had slipped away, replaced by the emotions of the twenty-year-old who visited Sam daily in his waterfront studio, the smell of cod permeating her clothes so her disapproving mother always knew.

For a second she wished she were in the studio again. It was a fragile longing that passed quickly. Had Sam not abandoned his artwork, gone into business, and married Bertha while Henrietta was in Europe, their lives might have turned out differently. Her regret had never vanished completely, nor had an embarrassing trace of spite toward her mother. The real blame lay within herself, she knew. The resulting pain was permanent.

The silver lining had been Alec and Neville. Nothing in her life rivaled Alec's memory or Neville's company.

Realizing how long she'd been silent, she forced a smile as they returned to Tremont Street's cold wind.

"I'd say it was a productive visit," she ventured, "in that it raised new questions. McLaren's workers seem devoted to him. Of course, they didn't see the private side."

She tried to ignore Fordham's disconcerting lack of confidence in her brother's innocence. His opinion hardly mattered. What mattered more was Sam Ingraham's opinion.

The time had come, Henrietta decided, to update Freddy on her findings. Knowing he delivered an anatomy lecture on Friday morning, she planned to call on him after attending her two scheduled committee meetings.

Despite her ambivalence it was difficult to dislike Myrth altogether. Not every wife remembered her husband's staff at Christmas, especially a well-born woman who had lost her place in society. Myrth had forgotten neither her manners nor her consideration for the less fortunate. Henrietta could not cast aspersions when the blame was as much Freddy's.

She found Freddy in his office at the medical school and persuaded him to accompany her. In the privacy of her carriage she told him of her visits to Mrs. Baker's and Ingraham Piano.

"I also plan to ask Willie McCurdy what he knows," she said. "He might be the child Mrs. Baker saw before the murder."

"Possibly." Freddy sounded doubtful. His optimism failed more each time she saw him, his listless visage aging his features.

At least the sun that warmed the interior of the barouche made for a pleasant ride. She instructed her driver to take them westward on Beacon Street to view the progress of the Back Bay expansion, designed to relieve the stench from the city's tidal marsh. Each day throngs of people scavenged earth deposited by railway cars to fill in the bay. Rubbish had been mixed with the more expensive gravel, leaving trifles for the desperate to sift through. Only after numerous visits to the homes of the poor did Henrietta understand the delight she saw now in the toothless smile of an elderly woman who limped from the pile, hugging a broken chair and dirty basket.

She turned to Freddy. "We should visit the place where you met Myrth. Someone might remember her."

"We met at Harkness's Livery," he admitted. "We didn't plan on a second engagement but met by chance a week later. She told me she was once an actress. Afterward we often met at galleries for conversation. I came to care for her deeply."

She saw the situation in perspective: her brother, for years beleaguered by a wife who complained often and praised rarely, his life changed by a chance meeting with an engaging woman who showed genuine interest in his scientific pursuits. To Myrth, he must have seemed intellectual and wise, while to him her attentions were enormously flattering.

Directing her driver toward Charles Street, she realized Freddy hadn't spoken in a while. She had never seen him so vulnerable, his faith at an ebb, his future uncertain. She chose her words carefully, hoping he would accept her help.

"It isn't as black as it seems," she said kindly. "Prominent men, including Oliver Wendell Holmes, believe in your innocence. Your family will stand by you. What alternative does Cora have?"

Freddy's spirits seemed restored by that small but credible hope. Gazing away from the river, he withdrew a photograph from his pocket with a look of satisfaction. "At least I still have this."

From her seat Henrietta could tell the *carte-de-visite* was of Myrth. The sepia-toned likeness revealed a coquettish aspect as she sat in a wicker chair, a fan shielding her face. The expressive eyes and high cheekbones visible over the folds of the fan hinted at a smile. The photograph was playful and coy in contrast to the severe tintype in her flat. It managed to appear suggestive though she was fully clothed from eye to toe.

"What is your father-in-law's opinion?" Henrietta asked curiously.

"Atwood is far more understanding than his daughter." Freddy returned the photograph to his pocket. "Rather decent of him."

"He has great respect for you."

"While he's willing to forgive my romantic indiscretions, he isn't yet convinced I didn't kill McLaren. I had cause."

"Many did," Henrietta reminded him. "It's up to us to find out who they are in case the police fail to do so."

"If only I'd met Myrth twenty-five years ago before McLaren entered her life," he said with sudden spite. "I can't say I'm sorry he's dead."

"You were quite taken with Cora twenty-five years ago, as Myrth was with Angus. I'd be careful making statements like that when you're the prime suspect. And McLaren wasn't the only obstacle," she said gently. "There isn't likely to be another murder to free you from matrimony. There are no happy prospects here. You hope for what can never be."

As their eyes locked she detected a profound regret. It was quickly replaced by a determination that warned her not to hope for more insight. He had already been unexpectedly forthcoming.

"Perhaps it no longer matters," he said slowly. "For all we know Myrth might have perished even as we search."

Henrietta reflected on the consequences of a possible suicide. Without Myrth the police would have only Freddy's word. "I doubt we've seen the last of her."

"Ultimately no one is going to care." Freddy laughed bitterly. "At present Myrth isn't a member of the upper class."

"Nor will she ever be again. A woman's tarnished reputation is impossible to repair." She looked at him meaningfully. "No one knows that better than Cora."

"Cora's as predictable as daybreak. Difficult as she is, it's a comfort in some ways. I know what to expect from her."

"Her emotions might not be as predictable as her behavior," Henrietta warned. "She's hiding her hurt and might not want to share her feelings. Anger is an easy defense."

He was silent for a moment. "Thank you, Etta, for your faith in me."

Their eyes met again, this time in awkward understanding.

"Our course of action makes sense," she resumed. "If we retrace Myrth's steps, maybe we can determine what happened."

Freddy's attention was drawn abruptly toward the Charles River. He let out an oath. Henrietta rapped on the ceiling for her driver to stop, motioning for him to pull to one side.

Through the mist she saw a long rowboat not far from Hoppin's Wharf, its mast furled, carrying half a dozen men along the river's surface. A pair of dragmen worked a weighted net that trailed alongside the boat while three men paddled slowly.

Henrietta felt uneasy suddenly. "Isn't that a patrol boat?"

"It's a Whitehall rowing boat. It looks like half the Harbor Police are on board. They're dragging the river."

For a moment she could not speak. "Searching for a body?"

"That's precisely what they're doing," he said in slow, measured tones. "They're using a trawl to look for her. They must suspect she's dead."

Henrietta watched in horrified fascination as the boat drifted on the river, its pace slow as the men waited for the tug on the net that would end the search. There was something ghastly about the process, its hideous portent incongruous with the autumn sun sparkling on the water.

"They might simply be taking precautions," she said to ease his fears. "The abolitionists are pressuring the police. They need to take public action to prove they're searching for a solution."

They watched, tensing each time the dragmen hauled in a catch. They brought up a broken wagon wheel, rusted plow, rotted wharf pilings, and the hull of a rowboat. A half-hour later they had found nothing more than the refuse of earlier ages.

Freddy turned away. "Perhaps there's no need for handbills after all. It might already be too late."

Five

With speculation about Myrth dominating her thoughts Henrietta found it impossible to focus on her upcoming literary salon. She couldn't send out invitations until she chose a topic, yet the subject she considered most worthy of discussion was Freddy's situation.

As she perused her shelves for inspiration her glance fell on a bust of Shakespeare. Statues were common enough decorations. With a piano in the McLaren parlor, why hadn't Myrth chosen Beethoven instead of Caesar? She hoped to learn something of value later this week when she and Freddy visited the livery where he met Myrth. *There must be countless examples of behavior far more outrageous in history and literature,* she reflected. Selecting a volume, she took it to the receiving room where she decided to feed her pets first.

Happy for company, Captain Kidd flapped his wings as she filled his dish with greens. She glanced into the pan Mrs. Biddle had left in its usual spot. Gingerly she lifted the dead mouse by its tail and dropped it into the alligator's tank. It was the best use she'd found for mice who met their demise in traps. The mouse was followed by small fish bought from a vendor happy to unload the tiny catch.

The task left her with mixed emotions, but the Caiman had to eat. While he shunned the company of humans, she enjoyed his unique beauty—the broad flat snout, webbed feet, and bony four-foot spine. She watched as he ate, mysterious and misunderstood. Deadly only when goaded, ready to swallow anything. Who was more like the alligator, Angus or Myrth?

She could have avoided Freddy's problems had she gone abroad with Neville. His latest letter from Florence contained news of literary exchanges with the poet Robert Browning and his wife. Henrietta remembered her days in Europe with longing. If not for England she wouldn't have met William, and Alexander and Neville would never have been born. Dear Alec, dead these thirteen years. She turned her concentration to the book.

An hour later, her perspective refreshed by reading a portion of *Decline and Fall of the Roman Empire*, she decided Myrth had the seductive powers of Claudius's niece. Agrippina charmed the emperor into marriage after he vowed never to remarry, then murdered him with poisoned mushrooms. Whoever killed McLaren had chosen a more certain method of murder than mushrooms.

Henrietta envisioned Myrth in a toga, lifting the bust of Caesar above her head. Distrust was common among emperors. Had Angus distrusted his wife, knowing of her liaison with Freddy, or did he suspect nothing until the end? Many females among the Roman nobility had hoards of lovers. She hoped Freddy wasn't one of a multitude.

She knew less about Angus. Was he to be pitied like the emperor Marcus, devoted to someone who mocked his virtue, or was he a cruel tyrant like Commodus? Henrietta doubted he had ever indulged Myrth's indiscretions. If he knew about Freddy and threatened Myrth, murder might have been an act of self-defense.

Even if Claudius and Agrippina had lived before the empire began its decline, Henrietta decided there was plenty here for an animated salon discussion. Elated, she closed the volume as Celia Chase appeared in the doorway.

"Something for the salon?" Noting the title, Celia looked intrigued. "What made you select this?"

"Have some tea. The salon won't include the rise of Christianity or the fall of Constantinople. Instead it will concentrate on murderous relationships, a most appropriate theme these days."

Celia appeared impressed. "Mrs. Biddle said Mr. Emerson has read essays here, and gentlemen as reclusive as Mr. Longfellow and Mr. Whittier have come. Who will you invite this time?"

Henrietta considered. "The question isn't who to invite but how to entice guests to speculate on possible suspects besides my brother."

"I've been following the account in the *Transcript*. I hope you don't mind. I know how painful it must be." The earnestness in her eyes convinced Henrietta she truly did.

"My brother wants to believe Myrth is innocent. I'd like to think she murdered Angus because she cares for Freddy," Henrietta admitted. "Her guilt might end their relationship."

"Maybe he's protecting her," Celia suggested.

"We don't know if she's being pursued. I don't want to see him sacrifice his reputation for a murderess. I'm sure others wanted Angus dead, maybe someone at the piano firm." Thomas Fordham flashed through her mind. "I hope you'll accompany me when I visit Willie's boss, Mr.

Penrose, to see if he was at work the day McLaren was murdered."

"Why not talk with Willie at the evening school?"

"He might not attend. He hasn't responded to my invitation, but I'm not giving up. Perhaps we could hold class here. Home schooling failed, but this might be just the site we need." Henrietta was happy with her inspiration until she remembered the porcelain figurines on the étagère that might tempt a young thief. "We'll set up a room upstairs. There's less clutter, and it's more suited for study."

"It sounds ideal," Celia agreed, "as does your salon topic. I hope it sheds light on the situation."

"I've tried to find women in literature who killed their husbands," Henrietta admitted, "but I found them mostly in history."

"That's because history holds more truth than fiction." A dark humor lit Celia's features. "Catherine the Great went to war against her husband. I've no doubt many women wish they could."

"Most would lose." Henrietta returned Celia's smile conspiratorially. Her frankness was encouraging. Whatever misfortune she had endured had not robbed her of integrity.

Celia's next question surprised her. "Is there no one you could call on to help your brother? You mentioned an old friend who was once familiar with local artists."

Henrietta tensed at her quandary. While Celia had met Sam at the piano firm, Henrietta had told her little of their connection, preferring to wait until they could exchange histories openly. Celia had her own past to protect.

Henrietta suspected she would have the discretion not to press the matter.

"That was forty years ago. Having a salon topic will suffice for now." She smiled. "I'm content to have the Romans take our guests' minds off this Godiva woman."

"I'm sure they will. I was thinking, it's been three months since you took me in. By now a shelter bed must be available."

The delicate remark made Henrietta evasive. "It often takes time to find space. I can ask Eleanor Wilkes at my salon."

She fell silent, knowing she had never intended to ask. She considered Celia an indispensable part of the household and hoped she shared the attachment. Henrietta suspected she would find it difficult adjusting to shelter life.

"It's unfortunate, I suppose," Celia went on without awkwardness, "that I must leave in the midst of this."

"It's no imposition for you to stay," Henrietta assured her. "Please don't think you've been a burden. You're a stimulating conversationalist and an agreeable companion. You've been invaluable in helping me understand Myrth. Even having met her, it's difficult to judge which portrait is more accurate, the flirtatious or the serious. Most models don't marry abolitionists. She's a woman of contradictions."

Henrietta hoped before the shelter issue arose again Celia would find teaching school too ideal to leave. Her upper class sensibilities were tempered with another side of life she had witnessed firsthand. Celia reached for her tea before stating an observation that convinced Henrietta her trust wasn't misplaced.

"Both Agrippina and Lady Godiva were women of noble birth like Mrs. McLaren. They have a lot in common, don't they?"

The pungent smells of beef and pork from vendors' stalls greeted Henrietta when she arrived with her dog at Faneuil Hall Tuesday night. She mounted the stairs to the second floor, her progress slowed by the crowds who came to hear the antislavery address. She was glad she had left Celia working on lessons.

Spotting Freddy, Fanny, and Fan's husband near the front, she carried Fudge past the rustling skirts of the women and the coattails of the men. She squeezed in between Fan and Freddy, who rose to give her a seat on the bench.

"Packed to the rafters," Freddy observed, "and the sides aren't evenly represented."

Henrietta noted the preponderance of woolen workshirts and felt caps over broadcloth frock coats and stovepipe hats. The imbalance didn't bode well for abolitionists who hadn't won the support of the working class. Factory girls and grandmothers sat beside bankers and ministers, concern in all faces.

The arrival of her minister at the rostrum created a solemnity in the assembly hall. *Its white columns and woodwork were suited as much to a sanctuary,* Henrietta thought, *as a meeting hall.* Reverend Belcher invoked mercy and wisdom from the audience before inviting Cora's father to the dais amid jeers. Walking with the strength of his convictions despite his age, Williston Brayman Atwood took his place at the podium. The booing resumed as he reminded them of their patriotic responsibility.

"Who'll provide for us if our sons go to war?" a man shouted.

Henrietta wanted to warn them commitment came with a cost. Alec believed the country must avoid division to remain strong. The war divided mother and son when he died of yellow fever at Jalapa. Did anyone consider these costs? A voice cut into her reverie.

"Who'll operate our factories?" a gruff voice demanded.

"All those youngsters you hire." Laughter followed the retort as heads turned toward the gallery.

Jasper Penrose watched from above, his gnarled hands hanging over the railing, his craggy face fierce. Although his coarse speech marked him as lower class, he managed a factory of size for the Ingrahams, who had hired children at his request. *If not for Penrose,* Henrietta thought, *lower class children wouldn't need a night school.*

A boy in a faded jacket and breeches pushed forward, blue eyes bright beneath an oversized cap, conspicuous even in the throng. She was startled to see Willie McCurdy here when he had work tomorrow.

"You won't keep me from going to war even if I do work for you," Willie called defiantly to Penrose. "I'm ready to fight."

There were chuckles and hearty murmurs while a female voice announced that such an attitude was precisely what was wrong with society. A more sinister thought crossed Henrietta's mind. She suspected Willie had witnessed something the day Angus was killed. It occurred to her whatever he saw might put him in danger. On the street he was an easy target.

Her reflection was cut short by a remark from the rear.

"I suppose our iron foundries shall be forced to survive by making rifles and cannons," a familiar voice retorted.

Sam Ingraham's sarcasm brought laughter from some. His expression hardened by determination, he stood beside his brother Albert, his countenance just as unyielding. Bertha sat with them, her face warped by bitterness.

"I don't intend to let business suffer over principles," Sam declared. "Neither Northern industry nor Southern heritage should be sacrificed to satisfy a few fanatics."

The contemptuous voices of other merchants rose in unison. Sam's attitude told Henrietta his relationship with McLaren had been adversarial. Political differences must have contributed to animosity at the firm. Perhaps Bertha considered Angus such an influence on voters she wanted his activities stopped. Henrietta pushed the idea from her mind. Her dislike of Bertha wasn't enough to blame her for McLaren's death. For that she must look elsewhere.

Her concentration was broken as the slap of spit hit the floor. Her look of indignation had no effect on the rakish young man leaning against the pilaster beneath the balcony. The brogue that followed his bitter laugh was as Irish as his penetrating blue eyes and black hair.

"You Yankees worry about slaves you never met, but you don't give a damn about the Irish who step onto your docks so weak they can hardly stand," he accused. "I'd like to switch places with them. At least I'd have a roof over my head."

"Tell him, Sweeney," someone shouted. "They're treated better'n we are."

As others concurred with bitter grumbling, Fudge responded with a low growl. Henrietta silenced him with a tap on the head. Despite the Irishman's vulgarity there was truth in his words. He must find the hypocrisy as overwhelming as she did.

Atwood recaptured the audience's attention quickly. In a grisly display he held up a withered ear cut from a captured slave.

"This," he announced, "was mailed to me with a note. The Southerner promises the same to any Yankee who crosses the Mason-Dixon line. This is why we mustn't lose support from our ranks."

"P'r'aps the men oughtn't share wives," someone called amid whispers and giggles. "Losing an ear's nothing compared to losing a life."

"Let it pass," Henrietta whispered as Freddy stiffened beside her. "You're surrounded by supporters."

But she did not feel supported by the crowd any more than Freddy. Applause mixed with derisive shouts as Atwood reminded them of the hanging of John Brown, the revolutionary whose raids ended with his capture.

"Brown deserved his fate," one argued.

"None of us deserves war." Atwood paused. "A great challenge lies before us. If we are to be tested we'll show them we're fit for the task."

Murmurs of agreement spread throughout the hall.

"History will justify our course against those who've committed a monstrous wrong," Atwood proclaimed. "Even now there are traitors among us who would sell their fellow men for a price."

A thunderous ovation silenced the dissenters. As Atwood encouraged the throng to consider the slaves' plight Freddy's tension eased. Henrietta focused on the audience. Many here felt as Bertha did. She studied the faces, realizing McLaren's killer might be present. With a community so divided she couldn't imagine his interest in abolition was a coincidence. She heard Sweeney's gritty voice.

"We're better off without Brown and McLaren," he muttered. "The Lord was looking out for the Irish when he took those two."

"I told you that when McLaren fired you," his friend said.

The Irish lacked sympathy for slaves because they competed for jobs, yet Sweeney's viciousness frightened Henrietta. He spoke with the resentment that gnawed at the soul until it destroyed perspective. It was a cold, calculated remark with a hostility born of deprivation. The remark a murderer might make.

She absorbed the discontent in the voices around her — the men's disapproval, the women's alarm. Like Freddy's, it was a situation with no simple solution. She was aware of Fanny's husband thrusting a newspaper toward Freddy. He opened it, scanning the pages. Before she could read the small headlines, he had shoved the *Advertiser* out of reach.

"What does it say?" she demanded, concerned by the urgency in his manner. "Must I purchase a copy to find out?"

"It's the editorial." Freddy's tone was frosty, directed not at her but at an invisible enemy. "It recommends I should hang by the neck until dead if found guilty. How much support will it take to prevent that?"

A fine mist fell as Henrietta walked home with Freddy and the Brownings. Many who left Faneuil Hall with them were too distracted to care about the hot corn sold by the young girls who called after them. As they left Dock Square in subdued silence, Garrison Morse fell in step with them.

"Not much doubt of us going to war, is there?" he said.

"I'm amazed that ear didn't sway them," Fan said feelingly. "Still, there are many who support you, Freddy."

Freddy shook his head. "Most want me to get the same fate or worse."

"Surely it isn't that grim," Garrison remonstrated. "Anyone want to join me in a brandy and listen to public analysis of tonight's assembly?"

"I think not tonight," Henrietta said. "Congratulations on your Compass Club induction. You get to wear the coveted ring."

He smiled. "And I'm barely used to wearing a wedding ring. I'm in hallowed company now."

"Now you'll have a voice politically," Henrietta said. "That's especially important after tonight."

Garrison left them at Tremont Row. They parted from Freddy at Pemberton Square moments later and continued in silence. Henrietta had preferred to let political conversation dominate. Now Fanny raised the concern on everyone's mind.

"Abolitionist support in Massachusetts is growing as far away as the Berkshires," she murmured. "Some who think Freddy's guilty might resent him."

"More people resent Angus McLaren," Henrietta said. "Just because the Compass Club chooses to direct the morality of our city doesn't mean the nation will follow."

"We'll know in six weeks," noted Fan's husband, a retired admiral.

At Spruce Street Henrietta bid the Brownings goodnight. Having identified a handful of suspects in McLaren's murder hadn't put her at ease. In a city where abolitionism was so divisive, they were surrounded by individuals whose anger might spur them to murder.

As she rounded the bend toward Chestnut a sudden rustling made her jump. She gasped as cold fingers closed around her arm.

"Mrs. Cobb," said a feminine voice in the darkness, "I believe I asked you to keep my visit confidential."

Six

Henrietta recognized the features in the pale gaslight. Myrth McLaren's face peered at her from within the dark cloak.

Fear engulfed Henrietta. At this hour all nearby windows were dark. Only a dim light filtered up the side road from Beacon Street. Henrietta tried to shake off her fear.

"I didn't expect to see you," she said.

"I'm glad I caught you," Myrth said coolly. "We have matters to discuss."

Their encounter suggested Myrth had been watching her movements. Henrietta felt too vulnerable to speak.

"It's imperative you keep my presence a secret," Myrth intoned. "I told you I was the murderer's target."

"And I said you must inform the police." Henrietta couldn't hide her desperation. "It's the only way to clear Freddy's name. He fears you're dead."

Wait until I tell him, she thought, then stopped herself. Perhaps that was what Myrth wanted. She did not trust this woman who remained in shadow.

Myrth's expression softened at his name, the light of evening erasing any trace of age from her features, her high cheekbones and enormous eyes magnified by the light's distortion.

"Did you tell him how much I care?"

"I did. You don't deserve his affection." Henrietta's courage returned with her indignation.

"If you knew the truth you'd refrain from making such remarks," Myrth returned.

"Four months isn't enough time to truly know anyone."

"It was enough for us. We're all at risk, Mrs. Cobb. It would be wise for you to stop inquiring after me, or you'll be forced to suffer the consequences."

On that note she vanished, as insubstantial as the light that enveloped them. Henrietta's relief at being alone was followed by resentment at Freddy's fondness for this manipulative woman.

Stepping into the light, she looked down Spruce Street. Myrth might have been a shadow. The encounter left Henrietta fearful of the animosity that had replaced Myrth's charm. People issued threats when they were desperate, and no pair was more desperate than Freddy and Myrth.

She and Celia discussed the unexpected meeting the next day before reviewing lesson plans for the school.

"It happened so close to home." Henrietta frowned. "Maybe I imagined it, but I can't help feeling Myrth intended me harm."

"She must have followed you."

"Which means she's watching my movements. I haven't mentioned her to many people." A silence more revealing than words filled the room. "I'll need to be careful in whom I confide."

Henrietta was shaken by the deception. She'd made very few inquiries—Mrs. Baker, Fordham, Sam, and

Freddy. Who had betrayed her? Freddy believed Myrth was dead, and she wanted to be able to trust Sam. She didn't know Mrs. Baker or Fordham well enough to judge their motives.

They were interrupted when Mrs. Biddle announced Willie McCurdy's unexpected arrival in the kitchen.

"Just when I thought he was avoiding me. Show him in, and bring the usual refreshments." Henrietta turned to Celia as the housekeeper departed. "The trouble with Willie is that he enjoys learning about mischief more than anything. He'll be your most difficult charge, but if we're lucky, he might know something of value to our investigation."

Willie McCurdy was cursing under his breath as Henrietta and Celia entered the receiving room. The boy stood before the parrot on its perch, stroking its azure and yellow feathers.

He turned and faced them on their arrival. "I'm trying to teach Captain Kidd new words, but he don't pay much attention."

Much like Willie himself. Henrietta repressed a smile. His street language could be no worse an influence on the parrot than that of the sailor who had owned him previously.

"He's so loud he often makes conversation impossible." She took a seat, gesturing to Celia to do likewise. "Sit down, Willie. Can I interest you in tea and lemon cakes?"

"Thank you, ma'am."

Willie's manners never failed to appear at the mention of food. He hopped onto the sofa, swinging his legs, assessing Celia. It wouldn't surprise Henrietta if food prompted his call.

"This is Mrs. Chase, our new schoolteacher," she said. "She hopes you'll come to class. Willie, there's something I must ask you. Were you near Sentry Hill Place two weeks ago?"

"I work days."

"Try to remember. I need to know who visited the house at the end of the lane around three. There was a gentleman carrying a walking stick--" Freddy was never without it-- "and a lady who might have been running."

"Couldn't see nothing if I wasn't there."

Willie was so evasive she doubted he would answer. His indifference to hearing the details was suspicious. Willie was enthralled by scandal. Lying came as naturally as breathing to him. If Willie missed work Monday, she reasoned, he had received money from another source. A call on Mr. Penrose would settle the question.

"It's a matter of life and death," she entreated. "You could hold the key to solving a murder. Someone saw a boy resembling you. And please stop swinging your legs in such an undignified manner."

He watched her blankly. "Must be a kid who looked like me."

No one looked like Willie with his dingy, crooked cap, familiar clothing, and boastful walk that couldn't contain his exuberance, but it was the stubbornness of the mouth and eyes that set him apart. She wondered why he had called today when he should be at work. He glanced up, his eyes shadowed beneath the battered brim.

"That might've been the week I collected for Grammy Sullivan," he admitted. "Ma wants the doc to listen to her cough."

In poor neighborhoods collections were sometimes taken to pay for a doctor, though visits often came too late. Despite her senility Willie's grandmother was generally healthy. Henrietta reached for the bell pull.

"You're still bringing home money?"

"Lots," he bragged. "Mr. Penrose is very fair."

"He hasn't been in the past."

Celia had observed Willie silently but attentively.

"A smart boy knows the value of an education," she said. "Even those who work need schooling."

"I'll try to attend, ma'am."

"I can picture you teaching others someday," Celia continued. "I understand you were rather outspoken at Faneuil Hall."

He regarded her suspiciously as the housekeeper brought a light meal. Watching him snatch a lemon cake, Henrietta asked Mrs. Biddle to bring her reticule.

"There's lots I could teach 'em," Willie agreed, his mouth full.

"I daresay you could teach us a great deal, Willie."

Henrietta caught Celia's eye and smiled. Willie was studying the oyster soup too intently to respond. As his legs hammered the carved rosewood of the sofa, she took some bills from her reticule, laying them by his plate.

"I hope the doctor can see your grandmother soon," she said, "and I hope to see you in class."

"Yes, ma'am." Willie looked up from his plate. "Can I visit your squirrel?"

Henrietta knew in time she would break down his silence. For now, bribing him with food and pet visits would ensure his return.

Returning to the spot where she encountered Myrth, Henrietta relived the experience that afternoon as she told Freddy of their meeting and watched his face flood with relief.

She tugged gently on Fudge's leash as they rounded the corner. "To think I felt safe walking alone."

"No reason not to. She's thinking of your welfare. She trusts you, remember."

"As she said, we're all at risk, and it's because of her," she reminded him. "She knows I could go to the police."

"We were all overwrought last night. That's Harkness's stable on the right." They were approaching a cobblestone courtyard along Branch Street's gentle descent. "I suspect he helped other blacks on their way north."

Henrietta wasn't surprised. Boston had been a haven for fugitive slaves who sought shelter through the Underground Railroad. The stable yard doors were open beneath a bronze horse head. Within the gates a groom brushed a chestnut mare, its coat gleaming in the sun.

"What was Myrth doing here when you met her?" she asked, watching a groom trim a horse's fetlocks.

"Her husband had no use for horses. Couldn't afford them anyway," he added disparagingly. "She liked to ride."

"As her portrait testifies." He was too deep in thought to acknowledge her teasing. "Let's start here where she has a connection."

He consulted his pocket watch. "All well and good, Etta, but I've work to do while I still have a position."

"Then talk with the stable hands while I find Mr. Harkness."

Henrietta approached a groom removing mud from the hooves of a bay to ask directions to the office. Harkness ran a clean stable, for the odors of urine and disease noticeable in neglected stalls were absent here.

She found the owner upstairs, concluding arrangements with a traveler wanting to board a pair of horses. The liveryman was a middle-aged black man, eyes alert through his spectacles. A worn but well-made jacket covered a spotless white shirt and trousers, his outfit bespeaking both businessman and laborer. His self-confidence made it clear he was not to be trifled with.

When they were alone Henrietta introduced herself. He stared at the dog by her side but said nothing in the disquieting silence.

"I hope to locate a woman who frequents your stable." She gave the name hesitantly. Maybe Myrth called only on occasion.

"Not a customer of mine," Harkness retorted.

"She was here with a gentleman. A striking woman with chestnut hair. I'm confident you would remember her."

He continued to stack ledgers on a table. "Can't say I do. Why's it so urgent you find her?"

"My brother is wrongly suspected in a slaying," she admitted. "She has evidence that could help him."

"If she has evidence, wouldn't she contact you?"

Her gaze fastened on several equestrian drawings on the wall behind his desk. One pencil sketch featured a woman with flowing hair leading a horse by the reins, her face averted. Henrietta had no doubt it was a preliminary sketch for the Godiva painting. A second drawing also appeared to be a rough illustration of Myrth.

"That's Mrs. McLaren in the pictures behind you," she said. "Can you tell me you've never seen that woman?"

Harkness didn't turn to look. "Those were hung before my time."

Henrietta's frustration mounted. "I was under the impression you had a long and impressive reputation here."

"That I do, Mrs. Cobb, but my reputation ain't built on fancy artwork."

"I'm quite serious, Mr. Harkness. My brother needs help."

"Your brother's no customer of mine either," he said tersely, wiping bits of hay from his hands, "and it don't sound from the papers like he's a friend to black men. It might come as a surprise to you, Mrs. Cobb, but I can read, and I do."

Her cheeks burned with humiliation at having her social consciousness underestimated. His reluctance to cooperate convinced her he was lying about his acquaintance with Myrth, but why? If there were any chance she had killed an abolitionist, he would surely criticize her openly.

"I don't know why you think I can find some fool girl I don't even know," he snapped. "I haven't time to answer questions about folk I've never met. If you'll excuse me, Mrs. Cobb, I've got to check on the ventilation shaft."

Henrietta heard the door close firmly behind her as she walked downstairs. Harkness was not about to inconvenience himself for someone who might have murdered an abolitionist. While he was reluctant to discuss Myrth, he spoke disdainfully of her when he did. His reaction made it impossible to tell if he liked her or even knew her.

She returned to the stable yard where the sun hung low over the building's upper stories, ivy invading its brick facade. Freddy must still be in the stables. She passed through the rough-hewn gates, following a walkway between stalls where the odor of horses mixed with the sweet smell of soap.

At the end of the stalls a man loitered, talking idly with a groom who prepared to soap down a horse. With a start she recognized him as the Irishman who had expressed strong opinions at Faneuil Hall last night. Inching closer so she could listen, she pretended to study the horses.

"The betting will be fast and furious," Sweeney promised. "What do you say, Abel? There's no better game in Boston."

"Off with you," snapped the groom. "I've no money to gamble. My wife'd tan my hide."

The groom tethered the horse and retreated into the yard, leaving Henrietta face to face with Sweeney. She felt a surge of excitement facing the man McLaren fired from Ingraham Piano. The Irishman was tall, his penetrating gaze making her uneasy. She picked up Fudge as he growled, waiting until Sweeney left before approaching the groom who returned with a bucket.

"Do you know that man?" she asked after a moment.

Abel reached for a brush. "Pat Sweeney's a ne'er-do-well who hangs 'round the docks when he ain't hanging 'round here. Tries to sell ropes and lanterns on the wharves, anything he can find or steal, but the captains won't have none of it." He lathered the horse with suds. "Sweeney's good for nothin' but jail, which is where you usually find him."

"It isn't surprising Ingraham Piano fired him then."

"I'm surprised they ever hired him," Abel said bluntly. "He's nothing but a petty thief."

Freddy returned to Henrietta's side, looking perplexed.

"No one's seen Myrth for weeks," he frowned. "They claim she was afraid of horses. Why the devil would she come here?"

"At least they remember her. Do you have any idea why Mr. Harkness would lie about knowing her?"

Freddy shrugged. "Maybe he didn't see us together. I've only a vague recollection of conversing with him."

"You probably had eyes only for Myrth."

Another conversation drew their attention, where a bent elderly woman clung to the arm of a handsome, much younger man. Wearing a frayed cap that must be forty years old, she held the leash of a small scruffy dog who bore a remarkable similarity to the woman herself. While her face was withered and her hands lined, her eyes were clear. She paused by the stairs leading to Harkness's office.

"To think I'm not safe in my own home," she said, indignant. "Why would anyone break in here? The police told me not to let strangers in, as if I'm that foolish."

"It's good advice, Aunt Hannah. As long as you follow it, I'll know I needn't worry."

Henrietta found his features startlingly familiar and was puzzled by the vague warmth she felt upon seeing a stranger. Henrietta watched until he was out of sight before she turned resignedly to Freddy.

"We've done all we can for now. Even if Myrth is guilty of murder, there's nothing here to help us prove it."

"That poor woman isn't guilty." The old woman's sharp tone startled Henrietta. "You've no right to assume such a thing. I don't know why the papers are so unkind."

Henrietta set her dog down, curious to hear more. She had no time to react as Fudge startled her by lunging at the mongrel. Regaining her balance, she snatched up the pug before he could reach the little dog who wagged her tail without concern.

"I'm sorry," she apologized. "He meant no harm."

"Come here, Gyp." The woman picked up and cradled her dog, her eyes on Fudge. "Male. Best to keep them apart."

"It's true, we can't believe all we see in print," Henrietta said, hoping to entreat her to linger. "I merely wanted to help."

"That kind of talk won't help," the woman said bluntly.

"See here, I know full well Mrs. McLaren isn't guilty," Freddy defended her. "She's as upright a woman as any I know."

The woman gave him a dark look. "Who might you be?"

"Frederick Pendleton Newell, anatomy professor at Harvard."

"Well, fancy that." The woman drew her dog closer. "The papers are saying dreadful things about you."

"As we agreed, much of what one reads in the papers is untrue." A thought struck Henrietta. "Do you know Mrs. McLaren?"

"Well enough to know she isn't a killer," she retorted.

"Do you know where she is?" Freddy asked quickly. "I'm anxious to find her."

"I imagine you are." She softened her tone. "I haven't seen her since her husband died, poor soul."

Her outspokenness vanished so abruptly Henrietta feared Freddy had spoken too eagerly. Maybe Myrth had mentioned him to this woman. If so, did she know of their relationship? Despite her frail build she had a solid Boston reserve as hard to penetrate as the brick walls of the livery above which she resided.

Henrietta smiled and introduced herself. "We appreciate your concern when others are so judgmental. If Myrth didn't kill her husband, who do you think did, Mrs. — ?"

"It's Burns. Could be anybody, couldn't it? Even the nicest people have enemies." Her pale eyes assessed Henrietta coolly.

"Mrs. McLaren couldn't have had many," Freddy countered.

Mrs. Burns proceeded to give the answer Henrietta had come to expect. "Heavens, no. She's a lady in every respect."

"The police see her as a suspect," Freddy countered. "I fear it's more likely she's met with foul play."

"I'm sure she hasn't, Professor."

Hannah Burns's confidence puzzled Henrietta. It was unlikely she could remain so calm in the face of gossip and uncertainty.

"What a shame she has to remain in hiding and can't visit the horses she loves." Trying a new strategy, Henrietta noted her look of surprise. "She met my brother here at the stable."

"Myrth doesn't ride. She fears horses," Hannah said. "She's so petite, you see. She came here to visit me. I live upstairs."

"Please ask her to contact me at once if she should call on you again," Freddy implored. "I care very much about her welfare. Let her know I'll do everything within my power to help her."

"You're very kind, Professor, but I doubt she'll return. I'll pass on your concern if she does." She sighed. "To think we're both widowed now. Come along, Gyp."

After remarking on the weather they parted on pleasant terms. Mrs. Burns's serenity was so incongruous with Freddy's anxiety that Henrietta's suspicions deepened. She was certain the woman believed Freddy's sincerity but knew more than she would admit.

Bewilderment clouded Freddy's face as they continued down Branch Street. "Why the devil didn't Myrth say she had a friend here?"

"Maybe Myrth was ashamed to be seen with her. Myrth was proud of being upper class, something Mrs. Burns isn't."

Henrietta didn't know what to make of this woman of seventy whose friend was a suspect in her husband's murder. A widow whose circumstances were reduced by poverty, Hannah was so evasive after learning Freddy's identity Henrietta wasn't sure she was as unaware of Myrth's whereabouts as she claimed.

"Myrth might have been visiting the day you met," Henrietta speculated. "We know she wasn't visiting the horses. We should stay in touch with Mrs. Burns in case she calls again."

Myrth's friend might prove a valuable acquaintance. It was more than coincidence that early drawings of Myrth hung upstairs. She was convinced Harkness had lied.

The question was why.

With her salon three days away, Henrietta was still debating how to organize the discussion when a letter from Mr. Thoreau arrived in the mail the following morning:

Concord, Massachusetts
September 15, 1860

My dear Mrs. Cobb,
Regarding your inquiry concerning the withered weed enclosed in your letter, the plant is Datura stramonium, commonly called jimsonweed or Devil's trumpet. It is not a city plant but wild, common to the Berkshires and other rural environs where it should remain. I advise against using such flora in a display.

Not only does the plant have an unpleasant odor, but it is highly poisonous. The fruit appears in autumn and contains black seeds which are deadly. The poison is also in the roots, wilted leaves being of particular danger. Despite the fragrant flower that blooms at night, the plant is fatal.

No more than a handful of letters I receive are worth the postage, but your case is an exception. No sane person would choose to keep jimsonweed except out of ignorance. The very idea forces me to question the individual's motives.

As to addressing your drawing room companions, my fondness for my own bean-field, combined with my aversion to large gatherings, leaves me reluctant to commit to a reading. In my cabin at Walden I had but three chairs: one for solitude, two for friendship, and three for society. I can only imagine the quantity of chairs in your salon represents a mob.

As to the practice of caging squirrels, it is not what I envisioned when I spoke of the unity of man and nature. While their maneuvers offer much entertainment, squirrels are no more intended to be kept than mankind was meant to be imprisoned in the cage society politely refers to as Respectability.

I've taken the liberty of destroying this singularly vulgar plant. I suggest you do the same.

Yours sincerely,
Henry David Thoreau

Henrietta read the letter twice, her emotions wavering between exasperation and triumph. Surely even Mr. Thoreau must condone the rescue of a helpless creature. As for her invitation, she shouldn't have expected more from someone who found solitude more appealing than company.

Thoreau had questioned Myrth's motives. Henrietta remembered Cora's reference to Myrth as a Devil's strumpet. How ironic that Myrth kept flowers with a similar nickname, and poisonous ones at that.

She had discovered yet another link between Agrippina and Myrth. Both were familiar with poisons.

The news had arrived in time for her salon discussion. Her day was already a success. Mr. Thoreau had made a monumental contribution whether he chose to appear or not.

A steady mist fell in Pemberton Square at twilight, giving a shine to burnished leaves that heralded the coming of autumn. Henrietta's barouche entered the crescent, rounding the enclosed green until it stopped at her brother's home. Anticipating a difficult evening, she had left Celia at home with Fudge.

As she mounted the steps she hoped Cora's father hadn't been invited. Along with a very welcome letter from Neville, the day's mail had brought the note she dreaded in which Mr. Atwood threatened to postpone school funding until Freddy's guilt was resolved. It strengthened her determination to clear his name.

Henrietta was shown into the drawing room where Freddy's and Fanny's families had gathered. She had barely taken her seat before deciding the mood inside was more unpleasant than out. The strain on the faces of Felicity and Prudence told her the hostility in the home hadn't lessened with time. At the dinner table Fan's children surrounded their cousins protectively before Cora could suggest another arrangement.

Fanny circumvented the tension with her usual cheer.

"I hear, Cora, you're working with the Music Committee for the prince's visit," she said over the first course of cold oysters. "Imagine the Prince of Wales visiting Boston! It's still uncertain who shall have the honor of the first dance. Our mother, rest her soul, was among the most elegant dancers of her day. If she were alive he would surely ask her to waltz."

While Fan was old enough when their mother died to remember her grace and accomplishments, it always surprised Henrietta that Fan's recollections were so much rosier than her own.

"Mother will help choose selections for the recital," Felicity supplied to fill in the silence. "We must consult our wardrobe. I doubt we own anything grand enough for the ball."

"We'll visit the seamstress. Yesterday's *Transcript* said fifteen hundred tickets will be sold." Prudence turned to their mother anxiously. "We will be allowed to go, won't we, Mother?"

"The newspaper, Prudence, is not fit reading for young ladies." Cora stabbed at the haddock. "As for the ball, we shall have to see how we are received in public by then. Few invitations come our way these days. It seems we are on trial at every tea table."

Prudence's face fell. Their mother concentrated on her dinner with obvious displeasure.

"Surely it isn't as bad as that," Fanny protested.

"Not quite." Freddy looked up, his tone terse. "The only reason I've not yet been hanged in the Suffolk County Jail courtyard is that Professor Holmes intervened on my behalf."

"With Holmes at the helm the sailing will be smooth," said Admiral Browning confidently. "It's not your fault tensions are on the rise. McLaren was popular. It's up to the police to ease the situation."

His attempts to relieve the tension didn't ease Henrietta's. She watched Freddy struggle to keep his composure at the mention of his romantic rival.

"They might do more to fight crime," Fan tactfully shifted the topic. "The Allingtons were robbed of their family heirlooms last night. I hope they catch the man who did it."

Henrietta had read in the papers of recent thefts on Beacon Hill. No one knew for certain a man had committed the robberies. Briefly she entertained the notion that Myrth had grown so desperate she had been reduced to thieving.

"Maybe the mystery of the thefts can provide a topic for one of your literary salons, Aunt Etta," Prudence said.

"Your aunt frequently chooses controversial topics," Cora reproved, "but we face enough controversy at present. Staying home might protect you from more."

Prudence blanched at the idea of one of her social outlets being taken away.

"Offensive remarks have been made about that vile painting," said Cora. "They say that woman has taken Frederick for a ride, made him frisky as a colt. Yesterday's *Morning Post* cartoon made him out to be a slave to passion. Not that I read such rubbish," she added for Prudence's benefit. "It was told to me."

Freddy finally turned on her. "I've heard the remarks. Does it ease your grief to embarrass our family by repeating them?"

Any argument on Corinthia's part was interrupted by the arrival of the maid, her face a ghastly white.

"What is it, Annie?" Freddy snapped.

"Lieutenant Tripp is here, sir," she faltered. "He wishes to see you at once."

Seven

"In the middle of dinner?" Corinthia said in dismay.

"I'll see the lieutenant now." Freddy looked from one to the other. "We'll face him as a family."

While the younger generation remained at the dinner table, their elders departed for the receiving room. Lieutenant Tripp bowed deferentially to the family as they filed in. He watched them take their seats in turn while Freddy made introductions. Henrietta's hope that Myrth's name wouldn't arise was short-lived.

"Is there word on Mrs. McLaren's whereabouts?" Freddy began.

Tripp shook his head. "I didn't expect any, Professor."

"Then why have you come?" Freddy demanded.

"We've compared the footprint in the McLarens' parlor with the pattern from your shoemaker. They're a close match, sir."

"Since we spoke inside the home, that isn't surprising."

"There must be thousands of men in this city with the same shoe size," Browning defended him. "If you measured mine right now I daresay you'd find another match."

"I merely wish to make Professor Newell aware he remains the most likely suspect," Tripp said quietly.

Henrietta felt the room grow smaller. In the sickening stillness she feared it was only a matter of time before the police discovered Myrth's visit to her.

"Often it's during investigations that we discover the full significance of events, Admiral." Tripp turned to Freddy. "Have you met with any recent accidents, Professor?"

"Are you accusing me of having struggled with the man? For heaven's sake, take a closer look." Freddy extended his hands for inspection. "There's not a cut on them."

Lieutenant Tripp examined Freddy's hands in a decidedly thorough fashion, Henrietta thought, turning over each in turn.

"What of this cut?" the lieutenant asked mildly.

"That's a scrape from a broken flask. I'd forgotten about it. You can see there's a scab."

Henrietta tried to defuse Freddy's escalating irritability. "If my brother killed Mr. McLaren, Lieutenant, wouldn't he also have killed Mrs. Baker to remain anonymous? He had time."

"If you visit my laboratory you'll find it full of sharp instruments," Freddy snapped. "I'd like to know how you plan to locate Mrs. McLaren."

"We're searching for her, but we aren't convinced she's in danger," said Tripp. "We consider her a suspect like you. You both had means, motive, and opportunity."

"That's rubbish. You've no right to make false accusations." Freddy's fists were clenched. "I'll have your job."

"Until we can question Mrs. McLaren, I'm afraid a shadow of doubt will remain on you both." Tripp was polite but firm. "Removing her portrait displayed poor judgment, Professor, not to mention little regard for your welfare."

An act, Henrietta reflected, *that showed how Myrth's influence had altered his judgment.* She hoped Freddy recognized the lieutenant was offering him a chance to turn Myrth in and save himself. Freddy had no chance to react before Cora's voice rang out distinctly.

"The portrait is no longer on the premises, Lieutenant," she said evenly.

The look of terrible triumph in her eyes was returned by fear and suspicion in her husband's.

"What are you saying?" he demanded. "What have you done?"

"I ordered the painting destroyed. I found it yesterday while you were at the medical school. It had no place in your study. While you seem to be bent on trampling the roots of my family tree, Frederick, I have no intention of letting you humiliate our family further."

Henrietta was stunned. Cora turned back to Lieutenant Tripp.

"I'm willing to help you close this case, Lieutenant, even if my husband is not." She glared at Freddy. "Instead of exposing her for the murderess she is, he's posted handbills on every lamp post in this city offering two thousand dollars for her return. Perhaps that will help us find the real murderer."

Fanny and Admiral Browning remained speechless. Feeling like a conspirator defending him, Henrietta said nothing. While she was unable to excuse Freddy's misguided actions, she knew he was innocent, but she had to find Myrth to prove it.

Freddy stared at Cora wordlessly before he marched from the room. The slamming of the front door reverberated through the house until the only sound was the hissing of the gas jets. Henrietta felt a pang of dread remembering Freddy kept the bill of sale for the painting at home. If Edith Morse had heard rumors of infidelity, maybe Cora had as well. She might have found the receipt and, in a moment of revenge, destroyed a valuable clue.

If Cora had discovered the deception and decided to confront Myrth, could she have reached the McLaren home before Freddy? If Angus were forced to defend Myrth, the scratch marks on his face could be Corinthia's.

The idea was horrible, unthinkable. Was it possible Cora had sided with the police against her husband to protect herself? Feeling sick, Henrietta regarded her sister-in-law with unwelcome suspicion. It was the last thing she wanted to believe and one of the first she must consider.

The air had turned considerably colder as Henrietta and Celia made their way through the city to Jasper Penrose's factory the following afternoon. By the time they reached Washington Street, the scent of hot chestnuts and soup on trays around vendors' necks warmed the air.

"I worry about Willie," Henrietta admitted. "Not only does he work with heavy equipment, but I suspect he knows more than he's saying about the murder."

Celia lifted her cloak so the hem wouldn't catch on leaves that had collected in the gutter as they crossed the street. "Do you think he's in danger?"

"If he could identify someone at the scene, he might be, especially if that person recognizes him." They watched a fishmonger's cart pass dangerously close to a coal wagon before they continued toward the waterfront. "Calling on Mr. Penrose will remind him there are those watching out for the working children."

"Willie's fortunate to have you as a guardian angel."

"Since he's less than angelic he needs a watchful eye. The newspapers criticize companies that hire children after a serious accident. It's only a matter of time until the law forbids it."

"I would see children leaving work when I lived on the street," Celia admitted. "It made me fear for my--"

She stopped abruptly as if the reference were too personal. They walked in silence, trying to ignore the street urchins staring at them, their clothing marking them as outsiders.

The ringing of metal resounded across cobblestone as they approached India Street. In contrast to Ingraham Piano with its elaborate facade and music echoing throughout, the first thing one noticed on entering Penrose's factory was its musty smell, insect-infested walls, and the noise that emanated from all quarters. Henrietta found it difficult to believe the same family that owned the Tremont Street factory owned this.

A worker directed them to Mr. Penrose. As they entered the casting room with its oppressive heat, sparks from the furnace spattered in their direction, threatening to catch on the aged wooden beams. Henrietta was relieved to see only adult men working in the area.

Hands on hips, Mr. Penrose surveyed a group of men soldering one of the cast iron piano frames the factory produced. Sensing her presence before she announced herself, he turned, wiping his brow with his sleeve. Under a mop of gray hair his keen eyes missed nothing.

"Mrs. Cobb, is it?" he asked, his voice hard and unrefined. "What would you be wanting today? Hope you haven't come to tell me how to run my business like you did on your last visit."

"I've come to speak with Willie McCurdy if I may." Henrietta smiled thinly. "I'd also like to ask about his work habits."

While Henrietta addressed Jasper Penrose Celia took in their surroundings.

"He hasn't shown up in two weeks," Penrose retorted. "That answer your question? If he expects to get paid, he'd better get back before I replace him."

"His grandmother's been ailing," Henrietta explained. "His mother usually sends a note when he's sick."

"He didn't seem sick at the Faneuil Hall rally. Even when he's here his mind's somewhere else. Best thing I could do is let him go."

"I hope you'll warn him beforehand so he can find other work," she reproved. "His family depends on his support."

"Dunno who'd take someone so preoccupied," he said bluntly. "Plays with wax in his pockets. Always threatening to go off to war. He'd be doing me a favor."

"I suspect he knows something about a murder."

"Wouldn't surprise me. That boy's headed for trouble, mark my words." His eyes narrowed with sudden comprehension. "The fellow with your name that's in the news, Newell. He a relative?"

"I'm helping clear his name of any wrongdoing," she said curtly. Penrose was the last person with whom she wished to discuss the matter, yet it was an ideal opportunity to inquire about Angus. "Mr. McLaren's death is a blow to abolitionists. Perhaps you didn't know him since he worked on Tremont Street."

"Angus worked hard, but work ain't the place for politics." He spoke with contempt. "Gives workers airs that are above 'em. They're probably glad they don't have to hear more of his talk."

She was ready to grasp any possibility. "It sounds as if the Ingrahams wanted to be rid of him, that he might have been a threat. Wouldn't that attitude raise police suspicions?"

Penrose laughed. "I doubt they'd look hard. Sammy and Al—you didn't hear me say that—are the chief's cronies. If anything was amiss they'd look the other way."

The Ingrahams' adversarial relationship with Angus saddened Henrietta but gave her hope. If others disapproved of his political leanings, surely someone had motive to kill.

"What did Fordham think of it?"

"Not much," Penrose said bluntly. "They didn't get along when it came to McLaren's wife. Ask anyone at Tremont Street."

She was glad she had asked Penrose. "Did Fordham dislike her?"

"He liked her too much, if you get my point." She found the lewdness in his tone enlightening, if repulsive. "There was bad blood there. Angus ruined Tom's marriage. Did it out of spite. The slaves Angus hired illegally were let go when Tom ratted him out. Neither was too nice, from the sound of it, always competing with each other. There're those happy to see Angus done in."

Were it not for the heat from the furnace, Henrietta would have shivered at Penrose's words. Could Fordham have been Myrth's lover? It gave him a motive to kill.

Penrose's description exposed Angus's negative side, reinforcing Garrison's impression.

"So your relative's in trouble." Penrose reached for a hammer. "Folks are too worried about war to care. I dunno what's worse, slaves who gripe when they've got food and housing, or Irish who complain even when they get paid to work."

Despite his aversion to the Irish he would hire them as long as they exchanged brawn for low wages, especially since the factory was built in an Irish neighborhood. Clearly, Penrose considered Willie's absence and McLaren's death minor compared to the prospect of losing a half-hour's work. A glance at Celia indicated she felt the same.

"Rather than fighting wars men ought to be fighting for better laws," Henrietta retorted. "People of consequence will not tolerate slavery, nor will they stand for children working."

"I don't see that they care all that much," Penrose shrugged, "when it's them who owns the factories."

"It's allowed in places like this where children are paid paltry wages to do men's work. How can we expect them to learn after a ten-hour day? They're too weary to think."

"Here they learn a trade." Penrose slammed the hammer on his worktable. It was clear the visit was at an end. "I don't own this factory. I just hire who I can with the money they give me. Take your concern back to Tremont Street."

As he escorted Henrietta and Celia to the door, they noticed the furtive glances of foundry workers who quickly resumed their chores.

"The Ingrahams must be pleased Mr. Penrose is able to hire children for so little money," Celia said once they were outside.

"I wonder what he thinks of the money the firm earns while he's relegated to this filthy foundry," Henrietta fumed.

While unpleasant, the visit had redirected her suspicions about McLaren's murder. The brash Irishman Sweeney had motive, but Fordham had begun to appear a more likely killer. Another call on Sam might be worthwhile.

"Penrose might not like the Irish," Henrietta said grimly, "but at least here there are no signs saying 'No Irish Need Apply.' And though I dislike him immensely, I'm afraid I can't pin Angus's murder on him, not when so many others have genuine cause."

The guests began to arrive for Henrietta's literary salon before one o'clock on Saturday and were shown upstairs to the drawing room. As they mingled congenially her confidence was bolstered by each new arrival. Those who came had chosen to ignore the scandal. She watched with satisfaction as the chairs filled with notable scholars and friends. Her guests had names of distinction and obscurity in equal proportion.

All shared a loyalty to her. There was much to be said, she decided, for the sound judgment that grew out of long acquaintance.

She watched familiar faces animated in conversation. Fanny chatted with the Morses, Edith radiant with optimism for the night school while Garrison listened intently. Celia conversed with Henrietta's friend Lavinia

Brattleby, unmarried and gaunt and filled with sincerity, and her brother Edgar, a playwright. His heavy spectacles and temperamental tufts of hair giving him an owlish appearance, Edgar extended to all an invitation to attend the opening night of his first play in two weeks.

The only surprise was that the guest Eleanor Wilkes had asked to bring was Bertha Ingraham. Henrietta knew Bertha disapproved of literary discussion and wondered if she came merely to see how Henrietta coped with scandal.

"I'm delighted you could join us, Bertha," she said. "I had no idea you possessed an interest in the classics."

"Literature is the foundation of a solid education," Bertha replied. "I try to be selective in my choice of readings."

Implying Henrietta might not be. After giving Bertha a warm introduction, Henrietta seated her beside Eleanor. Noting her nieces' absence with regret, Henrietta was grateful most guests had returned from vacationing on the beaches of Maine or, closer to home, Nahant or Naushon and were prepared to resume life as usual. She began the discussion promptly at one.

"Now that summer is over I'm pleased to welcome you back," she said. "I've planned a new season of salon topics I hope will inspire and intrigue you. Today our task is to compare two memorable figures from a work we've known since childhood. Our salon will focus on Edward Gibbon's *Decline and Fall of the Roman Empire,* and particularly on Marcus, the virtuous father, and Commodus, a son so evil his favorite concubine was compelled to arrange his murder."

In time, she hoped, the discussion would wind around to the possibility of a wife killing her husband in present-day Boston.

"I'm afraid these struggles are more common than we like to think," Admiral Browning said in opening. "Literature's full of ungrateful and wayward children. Who understood that better than King Arthur? One can only imagine being burdened with a son like Mordred."

"Commodus couldn't trust his favorite concubine," Henrietta noted, "and that's a sad state of affairs indeed."

"We consider women weaker than men," Garrison said thoughtfully, "but they're just as likely to kill if not more so. They're far more subtle. I'd wager it happens more than we know."

"Precisely the point." Henrietta appreciated Garrison's dependability, though his words made her picture Cora confronting Freddy in anger. Her fury suggested she could be capable of murder.

"Agrippina murdered Claudius so her son Nero could ascend to the throne," Bertha spoke up, "but Mrs. McLaren had no son."

It was the direction Henrietta had anticipated. She wasn't surprised Bertha had raised the idea of a mother's attachment to her son when her own emotions were similar to Agrippina's.

Edith bypassed the topic altogether. "Forgive me if I speak out of turn, but there's a parallel in our own circle. Mrs. McLaren disappeared right after the murder. There must be a motive, but we can't ask her since the motive vanished with her. We all read the newspapers." Edith shot Bertha a cool, quick glance. "I don't believe she's dead. I believe she's in hiding."

Garrison raised an eyebrow. "I call it damned suspicious when a woman doesn't appear at her husband's funeral."

"What about the abolitionists' enemies?" Edgar suggested, adjusting his spectacles. "There's no shortage of suspects. More people in Boston wanted McLaren dead than alive."

"We can't always know who to trust," Browning agreed. "The Faneuil Hall rally called to mind the traitor years back who turned over fugitive slaves who'd taken refuge in Boston. Had to be fifteen years or more. We never learned his identity."

"As I recall the betrayals gradually stopped," Edith said. "What was the name of that slave catcher? Horrible man."

"Orson. Damned turncoat," Browning said shortly. "Now that the Fugitive Slave Act requires slaves be returned to their owners, the scoundrel would simply be obeying the law."

If that didn't sober her guests, Henrietta knew a discussion of Freddy's plight would. Planting the seed at her salon was the first step in proving him innocent. *The empress Agrippina,* she mused, *was like Myrth.* Both were upper class, and each had fallen from grace but retained her ambition. Not only had Myrth pursued Freddy, she had consorted with actors at one time. Agrippina's son Nero often felt he was playing a role in a Greek tragedy. No doubt Myrth felt the same.

The time had come for Henrietta to play her card. "It's clear the police can't trust Mrs. McLaren. She hasn't explained why she kept jimsonweed flowers locked in her sewing cabinet. Poisonous plants have no business lying about."

The reaction she wanted came in murmurs and gasps. She saw no need to inform them the police knew nothing of Myrth's petals.

"I said from the first she's a woman of loose morals," Bertha said indignantly, "married to someone so arrogant he'd go to war over mere ideas."

"Principles are more than ideas," Edgar retorted. "Without them every state would claim the right to rule itself in any manner it pleased."

Bertha raised her chin. "I'm well aware my opinion is in the minority in this room, but it represents the majority of Bostonians. No sensible person can condone going to war over matters that aren't our concern."

"They're our concern just as jimsonweed is." Browning looked intrigued. "Maybe Mr. McLaren wasn't the only one Mrs. McLaren intended to do away with. The marble bust was effective, but apparently she had another means of murder at her disposal."

Garrison frowned. "How do we know it's jimsonweed?"

"Mr. Thoreau examined the petals," Henrietta said.

After a flurry of exclamations the naturalist's expertise with all things wild satisfied everyone into silence. All the women, Henrietta noted, listened intently, including Bertha.

"Poison is a woman's weapon," Celia agreed. "It's simple and clean. McLaren's killer chose a more deadly method."

"I'm not willing to exclude Mrs. McLaren from consideration," Edith said. "We know how the murder was committed. We ought to question what drove her to it."

"Often it's the behavior of men," offered Lavinia Brattleby. "No matter how harmonious a marriage seems, we can't know what happens when the couple is alone."

"Deceptive appearances can thwart judgment," concurred Fanny. "How can we judge the McLarens when we don't know them?"

"Look what Thackeray did with Lady Rachel Castlewood in *Henry Esmond*," Lavinia continued. "Henry viewed her as an angel of mercy while her husband saw her as possessive and aloof. We never know whether she's a woman of virtue unfairly treated by her husband or a cold wife without goodness or sentiment."

"One might wonder the same of Mrs. McLaren," Celia added, mirroring Henrietta's thought. "We don't know her as a person."

As the salon progressed ideas were proposed and rejected, suspicions raised and dropped for lack of evidence. The hours passed without conclusion but with discussion enough to make the most prejudiced guest reconsider his opinion.

Suddenly it was time for the sandwiches and stewed oysters the staff had prepared. As they adjourned to the table Henrietta was satisfied her strategy had worked. She had made it apparent Myrth had reason to do away with her husband, even if she didn't quite believe it herself.

She couldn't deny the possibility someone other than Myrth had killed Angus. A marble bust would be difficult for a woman of average height to heave at a tall man while taking aim. If she were weakened by bruises, McLaren would have had the advantage.

With dismay Henrietta realized she had talked herself out of the very argument she'd tried to make. Her guests knew Myrth had motive for murder and even the means, but much work lay ahead in clearing Freddy's name. In a city filled with political dissension, fortunately, her list of suspects was growing.

After the guests departed Henrietta and Celia went downstairs to the receiving room to tend to her pets.

"You have an advantage," Celia reminded her. "While we were merely speculating, you've met Myrth."

"But what do I know?" Henrietta poured out some greens for her parrot. "She claimed to be the killer's target but wouldn't say who it was. Why would she protect a murderer when she's a suspect? I wish I'd followed her." New insight gave her a sense of triumph. "The reason I didn't was that I believed her. I'd rather believe she had a lover who killed Angus, but unless she's a superb actress I'm convinced at least part of her story is true."

"Are you saying you believe she loved her husband?"

"She respected him. If she was the intended victim, our list of suspects changes. I haven't found anyone who disliked her."

"Why would she risk everything by coming to you? It was daring considering she had just left the scene of a murder."

"I felt she came out of concern for Freddy, but her story was so outlandish." Recounting the incident prompted a vision she tried to push from her mind.

"She might not have said who the murderer is," Celia said, looking troubled, "because she cares about someone more than your brother."

Henrietta felt a pang of dismay. While Myrth was now a widow, Freddy remained unavailable. If Myrth loved another, Henrietta should be relieved they had no future. Was Fordham fond of her as Penrose claimed? Dissension between the two might mean Angus suspected an attachment.

She rose to stretch, passing the alligator's tank. His eyes remained stationary, but she knew they followed her every move.

Celia looked thoughtful. "Did you notice Myrth's dress?"

Henrietta paused to consider. "Blue-green, a few years out of date but still fashionable. Well made and well cared for."

"When I lived on the streets I had one dress which wore out quickly. I wonder if Myrth took a change of clothing."

"Her flat looked as if she hadn't time to take anything. Unless she's staying somewhere she'll have only one dress." An intriguing idea struck her. "She was probably visiting Mrs. Burns when Freddy first met her. Why would she be there if she's afraid of horses?"

"Maybe she's taken shelter there." Celia's face brightened. "Could Mrs. Burns be protecting her, or is it too obvious?"

"If she's still in town someone must have seen her. I could borrow Freddy's picture to show about town and inquire for her."

"She might emerge only after nightfall. The streetwalkers would remember her."

"You have your hands full preparing for your first evening class next week, but it might be useful for you to take to the streets again." Henrietta hesitated. "If you don't mind."

Celia smiled. "At least this time, I won't be alone."

Eight

Hoping to catch Freddy at home early the next morning so they could talk privately, Henrietta was disappointed to find he had left for the medical school. *How many natural elements beside jimsonweed, she wondered* as she retraced her steps past golden elms, *could be used to kill?* More than she knew.

In a city where many disagreed with Angus politically she regretted having to include Sam Ingraham among the suspects. By his own admission he wasn't about to allow business to suffer. Still, effective management skills didn't make him a murderer.

She was disappointed again when she reached Freddy's office and received no answer to her knock. She was about to try the laboratory when he opened the door, looking startled. After a moment he invited her in. He might have been happier, she thought, to see someone who cared about his welfare.

"Freddy, we need to talk," she began, stopping herself when she saw he wasn't alone.

Across from Freddy's desk Oliver Wendell Holmes rose from his chair. The writer and physician bowed graciously, his presence compelling despite his diminutive stature.

"Forgive me for interrupting, Dr. Holmes," she apologized.

"Nonsense, Mrs. Cobb, it's delightful to see you," he smiled. "Just like you, I called unexpectedly on your brother with a bit of advice I hope will help."

"We're reviewing Hutton's teachings on uniformitarianism," Freddy said.

"You see, Mrs. Cobb," Holmes said with as much enthusiasm as if he were explaining the principle to a student, "to understand a truth, at least in geological theory, one must look at processes that work together today and apply them to the past. In Hutton's thinking the present is the key to the past. I believe the reverse is also true, that the past is key to the present. Remembering this might help release Professor Newell from his fears."

From his pocket Dr. Holmes withdrew an instrument. Henrietta recognized it at once.

"You see this tape measure," he announced. "There isn't an elm on the Common that hasn't felt this tape measuring the circumference at its base. Men, alas, have their own yardsticks by which they judge. How great is one's integrity? What is the breadth of honesty?"

"Philosophical questions for which there's no measure, unfortunately," Freddy said dryly.

Holmes shook his head with a smile that charmed Henrietta. "Some things can't be measured even by firsthand witnesses. You might feel all eyes are on you today, Frederick, but only you have seen the full spectrum of events unfold while you've answered to your conscience."

Holmes startled Henrietta with an idea related to her salon.

"Undergoing moral scrutiny is like entering a horse race," he continued. "One must be as fast as, if not faster than, the others to qualify for the next race. I don't wish to see one stumble cost Frederick his career and possibly much more."

"Focusing on my research has been a great source of strength through this," Freddy admitted.

"One mustn't forget family," Holmes reminded him. "I've no doubt Mrs. Newell will maintain her faith in you. Some morning before the last leaves have fallen, Frederick, we'll take a ride up the Charles in my water-sulky and talk more when you can see the day in a whole new light." He turned to address Henrietta. "Though I'm not your brother's physician, I feel it my duty to take care of him in whatever small way I can."

Holmes turned their talk to the Prince of Wales's upcoming visit before taking his leave. Henrietta waited for the door to close before looking to Freddy for a sign of relief or pessimism.

"I'm sure Dr. Holmes would rather not be involved in such matters," she ventured, "but he has no choice."

"The medical school has survived worse." Freddy shrugged. "Holmes seems more philosophical than annoyed and refrains from casting blame."

"I hope the police are as kind if they learn Myrth called at my house. I had a letter from Mr. Thoreau confirming my theory. The flowers I found in Myrth's apartment are poisonous." Briefly, she explained. "Mr. Thoreau informed me the petals are jimsonweed and very deadly."

"You had a reaction. It isn't as if she tried to poison you," Freddy said dismissively. "Did you ever think she might have used them on herself? Perhaps she's tired of running and has done herself in."

"She won't give up so easily," Henrietta retorted. "I'm certain she has a plan and a purpose. Mr. Thoreau told me to destroy the petals, but I kept them as evidence for the police."

"Pressed flowers aren't proof, Etta. They're brittle bits of weed that the police won't take seriously," he said impatiently. "Have you any idea how ludicrous this sounds? If you continue to trespass the police will charge you with theft."

"They'll thank me for helping their investigation. Don't you find it suspicious that she saved jimsonweed?"

"If it mattered, why would she leave it behind? She confided in you."

"She confided very little. Instead of waiting for the right moment to bring proof against her husband's murderer, she probably left town." She resented his patronizing tone. "At any rate I have a new idea for finding her. I'd like to borrow your picture to see if shopkeepers have seen her."

"She won't be shopping while in hiding," he said dubiously.

"Maybe a visit to Mrs. Burns can shed light. What if Myrth's taken refuge in her apartment?"

"I imagine the police looked there."

He is as calm as Hannah Burns was in dismissing the idea that Myrth had come to harm, she thought. She was suddenly aware of a subtle scent in the room.

"You've seen her, haven't you?" she demanded. "Myrth was here. That's why you were startled to see me."

Her trust violated, Henrietta fought back her indignation. What else hadn't he told her? He'd plunged heedlessly into this relationship and was now in the clutches of a most manipulative woman.

"My only reason for not telling you was to protect her," he insisted. "She truly wants you to like her."

"Her behavior makes that difficult. She knows who the murderer is yet won't identify him. When was she here?"

"She came last week and again today to reassure me that she's fine and she misses me," he said testily. "She asked me to keep her visit confidential and let her handle matters."

"And you accuse me of being ludicrous. The police consider you the main suspect. How could you let her leave without asking what proof she has? Why won't she admit who killed Angus?"

Henrietta was as stunned as she was perplexed by Freddy's stubborn silence. Could Myrth have known the murder was about to happen? She knew Freddy was due momentarily. She had invited him.

"I believe she's using you as a scapegoat, Freddy. It's unthinkable if she truly cares for you."

"Myrth loves me. I wonder if the same can be said of Cora. She destroyed the portrait, but I still have a photograph."

Freddy resumed his seat behind his desk. Henrietta watched his fingers rest momentarily on the front of the drawer, an idea developing. As if reading her mind, he spoke up.

"I'm sorry I can't let you borrow her picture, Etta. I don't want to the police to find her. If you truly care for me," he said shortly, "you won't involve them."

Frustrated, Henrietta fell silent. Her faith in her brother had shattered. "It's clear she doesn't want you involved. What kind of proof can she have? Why wouldn't she tell you who murdered Angus if she knew? Unless it's a name you'd recognize."

The idea slipped out before she realized it. The room seemed sickeningly close as their eyes locked.

"If she says she has proof, then she does," he said, "and she'll use it at the appropriate time. What matters is she's safe."

Henrietta stared at him. "Even if she is, are we?"

Henrietta waited anxiously in her study Wednesday evening for Celia's first evening class to end. Shortly after the mantel clock chimed eight Celia appeared, her face glowing.

"Mrs. Biddle is escorting the children home," she reported. "Most had never been in an omnibus much less a private carriage."

"You were doing well when I peeked in. Did they enjoy it?"

Celia's eyes were bright. "Whether they'll do the assignment remains to be seen, but they promised to return. Some have had no education or astonishingly little. They listened when I spoke."

Henrietta's heart leaped at the news. "I knew the idea had merit. Now word will spread, and we'll draw more children until the city is forced to address their needs. How did Willie fare?"

Celia's smile faded. "That was the only disappointment."

"Predictably absent. Perhaps he goes begging door to door. He's probably made enough to buy the Turkish Orientals my brother is so fond of while Freddy's reduced to roll-your-owns." The idea amused and distressed her. "I'm glad I appointed you teacher, Celia. You've a natural way with children."

When Celia didn't reply Henrietta felt certain the suspicions she harbored privately were accurate. She hoped she hadn't caused Celia undue pain in raising the topic. Opening the subject even if she wasn't ready would clear the path for later.

"Now we can resume the search for Myrth. Someone has seen her. Who notices women? Other women. And men, of course, but they don't talk. Freddy's reluctant to part with her picture." She paused, remembering the telltale scent in her brother's office. "Now that I have less reason to trust him, maybe I'll borrow it without telling him. It might not help anyway."

Celia was deep in thought. "It doesn't show much of her face. Still, there's something about Myrth one doesn't forget."

"Thomas Fordham apparently felt that way. Our best hope for finding Myrth is to talk to women on the street. They know me better than you, especially if we disguise you as a streetwalker, but before then we'll visit Mrs. Bannister's wig shop."

Mrs. Biddle interrupted them to announce Garrison and Edith Morse had called. Henrietta instructed her to show them in. Flushed with anticipation, Edith came straight to the point by asking how classes went.

"Celia, why don't you give them the news?" Henrietta said.

Celia reported the encouraging attendance and enthusiasm. "We'll see how they do when it comes to homework."

"I knew it had to work." Beaming with gratitude, Edith seated herself with Garrison on a settee opposite Henrietta and Celia. "You've made it happen."

"Many thanks for offering your home," Garrison said, "though the school still needs a permanent site. One in the neighborhood so the children aren't too tired to work the next day. How's Freddy getting along?"

"The police view him as the prime suspect." Henrietta was tempted to tell him they'd seen Myrth but thought better of it. The fewer who knew the better. "Celia and I are searching for Mrs. McLaren on our own."

"How can you outwit the police?" Garrison asked skeptically.

"We know something they don't." Henrietta told him of the encounter with Hannah Burns. "She and Myrth seem unlikely friends. One is a former actress and model, the other an elderly woman. One wonders what they have in common."

"Perhaps their husbands knew each other," said Edith.

Celia's face assumed a thoughtful look. "If I had Mrs. McLaren's acting experience, I'd put it to use. She might be in disguise. The first place I'd look for her is the last place one would expect to find her."

"Since she was once upper class she might try to hide among the lower classes." Henrietta felt her excitement growing.

Edith raised her eyebrows. "You are thorough. We won't keep you from your task. We just wanted to make sure class went well."

Garrison and Edith took their leave shortly after, and Henrietta and Celia resumed their plans.

"A shopkeeper might recognize Myrth unless someone's helping her so she needn't venture out." Henrietta looked at Celia with new eyes. Subtlety had never been her strong point, but here was an opportunity to inquire into Celia's past. "It must be extraordinarily difficult to obtain even the most meager provisions while on the run. You must have found the means."

"It is," Celia said, "and I did."

"No matter," Henrietta said after a moment, realizing Celia had closed the subject. "Myrth is a woman of contradictions, which is what makes her unpredictable."

"Willie McCurdy is also with his disappearing act."

"He's absent from work and truant from school but has money. All we know for sure is he wants to run off to war." Henrietta stood up. "We have two reasons to call at his home tomorrow — to see how both he and his grandmother are doing. I won't believe anything he says unless I see it with my own eyes."

Henrietta was glad she had found a pair of sturdy walking shoes for Celia to wear the next day on the ungraded roads near Fort Hill. They traveled to the waterfront mostly in silence while observing the advancing state of neglect in the area.

Her mother wouldn't recognize the area now. The neighborhood had given way to decay, and landlords seeking easy profits had divided the houses until only tiny quarters were left, unappealing even to those too desperate to refuse. As they neared Half Moon Place Henrietta thought of the squalor in which the McCurdys lived. Three boys in tattered clothing ran across their path, apples in their hands, an emaciated elderly woman pursuing them with curses while shaking her cane.

They turned into Broad Street and stepped under an archway that joined a pair of tenement houses. The path led into a tiny courtyard crammed with shanties. Clotheslines stretched between buildings, a testament that cleanliness was still considered next to godliness even here.

"There's no sun," Celia said in disbelief.

"That's because these homes are built in the backyard of the tenements between Broad Street and Fort Hill," Henrietta replied. "At least the North End shacks have light."

The dilapidated buildings looked as if they might collapse with the next northeasterly gale, but their snug placement rendered the tenants impervious to any stroke of fortune that might force them into better living quarters. *Except for fire*, Henrietta thought, *the landlord need not worry about the loss of property or, often less significant to him, the loss of life.*

The dozen privies lined up by the tenements overflowed with waste, fouling the air with a stench that made Celia's eyes water. Rubbish had been left to decay in the few feet of walking space. A battered staircase that looked as if it wouldn't hold the weight of an alley cat led to a row of hovels above. Beside the ladder leaned a plank that served as a drain, the wood clotted with filth.

"That's Humphrey Place up above," said Henrietta. "Mrs. McCurdy considers those who live there lucky."

"I think life on the street might be safer," Celia faltered.

Picking her way around the trash, Henrietta opened a door hanging on one hinge. They descended a flight of steps into a room that served as parlor, kitchen, and grocery where two women sorted through produce in bins on the floor. Henrietta led the way to the next room.

Celia hunched her shoulders to enter the eight-foot-square living quarters where Molly McCurdy, the fourth of five children, was slipping resignedly into a premature adulthood. Molly sat sewing by inadequate candlelight, her eyes bright and focused like her mother's must have been before alcohol altered her looks. Her grandmother, sitting in bed, hummed an unrecognizable melody, oblivious to visitors.

Molly looked up at Celia, polite but curious. Henrietta introduced them.

"Have a seat, miss, so you don't strain your neck." Molly motioned Celia to a chair with a broken leg.

"We can only stay a moment." Watching Celia sit gingerly, Henrietta studied the ancient woman in bed, drooling and seemingly unaware, her hands shaking. "Willie said your grandmother wasn't well. It appears the doctor came in time."

Molly's eyes were vacant. "No, ma'am, the doctor hasn't been. Gram's gout's not bothering her anymore than usual."

"But Willie came to our house collecting last week."

Molly's blank stare made Henrietta suspect Willie had used a feigned illness to prey on upper class sympathies. She watched Molly's expression waver as she contemplated whether Willie had latched onto a clever idea, one she would never try. Henrietta recognized in Molly's blue eyes the acceptance of one who had learned to live with the ebb and flow of adversity.

"We need the money," Molly admitted, "but the boys all work. Mother, too, when she's able."

"I was disappointed Willie wasn't at school last night," Henrietta said. "He's missed work also."

"He brings home money, so he's working somewhere." Molly continued stitching, dismissing Henrietta's concern.

Where had the money come from if Willie hadn't been at the factory? Henrietta hoped he wasn't handling dangerous equipment.

"I'll see he attends next week, ma'am."

"Thank you. In time your situation will improve, Molly," Henrietta said gently, wondering if it was fair to promise hope when many immigrants died before relief arrived. "These days are the hardest. I know there isn't much mirth here."

Molly's grandmother stopped singing and began to cackle with feeble laughter. "You made a joke," the old woman said with a toothless grin, her gaze wandering from the wall in front of her to the general direction of her visitors. "My, it's nice to have a visit from such a pretty lady."

Celia took the woman's hand and squeezed it. "I hope you feel better soon."

They took their leave shortly after, relieved to be back in the open air. Despite the refuse lining the alley it was preferable to the closeness of the small rooms.

"Such poverty's overwhelming," Celia said in a voice of awkward distress.

"The McCurdys are on the brink of starvation even when they're working," Henrietta admitted.

In places like this where virtue struggled to overcome despair, what chance did a boy like Willie have? It was no wonder his mind wasn't on schooling when the temptations on the streets outnumbered the virtues. Truancy and idleness in the company of other boys often led to thieving as a way of life.

And of all nine-year-olds she knew, none needed educating more than Willie.

Henrietta awakened suddenly in the night. She thought she had heard a dull thud, loud enough to disturb sleep but not enough to rouse her fully.

A ray of moonlight slipped between the drapes and rested on the mantel clock. Two o'clock. Too early for tradesmen or household activity. A second thud followed, softer this time.

There was no mistaking it. Someone was in the house who did not belong.

Nine

Instantly alert, Henrietta reached for her robe. Any visitor at this hour was no guest. She stepped into the hall and caught her foot on a table, banging it loudly enough to alert the entire downstairs. The misstep reminded her that the house was in darkness. She had brought neither lamp nor candle and would not stop to get one.

She proceeded down the staircase toward the back of the house. Her eyes adjusted to the darkness, light from the windows easing her path. A shaft of cold air penetrated the passage. She hurried to the ground floor through the kitchen where the door hung open. Stepping into the doorway, she looked into a silent yard.

The storage shed and potted plants cast shadows across the brick. There was only stillness under moonlight. The alley leading to West Cedar Street was dark. Whoever had been here was gone.

Shivering, she closed the door, the light behind her growing stronger. Celia and Mrs. Biddle squinted at her, Celia's hair tumbling into her eyes, Mrs. Biddle's secured in a nightcap.

"What's happened?" demanded Celia.

"Someone was in the house," Henrietta said. "We need to summon the authorities. I'm not sure if I'm shivering from fear or from cold." She looked at Celia ruefully. "I probably brought this on myself by jokingly blaming Myrth for the robberies. Now I'm the victim."

In the short time it took the detectives to arrive, Henrietta determined a fair amount of silver had been taken.

"But not all," she said. "The thief didn't find the valuable cutlery. I must have interrupted him."

One policeman took her report while the other examined the yard.

"There have been burglaries in the area in which the thief took china, silver, items he could carry," the detective said. "I'd like to inspect the lock, if I may."

The women watched as he fingered the doorknob carefully.

"There's no sign of forced entry. The lock is intact."

Henrietta frowned. "Are you saying he used a key?"

"It seems so." The detective looked thoughtful. "Who else has a key?"

"Only my brother," she said, "but he would announce himself."

"Other thefts are similar. No force was used, yet there was often no other key."

"Do you think the robber has a set of master keys?"

"That's one possibility," the detective said.

Not the one he is exploring, she surmised. He wiped his hands on a handkerchief before closing the door. The kitchen warmed up at once.

"Did you see the intruder?" he asked.

"I'm afraid I saw very little," she admitted. "If I hadn't heard a noise I'd never have known anyone was here."

"Mrs. Cobb made more noise than the burglar," declared Mrs. Biddle. "Neither Mrs. Chase nor I heard a blessed thing."

"You were lucky the intruder never made it past the pantry," the officer said. "Here's the source of the noise."

He indicated a broom lying lengthwise in the doorway.

"The new girl must have left it out," Mrs. Biddle exclaimed.

"Tomorrow I'll have a locksmith change this," said Henrietta.

After he finished the interview the detective joined his partner. They examined the area thoroughly, particularly the kitchen and pantry from which the silver was taken. After they departed Henrietta checked the back door to make sure it was secure.

"If the thief had a key," she mused, "I'm wasting my time."

"It's frightening, the idea of a stranger in the house." Mrs. Biddle tightened her dressing gown. "And a man at that."

"Especially when he might return," Celia agreed.

"No thief would return to a house he robbed the same night." Henrietta spoke before unchecked fear could take hold. "Tomorrow morning I'll summon Mr. Tyler to replace this lock. Then we'll find a better place to hide the key."

She felt uneasy at a stranger entering her home while everyone slept. Her hands felt chilled and waxy, and she wiped them on her pockets. Wishing she could do away with the memory of the intruder as easily, she returned the beribboned key to its customary spot on the hook beside the door.

After the locksmith had completed his task and a new hiding place was chosen, Henrietta decided to call on

Hannah Burns. This time she left Fudge at home, remembering the incident with Gyp, and brought Celia.

"For someone so anxious to defend Myrth," Henrietta said as they walked, "Mrs. Burns grew oddly reticent once she learned Freddy was an acquaintance. I'll need sympathy and a frank approach to learn more."

"The photograph you borrowed will help when we talk to the streetwalkers on Batterymarch Street," Celia reminded her.

"Borrowed is a generous word." Guilt returned as Henrietta remembered taking the picture from the desk in Freddy's unlocked office yesterday. Maybe it was only fitting that within twenty-four hours she had also been robbed. "I hope to return it before he realizes it's gone."

"I wonder what the upper floors are used for besides an office and an apartment." They entered the stable yard, its earthy smells strong in the autumn warmth. "Feed and tack? Storage?"

"A room where Myrth might hide?" Henrietta suggested.

In the narrow passage to Hannah's flat Henrietta was startled to see a pair of pencil sketches on the wall. The horses were so prominent she hadn't noticed the woman standing beside them on her first visit. The illustrations were rough and unfinished, but there was no doubt who the subject was.

The greeting they received was warmer than expected. The elderly woman straightened up when she saw her visitors, eyes pale but sharp, wispy hair fluttering about her face. Her little dog Gyp, so like her in appearance, was equally happy.

"Mrs. Cobb, how nice of you to call, and you've brought a friend." Hannah adjusted her spectacles and opened the door wider. "Do come in. Forgive the clutter. It's not often I have callers. One slips easily into bad habits living in solitude."

Henrietta introduced Celia before Mrs. Burns seated them in chairs with antimacassars laid discreetly over the arms to cover the threadbare upholstery. The simple but tasteful parlor was furnished with styles from half a century ago, the only accessories a mantel clock and figurines. From the corner a canary chirped a welcome.

"It seems we share an unpleasant experience," said Henrietta. "My home in Louisburg Square was robbed last night."

"You don't say! Such a fine neighborhood. This calls for a pot of tea." Shaking her head, Hannah hobbled away. "What makes a body steal like that? That man should be ashamed."

In the comfort of her flat the elderly woman was more at ease than on Henrietta's previous visit. Hearing her opening a tin in the kitchen, Henrietta studied the parlor but saw nothing out of the ordinary. If Myrth had stayed here, all traces were gone.

Hannah returned holding a tray laden with refreshments and china nicked with age. The yellowed napkins implied she had few occasions to use her linens. Henrietta felt flattered by the gesture. Hannah sat across from them.

"I have only a bit of biscuit," she apologized. "It's not every day I have the likes of Mrs. Cobb from Louisburg Square visiting."

"It's delicious, thank you," Henrietta said. "It's our fault for not announcing ourselves properly."

"Better spur of the moment than not at all. My house was ransacked something terrible, but the intruder didn't take a thing. Just put me to some trouble to clean it up." Hannah looked sympathetic. "I'll bet he found some fine things at your house."

"He apparently had a key, for the lock wasn't broken. Was it the same here?"

"As if he'd walked right in. Sounds like the same thief. Makes me nervous. I don't know who to trust."

Henrietta introduced a new possibility. "If she's in hiding, could Mrs. McLaren be desperate enough to steal for food?"

"The notion! Thieving is below her under any circumstance."

"You speak with such familiarity." She knew Hannah might be torn between her urge to chat and her desire to protect Myrth. "I was surprised she called on me after her husband's murder."

It was impossible to interpret Hannah's reaction. "Did she?"

"It was most alarming. She said her husband's killer meant to kill her." Appealing to Hannah's confidence might win her trust. "Do you know if she had any enemies?"

"I told you I don't," Hannah said smartly, as calm as Freddy had been, "but I'm relieved to hear she's safe."

"Mrs. Burns, I must confide in you." Henrietta might gain more through honesty. "Mrs. McLaren wants to help my brother. We want to protect her also. It's admirable of you to help her, but it's urgent that I speak with her."

Hannah set down her teacup with a perturbed expression.

"While I'm sure your intentions are decent, neither you nor the police know Myrth like I do," she bristled. "She didn't kill Angus. She's running because she got herself in a difficult situation, nothing against your brother."

"I want to think she's honorable. I hoped you might shed light on her character," Henrietta said carefully.

"More tea? She isn't the type to encourage enemies."

But Myrth insisted she had one. Hannah's sudden charm was out of character with her outspokenness. While her first loyalty was to Myrth, she might feel a secondary loyalty to Angus. Henrietta would have to be as shrewd as Hannah to break through her reserve.

"Did she ever mention a Thomas Fordham?" she asked.

Hannah thought for a moment. "I don't know that name."

"He worked with Mr. McLaren. Did she support abolitionism?"

"Not as much as Angus, but she believed in it."

"You seem certain she didn't kill her husband."

Hannah smiled thinly. "Are you married, Mrs. Cobb?"

"Widowed." She saw no need to admit the truth.

Hannah eyed her with new sympathy. "Then you understand. Angus was Myrth's husband. You see how it is."

At this juncture Celia was compelled to break her silence. "Marriage doesn't guarantee love," she said politely.

And jealousy could compel one to murder. Henrietta thrust aside thoughts of Corinthia.

"It's a shame you didn't know her better," Hannah said with a wistful smile, "for you'd know she wouldn't have done it."

"I never knew Angus either, but I know he was respected and hardworking. He must have been a fine husband." Henrietta waited for Hannah to contradict her. "It's surprising they had no children."

"A shame but not a surprise." Hannah laughed bluntly. "I know what it is to marry a Scot. It wasn't easy for Myrth."

Henrietta was surprised Hannah would divulge intimate information. "Did he indulge in drink?"

"No, he was too upstanding for that."

"I hope for Myrth's sake they were happy." Henrietta knew Freddy would resent the sentiment. "She had bruises during her visit."

"It happened sometimes. Angus met her when she was eighteen and a real lady. He was on his finest behavior. It wasn't always a good marriage but better than what she might have had. Myrth was grateful. She helped Angus rise in society. She was refined but penniless."

And completely vulnerable, Henrietta guessed. The revelation brought the marriage into focus. Yet her image of Angus was so contradictory it was hard to envision the type of man he'd been.

"Aren't those pictures along the staircase of Myrth?"

"Yes. Many were done when she modeled."

Henrietta was glad Hannah confirmed the model's identity even if Harkness wouldn't. "Did she talk about modeling?"

"That was long ago. As I recall, her career was brief."

Perhaps fearing she had revealed too much, Hannah turned her attention to the shortbread. Gyp sat patiently before Henrietta, eyeing the biscuit in her hand.

"I found the sketches in Mr. Harkness's office striking," said Henrietta, "but he wouldn't discuss them."

"That's his way. He was kind enough to give Nicholas his first job before the theater."

"Nicholas?"

"My sister's boy, Nicholas Trindell. I raised him."

Where had she heard that name? "Is that the man we saw you with when we met? He looked familiar."

"You might have seen him on the stage," Hannah said proudly.

Nicholas Trindell's roles must have been minor for Henrietta not to know his name, for she frequently attended Boston's playhouses. After an exchange on popular theater, she realized the subject had drifted beyond the point of value to her investigation, but she and Celia had spent a pleasant morning with Hannah while learning about Myrth's marriage.

While Hannah returned the tea set to the kitchen, Henrietta studied the photographs in the room. There was a formal picture, presumably of the late Mr. Burns and his sisters. She saw no pictures of Hannah's family except a small likeness of her nephew from years ago. Henrietta couldn't decide who Nicholas took after, for he looked nothing like the family pictured here.

Excitement rose within her as she recalled where she had seen the name. The recollection came with startling clarity.

Nicholas Trindell was mentioned in Angus McLaren's will as the recipient of the bust of Caesar used to kill him.

Henrietta could barely contain her excitement but refrained from telling Celia now. Hannah would return at any moment.

Why would Angus leave anything to the nephew of Myrth's friend, especially the murder weapon? While handsome, it appeared to be of little value. Still speculating on the matter when Hannah returned, Henrietta debated whether to mention it. She couldn't admit to having read McLaren's will without having her morals questioned.

"This is a charming likeness of your nephew," she said casually. "Was Mr. McLaren acquainted with Nicholas?"

Hannah glanced at her. "I don't think they ever met. He cared little for entertainment. I'm proud to say Nicholas has his first starring role in a play opening next week at the Boston Museum. Perhaps you've heard of *Florine*."

"I know the playwright. Mr. Brattleby is a friend."

"Fancy that! Perhaps I'll see you opening night."

"We'll be there to applaud your nephew," said Celia.

Exchanging civilities before departing, Henrietta reached for the doorknob while Hannah reminisced about friends who had passed on. As she listened Henrietta felt a waxy substance around the keyhole. She bent to inspect the lock. Despite a few scratches, the polished brass was immaculate.

"Have I locked you in?" Hannah asked.

"There seems to be some wax on the lock," Henrietta said.

"Pardon my oversight, literally. My vision isn't what it once was," the woman apologized. "Age, Mrs. Cobb, robs us of basic necessities. In a few years you'll understand."

"Your house is spotless, and tea was lovely," she assured Hannah, ignoring her warning about the encroaching years. "You have a charming collection of photographs."

"Thank you." Hannah picked up her little dog. "I don't know who'll care about them when I'm gone."

"Surely your nephew will treasure them," countered Celia.

"Yes, of course," Hannah agreed quietly.

They left with an invitation to call again. Henrietta kept her discovery to herself until she and Celia were on the street. They were still engrossed in the subject by the time they were settled in the study at Louisburg Square.

"Angus wouldn't leave a worthless bust to a stranger," Celia said.

"The irony is that it's the murder weapon. What's more curious is this robbery business," Henrietta mused. "The thefts weren't far from Branch Street, yet a brick rowhouse in Louisburg Square is a more obvious target than a flat in a stable yard. I doubt Hannah's robbery was random. It sounds as if it was more ransacking than robbery."

She watched her squirrel running in his wheel, repeating the rhythmic steps over and over. Like questions continually turning in her mind, each revolution returned her to the same point without any progress.

"Why rob Hannah?" asked Celia. "Could the thief have been searching for something?"

"She said nothing was taken, but she must have something of value. We know the thief didn't find what he was looking for."

"If he has a key," Celia said, "he can return at will."

"The same might be said of our home, even with a new lock. We're fighting more than one enemy."

Even after retiring for the night Henrietta couldn't erase Myrth from her thoughts. While Hannah insisted her character was impeccable, charm could disguise the most malicious motive. The little Henrietta knew about Myrth was contradictory at best. If she were the murderer's intended target, not everyone esteemed her highly.

She recalled Oliver Wendell Holmes saying the past was key to the present. If Hannah held the key to Myrth's past, she was prepared to allow only a glimpse of it. Sam Ingraham might have more insight. He had known Myrth and employed her husband. A talk with Sam could help determine the degree of conflict Angus brought the firm. Sam might know who painted Myrth. The artist's name had been little more than an unrecognizable scrawl, now lost forever.

With the picture of Myrth, they could ask women on the streets if they recognized her. Until Celia had a costume, Henrietta would limit her inquiries to daylight hours. Having lived on the streets, Celia could be in danger if she were recognized. Henrietta needed Sam's perspective before she would fully believe Myrth was in danger.

Henrietta allowed the weekend to pass before she returned to Ingraham Piano, enjoying the warmth of early October on Beacon Street. While she doubted her courage would fail her this time, her presence of mind was another matter. She waited only a moment before being directed to Sam's office.

Climbing the stairs, she came face to face with Thomas Fordham. He loomed over her, pausing on the step above, the muscle flicking in his cheek. Was it her imagination, or had his face flushed upon seeing her?

"Hello, Mrs. Cobb." He stared at her.

"Good day, Mr. Fordham. I've often wondered how the firm is managing without Mr. McLaren."

"From our perspective business is back to normal. There's no shortage of men willing to work."

"True," she conceded. "I'm sure Mr. McLaren replaced Patrick Sweeney very quickly after firing him."

Fordham's stare was blank. "Never heard of him."

"That was some time ago. I hope for Mrs. McLaren's sake Sweeney isn't the type to hold a grudge."

He started at the mention of Myrth. "The papers are filled with news but not about her. Now if you'll excuse me."

She watched him continue down the stairs. The idea that he was Myrth's lover seemed outlandish. He was too vulgar for someone so aristocratic. His manner wasn't that of a man enamored of a woman, but Jasper Penrose had painted a strong animosity between him and Angus.

Had Fordham felt so competitive toward Angus their conflict ended in murder? She thought it unlikely Fordham was helping Myrth hide, but he would remain on her suspect list.

She found Sam at his desk, reviewing a ledger. His head snapped up at her arrival.

"Good to see you again, Etta," he greeted her, rising.

Sam ushered her to a seat across from his desk. They talked superficially of his profession, his attention courteous yet impersonal.

"The piano's become so popular," he marveled, "South End homes are constructed with window nooks just for that purpose."

When her turn came, Sam listened politely as she related details of her charity work until she had exhausted her range of comfortable subjects. She noticed the only personal touch in his office was a daguerreotype of his sons in a bookcase.

"I'm happy you've found fulfilling work." He gazed at her intently, heightening the unspoken emotions between them. "No doubt Freddy's troubles bring you here today."

"I want to clear his name." *As well as my own.* The burden of exoneration weighed on her again.

"I'm sorry he's had such a hard time of it—all of you. Having little public support must make it difficult."

In his eyes she saw a sympathy that caught her off guard.

"Especially when the accusation is untrue," she said with sudden vehemence. "It's rubbish, Sam. I hope you believe that."

"Having known Freddy all these years, I found it hard to believe. Not that my opinion matters."

His opinion did matter. She sensed both warmth and distance in him, a potent combination. Their eyes locked in mutual remembrance of their past.

"I'd be happy to do whatever I can to help," Sam offered.

Perhaps she had judged him prematurely. She took a deep breath. "Tell me about Angus."

"He was a valued worker and humanitarian. Not a gentleman by our standards, but one in his own right."

"Did you enjoy working with him?"

"He was invaluable to the firm. Came over from Scotland as a boy and went right to work. Active in the Scottish Society." Sam shook his head. "He'd have made a fine politician. Not enough good men as it is."

She could conclude little from his replies. She felt the tension ease as he revealed more of his relationship with Angus.

"How did his abolitionist activities affect business?"

Sam hesitated. "His opinions were respected even if they weren't shared by everyone. He felt the police didn't do enough to help runaways by enforcing the Fugitive Slave Act."

She studied his face for a sign of duplicity and saw none. Any deception on his part was concealed in the professionalism that shielded his personal and commercial interests from scrutiny.

"Did you know he fired Sweeney, the Irishman who spoke at the Faneuil Hall rally?" she asked.

"Never met him. He isn't the type to fit in here."

"Angus must have felt the same." She paused. "I need to ask, Sam. Were relations between McLaren and Thomas Fordham strained?"

"McLaren stirred up the workers. Fordham's mind is always on business. I preferred Tom's attitude."

"What of Myrth? Did you ever see Fordham with her?"

Sam stared. "Once. Why do you ask?"

She considered how to phrase her inquiry. It would have been impossible for any man not to notice Myrth's beauty. She wondered if Sam saw Myrth as Fordham had. She thought again how gray her own hair had become and wondered if Sam noticed.

"Do you think Fordham fancied her?" she asked awkwardly.

"Many men did. She had an abundance of charm, but she didn't seem the type to act upon it." Amusement played about his mouth. "Even if she did pose for Boston's most remarkable work of art."

"That remarkable work was at Freddy's until recently, when Cora destroyed it." After careful consideration she dismissed her concerns about his trustworthiness and decided to confide in him. "I've seen Myrth, Sam. She visited me after the murder and then Freddy. She claims she didn't kill Angus."

Sam's brow creased. "Why in blazes hasn't she come forward?"

It infuriated Henrietta to have to repeat Myrth's excuses. "She says she's in danger and has proof someone else murdered Angus."

He looked skeptical. "All the more reason to turn herself in. Her hesitation isn't to Freddy's benefit."

"That's what makes this harder. Do you know why anyone would want to kill either Myrth or Angus?"

"For political reasons, I imagine. I don't know why anyone would want to kill Myrth. She seemed sincere and exceptionally thoughtful."

"I'd give anything to meet the artist who painted her."

"That won't happen, I'm afraid. He's deceased. He signed his name in a larger hand than his reputation warranted. The Godiva was his most famous work." Sam leaned back in his chair. "I wonder why Myrth hasn't returned, if she's innocent. She needs police protection."

While the chance was slim he'd recall anything of value, her disappointment stung. "It seems she would rather let Freddy take the blame. I hoped you might remember her from her modeling days."

"That was a quarter of a century ago, Etta. She's younger than we are by almost that much." Sam spread his hands. "I wish I could help, but I'm afraid I never crossed paths with your Lady Godiva or the artist who painted her."

She smiled at the memory. "Do you miss the creative life?"

"The arts are hardly a respectable profession for the son of a merchant banker." He turned away. "My paintings never built the reputation I'd hoped for. I found greater success heeding my father's advice."

They were back in the present, their conversation returning to an impersonal level. Henrietta invited Sam to the opening night of Edgar's play on Friday, and he asked if she planned to attend the Prince of Wales's ball. When she asked his opinion of antislavery activity in the city, he conceded he had been too busy to give the issue the attention it deserved.

"Ask me next year," he advised, "when it comes to war."

"I like to think it won't, but perhaps I'm deluding myself."

"Our economy can't continue to flourish if our businesses can't run. Southern states make up nearly forty percent of our business. I don't intend to lose our clients or our reputation."

Many in the North sympathized with Southern plantation owners. Still, Sam's lack of concern for ethical matters disappointed her. Forty years ago he wouldn't have viewed war as a distraction from business.

In parting she refrained from asking Sam why he allowed child labor at India Street where he didn't have to watch children struggle with machinery beyond their strength. Having to compromise her ideals to gain information about Angus depressed her. She was relieved to depart.

She crossed Tremont Street, searching for something of value in the visit. Sam's lack of knowledge about Myrth's life might mean there was little of note in her past. At least he had expressed support for Freddy.

Her visit had been of value in another way. Although Sam's office had contained a photograph of his children, there was none of Bertha. It was a petty victory, disturbing yet pleasing, and one that filled her with a lingering satisfaction.

Heading home in the shade of Walnut Street, she hurried past the Parkman residence, trying to ignore the memory of the grisly incident at Harvard that ended Dr. Parkman's life. She turned her attention to the elegant gait of the horse led by its groom up ahead. It was curious that Myrth feared horses. She and Hannah were an odd pair, with Harkness forming an even less likely trio.

Despite his denial Harkness must know Myrth from abolition rallies, well enough, perhaps, to be convinced she hadn't killed her husband. That logic directed guilt away from Myrth, a concept Henrietta wasn't ready to accept.

At least she knew the man named in Angus's will. Why would Angus leave a bust of Caesar to Nicholas Trindell if they'd never met? Perhaps Nicholas once played the role of Caesar and Myrth asked Angus to leave it to him.

An idea began to develop in her mind, fantastic at first but too compelling to dismiss. No wonder Nicholas looked familiar when Henrietta saw him outside the livery with his aunt. She had seen his likeness once before. The sight of the groom holding the horse's reins reminded her of the photograph in Myrth's sewing chest, a picture of a young man of fourteen or so beside a horse. A young man she now believed was Nicholas. There was a quality in the photograph that had reminded her of Myrth.

Then a thought hit her, stunning, yet it made sense. It came into focus with increasing clarity. The more she thought about it, the more real the possibility became that Myrth McLaren was Nicholas's mother.

Ten

Henrietta felt the same excitement as when she first saw Nicholas. Even then he seemed too young to be Hannah's nephew. There was only one picture of him in Hannah's flat, a larger one hidden in Myrth's. On some level she had associated him with Myrth.

No wonder Myrth turned to Hannah. She had trusted her enough to raise her son. The arrangement gave Myrth a way to remain in contact and explained why Hannah hadn't raised him as her child but assumed an aunt's role. Older, more experienced in the ways of the heart, less judgmental than those of Myrth's class, Hannah must have seemed the ideal person. *How sad,* Henrietta mused, *that Myrth never fully experienced the joy of motherhood – and ironic that her son chose the same profession.*

Hannah claimed Myrth had a better life with Angus than she would have otherwise. Perhaps Myrth found herself unwed and with child, disgraced in the eyes of society. Hannah said they hadn't met, but Angus must have known about Nicholas. It explained why the marriage wasn't always happy.

Did Nicholas know the truth? It was a rare individual who would share such a secret, but Myrth was rare indeed. For a wild second Henrietta wondered if Thomas Fordham had been the father. She doubted their relationship could survive such a powerful secret over time. Angus hadn't survived.

What did Harkness know? As a black man he understood oppression. Would he have protected Myrth? As a mother Henrietta knew with absolute certainty that Myrth would have done anything to protect her child. She definitely hadn't told Freddy about her son.

She very much looked forward to her evening at the theater where she would see Nicholas Trindell in person.

Henrietta could hardly wait to tell Celia her discovery, but since Celia was out questioning shopkeepers about Myrth's whereabouts when she arrived home, she penned a reply to Mr. Thoreau instead:

Louisburg Square, Boston
October 2, 1860

My dear Mr. Thoreau,

I thank you for your prompt reply to my letter regarding jimsonweed. While I appreciate your wisdom in botanical matters, you can hardly expect a Bostonian to recognize a wild and dangerous plant.

I am attempting to aid my brother who has been implicated in a murder he didn't commit. It's my hope that your letter will be of value in seeing justice done. I too wonder why someone would keep a plant so deadly. Perhaps my acquaintance was unaware of its potency and kept the petals for sentimental reasons rather than for harmful intent.

I plan to ask her that very question as soon as I find her.

Yours most sincerely,
Henrietta Newell Cobb

As she laid down her pen she felt a cold touch against her hand and looked down to see Fudge beside her, his tail wagging at the chance for attention. She felt guilty for having been remiss in not walking him more. Knowing she had spent more time away from home than usual, she stroked his head patiently.

Yet it was urgent that she find Myrth. Her gaze fell on her desk where she expected to see the pale petals. Alarm surged through her as she stared at an empty spot.

The jimsonweed petals were gone.

Her search had revealed no trace of the flowers by the next day. Fear became reality when her parlor maid remembered Freddy had called the previous day to retrieve something from her study.

"What he claims he forgot never belonged to him," Henrietta fumed to Celia. "He knew I'd be out visiting Sam because I dropped him a note telling him. I should have suspected him from the start. I trusted him again and wrongly."

"It's of little consolation, but I imagine he would say the flowers belonged to Myrth," Celia ventured.

"And Thoreau would say they belonged to Nature. When I took them I had no idea how important they would become."

Henrietta still harbored a sense of resentment that evening when Mrs. Biddle surprised her with news of an unexpected caller.

"A Miss Annie Jackson." The housekeeper's face darkened. "Says it's a matter of life and death. Sounds daft to me."

"I don't know the name, but I'll certainly see her at once."

Henrietta and Celia found Annie Jackson in the receiving room, still bundled in her cloak, talking to the alligator. The young woman with neatly coiled hair turned as they arrived, eyes alert. Her build was slight but her appearance robust, probably the result of her job combined with domestic burdens. Henrietta's heart leaped as she recognized her from Ingraham Piano.

"What a creature he is." Annie smiled at the alligator. "Looks as if he wouldn't mind taking a nibble."

"He's curious about people and has bitten at least one," said Henrietta, "but he won't have the chance to bite another."

"Caution's wise, I always say. I'm sorry to call uninvited. I don't know if you'll remember me, but after I saw you at Ingraham Piano a second time, I had to talk to you."

"You worked for Mr. McLaren." Henrietta gestured to a chair. "What brings you out on such a rainy night?"

"I heard Mr. Fordham tell you politics weren't a problem at work." She looked at Henrietta with anxious eyes. "The dead should be able to rest in peace. That's why I had to tell you it isn't true. Mr. McLaren did what he believed in, but the bosses didn't like that freedom talk. They were so loud I heard them arguing plain as day even though it's not polite to listen."

Henrietta's heart pounded as she tried to remain calm. "Arguing with Mr. Ingraham?"

"With Mr. Samuel, ma'am." Annie's face was pale. From her first word it was clear she wouldn't stop until she had said all she intended. "They were shouting something awful. He said such talk would lead to war, and he didn't want no more of it at work, but the next day Mr. McLaren told us class never determined morality or bought kindness."

So Fordham had lied in claiming his superiors weren't antagonistic toward Angus. Had he concealed the truth to protect his bosses or himself? Thousands in Boston hated abolitionism. Why was Angus singled out over more powerful men? The Secret Six who conspired with John Brown to end slavery were more logical targets.

"Did you know Mrs. McLaren?" Henrietta asked.

Annie's expression turned fervent with emotion. "Oh, ma'am, she was an angel. At Christmas she remembered us with turkey to feed the family. Last year she sent each lady a lace handkerchief. You'd never find the Ingrahams doing that. Not to speak badly of them, mind, but she was special."

Perhaps for Myrth the charitable gesture was an imitation of the life she had once lived, allowing herself the annual indulgence of behaving as if she had plenty.

"I'm sure the police will find her. I understand relations between Mr. Fordham and Mr. McLaren were difficult. I heard each attempted to ruin the other's marriage."

Annie's eyes widened. "I hate to speak bad of Mr. Fordham, but I think he hated Mr. McLaren. Mr. McLaren was angry Mr. Fordham told the bosses he'd hired runaway slaves, so he hinted that Mr. Fordham spent too much time with a female worker, if you know what I mean. She don't work there no more."

"Was there anything to the rumor?" Henrietta pressed.

"Oh, it was true enough, on account of Mr. Fordham sometimes goes around with a brick in his hat." Annie explained upon seeing Henrietta's puzzled expression. "He drinks too much. But word got back to Mrs. Fordham. That was the sad part. It caused a terrible row. Ruined their marriage." She shook her head distastefully. "He said things that were uncalled for just to hurt Mr. McLaren."

"In retaliation, you mean. What kind of things?"

"Rude things about Mrs. McLaren." Annie lowered her voice to a whisper. "About the private parts he shouldn't have been noticing. He would — incinerate things."

"Insinuate things?" Henrietta's thoughts had headed in the same direction. "Was there any truth to it?"

Her eyes flew open. "No, ma'am! Mrs. McLaren only came by at Christmas. She didn't like Mr. Fordham. He only said those things to get Mr. McLaren's goat."

Annie's admission defused the likelihood of any relationship between Myrth and Fordham. It had seemed preposterous, Henrietta acknowledged. Dissension at the firm was another matter. She wanted to believe Sam's claim that he didn't know Sweeney. Fordham never admitted Angus fired him. How much of what either said was true? It was a safe bet Annie knew.

"Do you remember a Patrick Sweeney who worked for Mr. McLaren?" Henrietta asked. "It would have been some time ago."

Annie made a face. "That rotter. Shouldn't've been hired in the first place. Sweeney was a lazy good-for-nothing. Bothered the girls something fierce. We was relieved when Mr. McLaren fired him."

"Was Sweeney angry enough to want to get back at him?"

"I'd be shocked if he were that ambitious, really."

Sweeney remained firmly on Henrietta's list of suspects. Another was also in question. "I'm sure Sam Ingraham didn't like controversy over runaway slaves."

"No, ma'am, especially when we sell to plantation owners from South Carolina." She lowered her tone confidentially. "They threatened to stop buying from us if Mr. McLaren didn't settle down. I guess I can see their point. Mr. Ingraham wants to keep selling pianos after the war."

"Understandably."

Henrietta's spirits fell. The threat of a boycott must have created unimaginable tension. If Sam kept Angus as an employee, he risked losing Southern business. If he fired him, he faced the loss of wealthy customers in the North. McLaren's death eliminated the risk of either.

Annie seemed less anxious now. "I don't want to get anyone in trouble, ma'am, 'specially myself," she said softly. "My father can't work right now, and we need the money. I had to tell somebody, and since you asked, it only seemed right. Wouldn't be fair to Mr. McLaren's memory if I let everyone think things was fine when they wasn't."

"I won't tell a soul at the factory," Henrietta promised. "I thank you for coming forward, Annie. You did the right thing."

"I thought it would help your family, too," Annie confessed, "when your visit came right after Mrs. Newell's."

Henrietta was sure she'd misunderstood. "Mrs. Newell?"

"Your sister-in-law. She was a bit like a piano herself, real big and square, begging your pardon," she added quickly, "but lovely, like yourself."

Henrietta was stunned. What reason did Cora have to call at the firm? Had she suspected Freddy of having an affair as Henrietta feared? She exhaled slowly at the unexpected news.

"It's awful to say," Annie said sadly, "but it's pretty bad, isn't it, when everyone's acting sorry Mr. McLaren's gone, and really I think some of them are happier without him around."

Two nights later Henrietta seized the chance to witness Nicholas Trindell's opening night performance at the Boston Museum. Shortly before the purple curtain rose she offered Celia an explanation of the contradictory name of the theater where actors as notable as Edwin and John Wilkes Booth had appeared.

"You would think the foyer would be grand enough to convince the public it's a dignified establishment, but the euphemism is still needed for those who find theater scandalous." She turned to Edgar Brattleby on her other side. "I'm honored, Edgar, to be present at your debut."

"I'm pleased so many from our salon are here. I rewrote part of *Florine* after being inspired by Freddy. Not that I wish to benefit from his misfortune," he hastened to add.

"It might as well inspire someone." Henrietta studied the playbill. "I look forward to seeing Nicholas Trindell. I'm acquainted with his aunt. What sort of fellow is he?"

"An excellent sort, I'd guess. No airs, talented yet genuine. His charming wife is with child. This is his largest role to date."

So Myrth had a grandchild to look forward to. Seeing Freddy and Corinthia in their box by the orchestra pit, Henrietta exchanged a glance with him hostile enough to convince her he'd stolen her jimsonweed. He must know she took the picture of Myrth from his office. What a fine pair they were, reduced to thieving from each other.

She consoled herself with the plan for tomorrow night, when Celia would don her disguise, and they would go inquiring for Myrth. To date no one recognized her, but Celia had spent days preparing for her role as a streetwalker. Henrietta hoped the irony of pretending to resume a lifestyle she had managed to escape wouldn't prove overwhelming.

The curtain would rise in seconds. Gazing into the audience, Henrietta noted the theater was nearly full. She was surprised not to see Hannah in the crowd. Scanning the faces in the back, she received the biggest shock of the evening when she spotted the face of a woman seated in the second row from the exit door.

If it wasn't Myrth, it was someone who looked amazingly like her. From this distance she couldn't be positive, for the woman's veiled hat and fastened cloak allowed only a cursory glimpse. Myrth was equally as alert. From her frozen stare Henrietta knew the recognition was mutual.

As she debated what to do, the lights dimmed and the strains of the orchestra faded. The playhouse was plunged into darkness as the curtain rose, exposing a battlefield on stage. Should she rise and disturb those around her? There

wasn't an empty seat in her row. She risked offending
Edgar by leaving.

She glanced into the darkness behind her. The back
rows had vanished in the theater's depths, the encounter
as unexpected as their first. Henrietta wondered if she had
been mistaken. Turning back to the stage, she realized she
had missed Nicholas's arrival. Tall and compelling, he
created a charismatic presence. His manner, as elegant as
his walk, made him seem destined for the theater.

Myrth might be leaving the building at this very
moment. The only way to know was to follow her. Hoping
for a forgiveness she knew was doubtful, Henrietta
collected her rustling skirts as quietly as she could and
edged past those in her row, whispering apologies.
Leaving the auditorium, she rushed across the hallway
past an astonished usher. She ran down the grand staircase
to find the foyer silent and empty.

Two rows of columns stretched before her, running the
length of the entrance hall. The softened gaslight cast
elongated shadows across the carpet, making the
scrollwork appear cold and menacing in relief. She slowed
her pace as she walked past the Copley and Stuart
portraits high above her.

"Mrs. McLaren, please, I must speak with you," she
intoned, her voice echoing in the stillness.

A gust of cold air from the doorway told her Myrth
had eluded her. She glanced out, looking left and right as
she had the day they met, with the same disappointing
result. The fear she felt during her meeting with Myrth
was replaced by an urgency to confront her and demand
the truth.

She returned to the auditorium despite cold stares from left and right, noting alarm in Celia's face and outrage in Edgar's.

"Myrth was here," she whispered to Celia. Composing herself, she faced front. Later she would explain to Edgar.

Her unsettled emotions made it impossible to focus. Myrth showed audacity in appearing at a social event when the police were searching for her. A playhouse was the last place they'd expect to find her, which was why she could risk coming to see her son. She might be in hiding, but she wasn't entirely in mourning.

The play's 1812 military setting and honest sentimentality gave it an immediacy that found its mark with the audience. As Edgar predicted, Nicholas gave a fine performance as a lovelorn soldier who lost his sweetheart along with his life. Henrietta's theory was substantiated as she looked for a likeness of his mother in his face and found it.

When the gaslight returned for intermission, she looked back, not surprised to see Myrth's seat empty. She turned to see Edgar glaring at her with displeasure.

"Please accept my sincerest apologies," she begged. "I thought I saw someone I knew."

Briefly she divulged as little information about Myrth's reappearance in their lives as possible. She fell silent while Edgar turned to accept felicitations from well-wishers. Quietly she related her tale to Celia, who was equally amazed. As they joined the others making their way out of the theater, she saw that all that remained of the back seat's occupant was a single rose tied with a ribbon. Picking it up as they passed, she looked for Hannah without success.

"The rose must be intended for the star," Celia surmised.

"Freddy hasn't the nerve to bring Myrth a rose with Cora here. A hall filled with acquaintances is hardly an ideal trysting spot. Later we can congratulate the star and ask him a few questions, once I've made amends to Edgar."

In the foyer Henrietta stood studying the crowd when cool fingers grazed her own. Fearing Myrth had come back, she jerked about to see Fanny, gripping her sister's arm in relief.

Concern flooded Fan's face. "You look as if you've seen a ghost."

"You'll think I have. Mrs. McLaren was here this evening."

Fan registered disbelief as Henrietta disclosed the details of recent developments. Sheltered between twin potted ferns, with Celia blocking the entrance from unintentional eavesdroppers, Henrietta confided what she considered her biggest discovery.

"I'm convinced Mrs. McLaren had a son."

She was impressed how admirably Fan concealed her shock. "Of course I won't say a word to Freddy. No doubt it happened so long ago Myrth hasn't told him."

Henrietta stopped short of telling Fan Nicholas Trindell's true identity here in the theater where he would take the stage for the final act. She disliked deceiving her sister, but she could hardly tell her about the jimsonweed without admitting her own theft, even if she did plan to return the photograph. The waterfront excursion she had planned with Celia was decidedly too dangerous for Fan.

"You've made progress," Fan murmured in awe. "I don't know how you do it. I wonder why Mrs. McLaren came here at all."

Henrietta hoped Fan's ruminations wouldn't help her connect Nicholas with Myrth. Across the foyer she could see Corinthia conversing with friends while Freddy stepped outside.

Excusing herself from Fan, she slipped toward the door. Freddy stood in the moonlight, meditatively smoking a cigarette. He spoke without looking in her direction.

"I believe you have something of mine."

"I can say the same," she countered. "Shall we trade?"

He squashed the cigarette beneath his heel. "The jimsonweed means more to me than the photograph. As long as I have it, you can't take it to the authorities."

"You still think it proves nothing? It could free you from suspicion." She stepped closer as a passerby paused to read the marquee. "Why not tell the police?"

"Time will prove her innocent of murder. In the meantime I don't give a rat's tail for society's opinion."

"Did you intend to meet her tonight with Cora here?" Seeing his puzzled look, she explained. "Myrth was here. I saw her."

His countenance paled. "That's impossible," he mumbled. "She couldn't be. I never told her I was coming. Are you sure?"

"I was the cause of the disruption a minute into the play." She reddened at the memory. "I pursued her to the exit."

"Why would she come here?"

"I have some notion about that. I hope from now on you'll be as honest with me as I've been with you."

"The definition of honesty doesn't include stealing."

"As you well know. I'd advise you not to rub your eyes when you touch those petals unless you're ready to test the effects."

Henrietta resumed her seat in the theater more frustrated than when she left. She'd never believed Freddy was connected with Angus's death, but she never thought he'd lie to her. Since learning Myrth visited his office she had to wonder what else he hadn't admitted.

His wife's behavior was equally as suspicious. Corinthia had no earthly reason to visit Ingraham Piano other than to confront McLaren about his wife's affair with her husband. Since Angus was already dead, that couldn't have been the reason for her call.

At the close of the play Henrietta remained seated with Celia as Edgar received a continuous stream of accolades, his sister Lavinia beaming with pride. Henrietta tried to ignore Freddy but couldn't help noticing when he and Cora left their seats. It must have been a major concession on her sister-in-law's part to appear in public.

"Corinthia seemed more attentive to Freddy tonight than she has in some time," she observed.

"Maybe she's giving him a second chance," Celia suggested.

Or maybe she wanted to minimize the likelihood of becoming a suspect. Had she learned something on her visit to Ingraham Piano that changed her feelings? Maybe she'd gone to talk with Sam about relations between the McLarens. But Cora never discussed personal affairs with those she barely knew. That included Sam.

"If the play was inspired by Freddy," Henrietta sighed, "let's hope his fate isn't as dreadful as the hero's."

As the last of the well-wishers departed, Edgar and Lavinia went backstage. Most of the actors had emerged in street clothing before Nicholas appeared amid cheers. This was what Henrietta had waited for. Her moment was stolen by two attractive young women who approached him. It was obvious he enjoyed their attention despite the fact his wife was with child. The moment revealed a stunning similarity between mother and son.

Leaving Celia in her seat, Henrietta waited until the women left before stepping up to Nicholas.

"What an engaging performance, Mr. Trindell. Truly outstanding." She congratulated him and introduced herself.

He thanked her, studying her inquisitively. "Have we met?"

"I'm a friend of your aunt's," she explained. "Edgar Brattleby is one of the more vocal guests at my literary salon."

"I imagine he is." His blue eyes regarded her with new interest. "He has a promising future in theater."

"He's one of many supporters here tonight, including Mrs. McLaren."

He looked startled. "I'm sure she has more pressing concerns at present than seeing a stage production."

"I thought the same, yet she left this rose for you when she left unexpectedly," she said without a trace of embarrassment. "I met her through my brother. He knows her well."

"Indeed," Nicholas said in a tone so polite she wondered if he'd been too immersed in rehearsals to have heard of Freddy's indiscretions. Either that, or his acting was truly superb.

"It's an unfortunate situation." She took his nonchalance as an indication to proceed. "She and your aunt are so different, it's hard to imagine them sharing such a close friendship."

"They've been friends since I was a child."

"I'm surprised your aunt isn't here. I know she planned to come. Mrs. Burns is a lovely woman. You must be very close."

"As close as a son. Aunt Hannah raised me." His smile held a touch of affection. "My mother died in childbirth."

"That explains why your aunt has no pictures of her." From his expression she couldn't tell whether he knew Myrth's true identity. "You must know Mrs. McLaren quite well."

"She's always been kind to me."

Another report of Myrth's unblemished conduct was hardly surprising, especially if she was Nicholas's mother. He wasn't as evasive as Henrietta had expected, but he was an actor by trade. She raised each new point with caution, judging his reactions. "What do you think of the newspapers' opinions?"

He shrugged, this time with slight irritation. "It's rubbish. I doubt she's capable of telling a lie."

Yet Myrth was capable of concealing the truth. Henrietta wondered if Nicholas was as skilled at lying.

"On the occasion I met her she was very forthright," she said frankly. "I hope she's able to come out of hiding soon."

Nicholas watched her with a guarded expression. "She's never mentioned you. I didn't realize you knew her that well."

Henrietta took a deep breath.

"Well enough to know her maiden name was Trindell."

Eleven

Nicholas stared at her, his eyes hardening. He had failed to conceal his shock sufficiently to deny the fact. Now he was trapped. Her silence unnerved him further.

"How do you know this?" he demanded under his breath. "Neither my mother nor my aunt would have told you that."

Henrietta hadn't thought of a response. She was relieved she wasn't telling him anything he didn't already know, although she would have done almost anything to learn the truth. Telling Freddy would be hard enough.

"My brother is close to your mother, as I mentioned," she confided gently. "He also knows a bit about Angus McLaren."

Bitterness wrinkled the corners of his mouth. "What of it? McLaren was nothing to me. It was my mother's misfortune to have married the brute. She paid for it dearly."

The venom in his tone startled Henrietta. She spoke with more sincerity this time. "I'm deeply sorry. I would have helped if she had let me. I wish I'd met her sooner."

He took a step back, his expression hostile. "I'm going to pretend this conversation never happened. Unless you can tell me where she is, I don't want to discuss this further with you. I intend to speak with my aunt at the first opportunity."

But not before I see her, Henrietta vowed. "I shall say nothing to anyone." *Except Freddy,* she amended privately. "I must congratulate you again on a fine performance. Your Shakespearean background was truly in evidence tonight."

He glared at her. "I've never done Shakespeare."

His reply confirmed a new suspicion that had begun to form in her mind. "No one would ever know," she replied serenely. "You have a tremendous talent for drama."

Turning his back on her, Nicholas joined the other actors gathered onstage. Henrietta returned quietly to Celia.

"I could see the truth in his face," Celia said.

"He's pretending not to know her whereabouts. If he did I'm sure he would never admit it," Henrietta said. "I'm not subtle enough, I fear. I should have left it to you to ask. He claims he hasn't done Shakespeare."

"Why would McLaren leave him a bust of Caesar? What could have endeared him to Angus?"

Henrietta smiled as they walked slowly up the aisle. "I doubt the bust has sentimental value. I believe Angus purposely left Nicholas something small and insignificant."

Realization filled Celia's face. Henrietta remained silent. Their confrontation had changed her view of Nicholas Trindell. Now that she knew he was Myrth's son she saw many reasons why he would dislike Angus, perhaps enough to want him dead.

McLaren had abused his mother physically and emotionally, probably refused to let her raise her son, and excluded him from any inheritance. Angus's will made it clear that if Myrth were to die first Nicholas would receive nothing, while if she outlived him her son might inherit the estate, an appealing prospect to an impoverished young actor with a wife and a child on the way.

The relationship made her question Myrth's claim that she was the target of the killer. Had she lied to direct suspicion away from her son? So few knew his true identity, the police would never suspect him. Perhaps Myrth feared the truth would be revealed eventually, and she was taking steps to protect him.

"I doubt Myrth's stayed with Hannah all this time," she speculated, "even if she did at first. Hannah wouldn't have been so quick to defend Myrth if she were hiding her. Discussion invites curiosity, and that's the last thing she wants. Even if I could find Myrth I need the jimsonweed to bring her to justice."

"She was within reach tonight," Celia said. "It's as I said. She'll appear where no one expects her."

"I'm inclined to think her appearance tonight isn't a testament to Edgar's literary genius." Henrietta sighed. "I've had enough acting for one night. Even Freddy acts confident when he must be terrified. Never mind. Tomorrow night your acting skills will rival theirs."

It was nearly twilight when Henrietta and Celia made their way to Batterymarch Street, dark enough for the lamplighter to be tending to his duties. They wished him a good evening as he hooked his ladder on the lamp-irons, climbed up the rungs, and lit each lamp in turn. The gas jets came on slowly, penetrating the gloom of the side streets.

Henrietta wondered what he must think of them. She and Celia were an odd-looking pair, one in upper class attire, the other an apparent charity girl. With her wig of blonde curls and a fraying cloak purchased from a rag man, her face gaudily painted, Celia seemed to relish her role.

"I used to wonder how it felt to live this way," Celia said. "It's easy to imagine, dressed as I am and made up to be attractive."

"I think we've made you less attractive." Henrietta eyed her critically. "But the look suits our purpose and explains my presence as a shelter worker. Are you ready?"

"In three weeks on the streets I became familiar enough with their speech to imitate it." Celia sounded confident. "I hope I can convince them I'm of their class, if not of their profession. I was timid then. Having you with me makes it less frightening."

It was refreshing to see her humility fading and her courage emerging. "I'd never let you do this alone," Henrietta assured her. "The streetwalkers don't appreciate competition. They understand the value of money."

"They also understand vengeance. If I say I want to find Mrs. McLaren because she owes me money, they might help us."

"It depends on the woman," Henrietta said tersely.

She was grateful the mild temperatures made the night ideal for their venture. Despite her anxiety she was determined to seize the opportunity while she could with Myrth's photograph in her pocket.

At the end of Custom House Street she spied the night watchman on the pier. His presence made her feel less vulnerable. Near the waterfront were the sailors, drunkards, and prostitutes. She realized she and Celia were close enough to Half Moon Place for a visit to the

McCurdys. The prospect of the night ahead made visiting an appealing alternative.

In addition to locating Myrth, they had to find Hannah Burns. Henrietta had called three times today without success. The silence in the flat made Henrietta uneasy. If Nicholas had reached his aunt first, Hannah might be avoiding her.

"What about those women off by themselves?" Celia said.

Henrietta turned to see two big-boned women in tattered cloaks with rough faces huddled by an oyster cabin on the pier. By the similarities of their features she judged them to be sisters.

"They might be willing," Henrietta agreed.

As they drew near, the women watched them warily.

"A word, if I might," Celia began in a friendly tone. "I'm looking for a lady I worked with a while back, before she changed her profession. Here's her picture. Do you remember seeing her?"

They scrutinized the picture in the pale gaslight.

"Looks familiar," the taller of the two said. "What d'you think, Mary?"

As she studied the women Henrietta decided that rather than birthrights their similarities were the marks of a lifestyle that had not been kind. They were considerably older than most streetwalkers.

Mary studied the picture. "Pretty. If I had eyes like that I wouldn't cover myself with a fan. We seen her last week, mebbe, near Broad Street. 'Member, Aggie? Her coat was shabby, but it was her walk, dignified like, that showed she was quality. It was after dark. I couldn't think what would bring such a fine lookin' lady out that way at night." She handed the picture to Celia, her face concerned. "In trouble, is she? Poor thing. A pretty face don't do a girl no good if she can't find herself an honest man."

Celia pressed a small loaf of bread and jar of preserves into the hands of each as they looked on in astonishment.

"Thank you for your help. My friend and I will find her."

As Celia turned to go the quieter of the two grabbed her arm. "Here, miss," she muttered. "I dunno what your line of work is, but you're too kind for the likes of this street. See Central Wharf and Long Wharf across the way? The men with money go there. You'd make big money if you was to work there."

As Aggie led Celia aside to point out the landmark, Henrietta remained with Mary.

"Nights gettin' colder now," Mary complained. "It's hard, this life, when you get to be our age."

Henrietta had started to suggest the pair seek refuge at the shelter when boisterous laughter interrupted them. A quartet of men approached from Water Street, one of whom was familiar from a distance. From where Henrietta stood it was impossible to tell whether Patrick Sweeney was drunk or not or whether he saw her in the shadows. His manner turned bolder and his words more deliberate when he saw Celia. Henrietta watched with alarm as he struck a confrontational stance.

"Well, if it ain't Miss Blue-blood out slumming," he said with biting sarcasm. "I know you even in disguise."

"You've made a mistake," Celia said.

Henrietta moved forward. Before she could say a word one of Sweeney's companions seized her arms, the liquor on his breath assailing her senses. She struggled to free herself, but his grip was strong. Mary and Aggie huddled together in fear.

"I seen you showing that paper around. Fancies herself an abolitionist." Standing with his face an inch from Celia's, Sweeney studied her with disgust. "Wants to help Southern folk but don't give a damn about those in her own backyard."

"That isn't true." Celia's face reflected growing fear.

"It's a photograph," Henrietta called. "It isn't what you think."

Sweeney yanked a rope off a pickle barrel on the corner. "It's time we taught Fancy Nancy a thing or two."

From out of the darkness a rock was thrown, narrowly missing Celia's head. A second struck her shoulder. Sweeney wrapped the rope around her throat swiftly, pulling her against him. Gasping for air, Celia reached back frantically, gouging his face with her fingers.

"Sweeney, let her go."

A bold voice came from behind Henrietta. She felt the hands release her. Turning, she saw Garrison Morse emerge from nowhere.

"Unhand her now," he commanded tersely.

Celia shook herself free and ran to Henrietta, panting as she tried to catch her breath. Sweeney took a step toward them but stumbled, catching himself before he fell. Garrison drew back his arm, preparing to deliver a punch. Sweeney stared at him before turning away and slinking into the depths of Water Street with the others. Garrison turned to the women.

"Did he harm you?" he asked Celia.

"No," she said, shivering, "but he frightened me."

"I'm glad you appeared when you did," Henrietta told him, clinging to Celia's arm. "I was afraid he'd incite a riot."

"Sweeney's not trustworthy. He's the type that frequents this area," Garrison said. "With the School of Industry on the waterfront I see my share. What surprises me is you being out here at this hour."

Henrietta was forced to relate their attempt to locate Myrth, aware that Mary and Aggie were listening curiously.

"We didn't come to convert any latent abolitionists," she finished. "I thought men might solicit Celia, not accuse her of being an activist."

As her heart slowed she considered the improbability of what she had witnessed.

"I don't know how Sweeney recognized you," she admitted to Celia. "You weren't with me at Harkness's Livery the day I met Hannah Burns. Where has he seen you before?"

Celia rubbed her shoulder, her composure still shaky. "We've never met. I'd remember."

"I'm grateful you came by, Garrison," Henrietta said softly. "I don't want to think what might have happened if you hadn't."

"It's fortunate I had to return to the school this evening."

"It's good you didn't have to use force," she added.

"It would have been a shame to damage my Compass Club ring. It took so long to earn it." He smiled tersely and extended his elbow. "Now I'll see you ladies home before there's another instance of mistaken identity."

Leaving Celia home to recover, Henrietta set off for the livery the next morning to discover why Hannah hadn't attended Nicholas's opening night. She hoped Hannah hadn't fled the apartment. While Hannah complained of having too few callers, Myrth gave Henrietta reason to visit.

Those who had more secrets than visitors frequently enjoyed conversation. Henrietta planned to tell Hannah she had seen Myrth in the theater and that she had been in the Broad Street area. Hannah's reaction might reveal whether they remained in contact.

The air was still by the time she reached Harkness's Livery. The stable hands seemed more flustered than usual when she arrived. She went upstairs and knocked, waiting for a reply. Instead of Hannah it was Harkness who opened his door.

He glared at her. "If you've come to see Mrs. Burns you won't get an answer from her."

Was Hannah evading her? "Has she moved?"

"In a manner of speaking. Heaven's where she's gone."

She was speechless for a moment. "When did this happen?"

"Can't say. I'm waiting for the coroner."

"How did she die?"

"Weak heart, I s'pose. Age does that."

"I called yesterday, but there was no answer." She wondered if Hannah was already dead. "Who found her?"

"I did." He hesitated long enough to make Henrietta wonder if he'd told the truth. Had Myrth or Nicholas called?

"Has her nephew been notified?"

"The police are telling him now."

How sad Hannah hadn't lived to see Nicholas achieve theatrical success. The actor obviously felt genuine affection for the woman he considered an aunt. It struck her as odd that Hannah's heart failure came without warning.

"Was she feeling well yesterday?" she asked.

"Didn't see her. Day before she seemed fine."

"Did anything unusual happen yesterday?"

"Some nights there's kicking in the horses' stalls. One of the grooms might have gone to check."

"What will become of her dog?"

"I presume her nephew will take him."

"I'm truly sorry. I'd like to pay my respects if I may."

"Do it at the funeral. I'm not unlocking the door for anybody but the coroner." Harkness stared at her squarely. "You started coming round here awful sudden. What kind of friend is that, I ask myself?"

Knowing he had reason to suspect her brother, she relented. "I'll see you at the funeral. Thank you for helping her."

Henrietta made her way downstairs slowly, unnerved by this unexpected blow. While she believed Hannah had secretly aided Myrth, her own end was ironic and bittersweet.

As she stepped into the cold daylight the sight of Patrick Sweeney seated on a crate in the stable yard made her recoil. As their eyes met she detected a wariness that told her he was sober enough to remember last night. There was no hint of drunkenness now.

"I won't hurt you," he said quietly.

"Why should I believe that?" Henrietta demanded.

Her courage failed her as she addressed the man who might have murdered Angus McLaren and almost brought the same fate upon Celia. Sweeney had openly expressed his attitude toward abolition, feelings probably intensified by the fact that Angus fired him.

"Celia could have been stoned to death." She trembled in spite of her anger.

"I didn't plan that," he conceded. "I'll make it up to you. I have information that will interest you about the woman in that picture."

The mention of Myrth startled Henrietta as did the fact that Sweeney had recognized Celia. Here was a chance to ask how he knew her. Sweeney was as likely as any shopkeeper to know Myrth's whereabouts.

"Coming to visit Mrs. Burns?" he continued.

Sweeney wasn't as aware as he thought.

"She passed away suddenly," she said, surprised by her own voice. "I wanted to pay my respects, but Mr. Harkness won't let me see her."

Looking startled, Sweeney removed a ring of keys from his pocket. "No point in you coming here for nothing."

He selected a key and started up the stairs. Henrietta followed, wondering why Sweeney had a key to Hannah's. She was too eager to get inside to ask.

They walked upstairs in silent stealth. Unlocking Hannah's door, Sweeney held it open as she entered the apartment. Hannah's little dog ran to her, panting and shaking, her tail wagging. The canary sang in his corner.

The parlor was just as Henrietta remembered it. An acutely unpleasant smell emanated from the bedroom. She found the frail woman sprawled on the bed in a strained, uncomfortable pose, eyes half shut, mouth open. From Hannah's agonized expression she appeared to have suffered a seizure. If her heart had failed, death had not been painless.

The sight made Henrietta weak. Leaving the bedroom, she went to the kitchen for water. On the table a tin canister sat beside a cup wet with tea leaves. Hannah's final cup. She inspected the canister. The fact that Hannah hadn't returned it to the cupboard probably meant she hadn't felt well before turning in.

A strange odor made Henrietta's nose run. With her handkerchief she wiped a bit of tea leaf from the corner of her eye. What had Hannah been drinking? The leaves in the canister appeared to be chamomile, suitable for someone feeling ill.

A shuffling in the doorway told her Sweeney had followed her. She had almost forgotten his presence, an unwise thing to do. He sat down at the table, putting his feet up.

"Thank you for letting me in, Mr. Sweeney." Henrietta felt like a criminal trespassing where she didn't belong.

"I seen you visiting." That, she assumed, was how he recognized Celia. "Figured you was a friend."

She took a seat across from him. "Did Mrs. Burns have many?"

"More than your brother does." His eyes were bright. "You've been asking questions."

She stared. "What of it?"

"I know things you might want to know. What's it worth to you?"

Never before had she been approached so directly to purchase information. She shifted in her chair.

"It depends on the information," she replied. "I'd rather reimburse you in other ways—goods and services, for example."

Sweeney chuckled condescendingly. "What kind of services?"

"Foodstuffs, provisions for your family. Surely you know someone in need. I'm not accustomed to paying for answers to simple questions," she said coldly. "Others also watch."

"I'm more observant than most."

"I've no doubt. If the police can't find Myrth McLaren, what makes you think you can?"

"I know she stayed here for a time."

Her heart pounded. To think Myrth sat at this table where Henrietta attempted to coax information out of Sweeney. She resented being at his mercy. If he were older he could have been the traitor who conspired to return runaway slaves to their owners. Sweeney found his niche in crime.

"When? Where did she go?"

He considered in a maddeningly slow fashion. "The answer's worth more'n bread and cheese."

"She must have been here often for you to notice."

"She came here before she was a fugitive." His tone was derisive. "Acted high and mighty, like she was too good for me."

More likely she rejected his advances, and he sought to even the score. He already hated her husband. If he had observed her here with Nicholas, could he have guessed their relationship? It gave him an opportunity for blackmail.

Studying the piercing blue eyes, she wondered what Sweeney knew. Suddenly aware of a burning in her eyes, she gazed at the handkerchief she had laid on the table. Tea leaves.

"Excuse me, Mr. Sweeney. I need some water."

She rose and turned to the sink, rinsing her eyes with a clean cloth from a hook. She felt thirsty and feverishly hot. Keeping her back to him, she took tea leaves from both the wet cup and the dry canister, careful to keep them separate and away from her eyes. A fear heavy with dreadful possibilities swept through her. She placed the wet leaves in the folds of her handkerchief, the dry folded in a paper from her reticule.

Her reaction was identical to the one she'd had in Myrth's flat when she rubbed her eyes after touching jimsonweed. A plant that belonged to a woman Sweeney saw in this apartment, a woman Hannah considered a friend.

Henrietta studied the cup with rising horror. Myrth made her presence felt even while hiding. Why would she murder the woman she trusted to raise her son? It made less sense than Sweeney having a key.

Someone had substituted jimsonweed leaves for chamomile. If only dogs could talk. The terrier before her had been a silent witness to something terrible, something that mustn't go unpunished. The canary was no help either. Henrietta replaced the canister, glad she had taken samples before the police came. She hid them in her pocket. Being caught with them wouldn't help.

Before she turned back to Sweeney she heard footsteps and voices in the parlor.

"In here," Sweeney called, removing his feet from the table.

Harkness's expression darkened as he entered the kitchen with a pair of policemen.

"How'd you get in?" Harkness demanded.

"I'm not the only one with a key," Sweeney said. "I used to get Mrs. Burns's groceries."

"Be on your way, Sweeney," one officer commanded.

"Get out before I throw you out," Harkness growled. "Don't let me see you here again. I'll change this lock tomorrow."

"I can recommend a locksmith," Henrietta volunteered.

"That warning applies to you, too."

Harkness glared at her from beneath threatening eyebrows as they returned to the parlor. The Irishman left without a fuss as an elderly man hobbled in, clutching a black bag unsteadily. Hannah Burns's physician had to be at least ten years older than his patient.

"Dr. Ebenezer Walton, Mrs. Burns's doctor," he rasped to the policemen. "Might I see her?"

"Weak heart?" questioned an officer.

"No doubt," the doctor confirmed. "Ladies of that age often suffer that fate. Gentlemen, too."

"Let's have a look," the officer suggested.

"I'd like to hear what Dr. Walton has to say after he examines Mrs. Burns," Henrietta spoke up. "As a friend I have reason to believe she was in danger."

The doctor gave her a rheumy squint. "Of what sort?"

"I believe she was poisoned."

"Nonsense. She hadn't an enemy in the world." His frown deepened as he studied her. "What makes you think so?"

Henrietta explained her suspicions regarding Myrth. Dr. Walton's disdain was evident in his craggy face.

"It's unlikely anyone would use jimsonweed when other poisons are readily available." He laughed shortly. "A writer like Mr. Thoreau hasn't the credentials to determine cause of death."

Taking the doctor and a policeman to the sink, Henrietta showed them the tea leaves and described her reaction. The officer turned to Harkness who listened intently.

"You must know of the search for Mrs. McLaren," he ventured. "Ever see a woman by that description here?"

Harkness shook his head. "Read it in the papers. I have too much to lose by housing fugitives."

His hand trembling, Dr. Walton gave the canister a cursory inspection, returning it to the counter with a shake of his head. If they relied on him to confirm Henrietta's fears, her suspicions would certainly be dismissed. She trusted neither his eyesight nor his sense of smell. He had proclaimed his diagnosis and wouldn't tolerate having his word questioned by a woman.

"Nothing but chamomile," he announced.

As she expected the policeman deferred to the physician.

"Mrs. Burns was an old woman with a weak heart who recently suffered the shock of a burglary," the officer told her kindly.

"She had recovered nicely when we last spoke of it."

"Killers don't use tea leaves. We'll look into it, Mrs. Cod."

"Cobb," Henrietta retorted as the police went into the bedroom.

Between the thefts and McLaren's murder, the police had no time to pursue her theory. Jimsonweed wasn't a common murder weapon, but a woman might use it. Who else knew Myrth had the plant? Only Thoreau and Freddy.

Was it potent enough to kill? If not, it was easy enough to rent a carriage, visit the Berkshires to procure some, and return within days. Harkness might have rented Myrth a carriage.

Gyp lay just outside the bedroom, watching the police with mournful eyes. Henrietta trembled as she waited in the parlor. It seemed likely Freddy would go to jail for a crime Myrth committed. At least he wasn't implicated in this murder.

She suspected Hannah depended on street vendors for groceries. Still, Sweeney's claim that others had keys might be true. Nicholas and Myrth came to mind.

Nicholas could have murdered Angus, especially if Myrth were the target. She would undoubtedly lie to protect her son. Hannah said there was no forced entry when her home was ransacked. The thief had no reason to kill her. No common thief took time to brew jimsonweed tea.

The trail of logic ended, as it always did, with Myrth.

Twelve

"Why would Sweeney admit seeing Myrth at Mrs. Burns's home? Why expose her now?"

Settled in the receiving room that evening, Henrietta didn't find Celia's question surprising.

"For money. Knowing Freddy was a suspect, he thought I'd be willing to pay for information after he saw me at Hannah's."

Extending her finger as a perch for Captain Kidd, Henrietta watched the parrot step on, as trusting as Hannah had been.

"But how trustworthy is Sweeney?" Celia asked. "The information we need is in the hands of someone unscrupulous enough to put a price on others' lives."

"The grooms said Myrth rebuffed him repeatedly. Having jimsonweed makes her a suspect, but why would she want to harm Hannah? My reaction to the tea leaves was the same as I had at Myrth's after handling petals. Someone switched jimsonweed for chamomile."

"Maybe Myrth knew nothing of its potency but knew someone who did."

"But I found leaves in her sewing chest. She must have taken the rest." Henrietta set down her teacup. "Even if she didn't kill Angus, it's possible a lover did."

"Knowing Nicholas is Myrth's son gives him reason."

"What we learned last night gives us new direction." Henrietta broached a subject she had wanted to bring up. "How did it feel playing that role?"

Celia smiled wanly. "Foreign yet familiar. Before I met you I'd lived on the street for six weeks after I got off the train. I thought I would find work as a maid or governess, but who would hire a woman without references? People assumed I was a fallen woman."

Henrietta listened intently. "How did you get by?"

"From hand to mouth." Celia seemed at ease with the memory. "I spent everything to get here. After my suitcase was stolen I was filthy and too ashamed to ask for work. My own husband wouldn't have recognized me. I'd begun to despair when you found me."

Here was the admission Henrietta had wanted. Celia had a husband somewhere from whom she was running. She knew more revelations would come when Celia was ready.

"Thank you for telling me," Henrietta said. "This house has been empty a very long time. I'm glad you stayed."

Celia shivered, her eyes sympathetic. "I'm grateful for your help. I've wanted to tell you about my past. So often I've compared myself to Myrth and wonder what her life is like now."

"I'd give money to know." Henrietta gave her a crooked smile. "If Sweeney has his way perhaps I will."

The morning cold was reflected in the faces of those attending Hannah's funeral. *October days were variable,* Henrietta reflected before the service, *either rich with golden light or bleak without sun. This day it's the latter.* She drew her collar higher, seeking shelter from the wind.

"Nothing is sadder," she told Celia as the minister started toward the grave, "than a funeral with few in attendance."

She was glad Fan had come and surprised Freddy hadn't. A dozen mourners, including Nicholas and Harkness, gathered in the Old Granary Burying Ground amid rows of slate markers, their rounded tops rising from russet leaves. Hannah would spend eternity surrounded by John Hancock and other patriots, remembered only by a child she had raised as her nephew and some aged friends who might soon be gone also.

Following the service mourners extended words of comfort to Nicholas before leaving for the warmth of their firesides. Harkness offered his sympathy as the minister engaged a gentleman in conversation. Celia and Fan stepped aside after Harkness left, and Henrietta approached Nicholas.

"I'm sorry about your aunt," she said. "I'll miss her. Is there no other family?"

"When one is eighty there are few left to mourn," he said in a bitter tone. "My wife is in confinement with child, but there's a cousin here. I'll see the date is inscribed on the stone. It's the final respect I can pay, that and taking her dog."

"And the canary?"

"My wife dislikes birds."

She made a mental note to look into the matter. "It's a shame your aunt didn't live to see your child, and of course Mrs. McLaren isn't here," she felt compelled to add.

When he didn't reply she continued. "Have the police determined the cause of death?"

"Heart failure. Predictable at her age."

A reasonable expectation for a woman who was elderly but otherwise healthy. There was no reason to find her death anything but natural, except for the tea leaves. Henrietta resolved to send them to Thoreau on her return home.

"I have reason to think her death was deliberate," she admitted.

Nicholas stared. "You think she was murdered? By God, death follows you everywhere."

"I think she was poisoned. Did you know your mother kept jimsonweed?"

"I've no wish to discuss family," Nicholas retorted.

"I hope in time we can discuss this," she said gently. "I want to see justice done."

With that he returned to the minister. The older gentleman pointed out as Hannah's cousin was the last at the grave. Before he left Henrietta introduced herself.

"I understand you were related," she said.

"We were," he said politely, his hat in his hands, "though I hadn't seen Hannah since she moved here with William years ago."

"It's a shame her sister died so young."

He looked at her strangely. "Lost three of my own in infancy. It's to be expected." He replaced his hat and bowed to her. "My condolences."

"And mine to you."

So Hannah had told the truth about having a sister. After the cousin left Celia and Fanny returned.

"It's troubling that no one takes your theory seriously," Fan said. "If Mrs. Burns suspected she was in danger, maybe she kept a diary that will answer the questions that outlived her."

"I'll ask Nicholas about it later," Henrietta said. "I also want to know why Freddy isn't here. First, Celia, we'll get you home. You have lessons to prepare. Our committee still funds the school even if Mr. Atwood remains reluctant." Her forced optimism failed to reach its mark. "I promised I'd retain hope until there's no longer reason to. I intend to do just that."

Her brother was occupied with a collection of bones in his laboratory right where Henrietta expected to find him. When she arrived he was examining them with the attention a jeweler might give a fine stone.

"I expected to see you at Mrs. Burns's funeral." When he barely acknowledged her she continued. "I'm surprised you'd miss the chance to see Myrth."

"She'd never come with people present."

"There weren't many, which made your absence more obvious. If she were innocent she'd come to a friend's funeral."

"Not when her own could be next." Freddy's voice was tinged with impatience. "I'll pay my respects tomorrow. I expect Myrth will visit when she can do so without fear of discovery."

"Perhaps her jimsonweed is what caused the funeral."

"That's ridiculous." He glared at her before turning back to the femur in his hands. "Mrs. Burns died of a heart attack. I wish you would believe me if not Myrth."

"How can we believe her?" Henrietta exclaimed. "She earned her living on the stage. Now she's playing with our emotions."

He set aside the bone and turned to her patiently.

"She's too honest to play with emotions, just as I am. I hope one day Lieutenant Tripp realizes she hasn't told me her whereabouts and will cease calling."

Henrietta was alert. "He called again?"

"I'm surprised you didn't see him as you arrived. Same old evidence, no new suspects." He picked up a smaller bone but laid it down, his attention now fully on the conversation. "The last thing the police want is the unsolved murder of an abolitionist."

"They need a scapegoat." She rushed to his defense. "You must tell them what you know. Don't jeopardize your future for this woman. She wouldn't do so for you."

A muscle twitched in his cheek as he weighed his promises against principles. She considered telling him about Nicholas but couldn't find the words.

"If only you would see her as I do," she said plaintively. "This is worse than anything you managed to get into as a child. You always were a troublesome sibling."

Her attempts at humor fell flat. She chose her words carefully. Few insights would change his mind if Tripp's visit hadn't.

"It may at some point become necessary for you to choose between your future and hers," she reminded him gently in parting. "It's evident to me that those paths are separate."

Her thoughts lingered on Freddy as she prepared for bed the next night. Would he feel differently if he knew Myrth had a son? Behaving honorably for Freddy wasn't merely restoring loyalty to his wife. He felt obligated to protect a woman in jeopardy despite threats to his own safety.

Yet it was Myrth who feared being blamed for murder. Was she protecting Freddy? Henrietta hadn't seriously considered the possibility of his guilt until now. The idea chilled her.

The mantel clock told her it was nearly eleven. This was the night Freddy planned to visit Hannah's grave. Anticipation coursed through her mixing with caution. The Old Granary wasn't far. If she dressed now she might catch him. Donning her clothes once again, she slipped outside and headed toward Park Street.

Freddy's walk would take less time than hers. She quickened her pace. Only a few pedestrians and carriages made their way along Tremont Street as she passed through the iron gates of the cemetery. At first glance she was disappointed to see only headstones until a furtive movement near the back caught her eye.

A hooded figure moved in the shadows of the Paul Revere monument near Hannah's grave. Henrietta hastened between the tombstones, sure of her identity. Their encounter after the Faneuil Hall assembly had terrified her. This time Myrth was the frightened one.

"Myrth, wait," Henrietta commanded. "I must speak with you."

Myrth paused as if she were too weary to run. Henrietta stopped, fearful of frightening her yet worried she might be concealing a gun.

"You said you would return," Henrietta said gently. "Don't we have some things to discuss?"

The woman before her had changed. She looked wary and haggard, her eyes shadowed.

"I expected to find Freddy here," Henrietta faltered.

"We arranged to meet tonight, but I was delayed," Myrth admitted. "He left a note at Hannah's grave."

"Did the police keep you away?"

"I warn you, you'll never see me again if you turn me in."

Myrth was shaking with more fear than Henrietta felt. She thought quickly. Much depended on her handling of this unexpected opportunity.

"You needn't fear me," Henrietta promised. "Won't you consider staying with me until this is resolved?"

"When will that be? Hannah didn't die of a heart attack as the newspapers claim," Myrth said bitterly.

"I know she was killed, but why? By whom?"

"For knowledge we shared. The same person who wants my life took hers. It's a warning to me. I'm the only target left."

Henrietta realized how vulnerable they were in this open ground, where even a tall man could go unnoticed among headstones. She lowered her voice.

"Why won't you confide in the police? Your silence only protects the killer."

"I can't face disgrace again," Myrth blurted out. "It cost me everything."

"It could cost Freddy his life if you don't tell them what you know. If you're innocent the police will protect you."

"If only I knew who to trust," Myrth fretted.

As the wind blew Henrietta drew her cloak about her. Leaves rattled in the cold, their branches throwing clawlike shadows over the ground.

"You said you have proof of the killer's identity."

"I gave it to Hannah for safekeeping." Myrth's tone was despondent. "I fear it's been stolen."

Henrietta's heart sank. As if sensing her indignation Myrth hurried on.

"My life was in danger. I didn't think Hannah's was. I've made terrible mistakes that Angus and Hannah have paid for."

"Don't let Freddy be a victim," Henrietta urged. "You're at risk without police help. You have a long life ahead with a grandchild to look forward to."

Recognition dawned in Myrth's eyes.

"Doesn't Nicholas deserve better?" Henrietta asked softly. "I'm a mother, too. I know what it is to lose a son."

Myrth barely appeared to breathe. "Does Freddy know?"

"I haven't found the right moment to tell him."

"I hope you don't." Myrth closed her eyes briefly. "I couldn't bear the humiliation."

"He risks his life to meet you in secret. Why remain in hiding? If you don't contact the police I'll be forced to tell them I've seen you."

"If you do they'll no longer trust you. We're all at risk."

"Especially your son," Henrietta accused. "You care more for his welfare than Freddy's. Did he kill Angus?"

Soft footsteps from the street drew their attention. A darkly clad figure emerged from shadow, probably a watchman looking for thieves. Without another word Myrth disappeared into the shadows.

"Myrth," Henrietta called.

Her cry met with silence. She saw it wasn't a policeman but a passerby who walked on. Myrth had tricked her once again. She ought to have shouted for help while she had the chance. If Myrth had been the target, Henrietta had found no one who disliked her. Had she made a false claim to throw suspicion off her son?

As the bells chimed midnight Henrietta turned toward Beacon Street, thinking of the concerns she expressed to Neville in her last letter, comforting herself with the encouragement from him that came in today's mail.

She was beginning to feel Angus's killer was a skilled actor by nature as well as by trade.

It had been little more than a week since Henrietta wrote Thoreau, but another correspondence was in order. Flash rattled about in his exercise wheel as she took up her pen.

Louisburg Square, Boston
October 12, 1860

Dear Mr. Thoreau,

I write today with a heavy heart. A woman has been laid to rest in our city. While the police believe her death was caused by a heart attack, I suspect jimsonweed.

I had the same reaction in her apartment as when I initially handled jimsonweed. My eyes experienced a strange burning, and I had a rare thirst and feverish skin reflecting symptoms of poisoning.

I enclose two samples for your analysis. The dry leaves within the blotting paper are a different consistency than the wet which I've enclosed in a pouch. The wet leaves are remnants from the deceased woman's final cup of tea.

Hoping your reply resolves the matter once and for all in the eyes of the authorities, with deepest thanks I remain,

    Your humble reader,
    Henrietta Newell Cobb

The church bells sounded less ominous after dawn when Henrietta walked Fudge along the paths dividing Boston Common. The night had delivered the thin coat of snow yesterday's leaden sky had promised and enough of a chill to make her wish she had brought her pug's woolen coat.

In the morning light her convictions melted away like snow under the sun's first rays. She felt torn by Annie Jackson's revelation of Sam's hostility toward Angus. Even with her brother's life at stake she didn't relish pursuing a disillusioning truth about someone she once cared for.

She doubted another lover killed Angus. While Myrth would protect her son, Fordham's motive for wanting Angus dead remained solid. Even if one of them was guilty it didn't explain three murders.

Henrietta wondered if Hannah's killer found what the thief wanted. The waxy feel of the doorknob was too coincidental. Did Sweeney kill Hannah for the proof Myrth entrusted to her? His motive was as strong as Fordham's.

The questions haunted her as she walked between Dr. Holmes's elms, their bare branches reaching skyward as if asking the same questions and receiving no answers. If only she could get Willie to admit what he knew. He had managed to disappear the past few weeks.

Her introspection deepening, she headed home to feed Ozymandias. She had never tested the alligator's patience and would not now. She headed up Charles, where snow-topped rowhouses and wrought iron fences glistened with the early light. On Chestnut two policemen were inspecting footprints in the snow at the Deven home. Another burglary.

By the time she turned into Mount Vernon suspicion nagged at her, more convincing as it developed. A thought struck her, one so awful it took her a moment to realize Fudge stood waiting for their walk to resume.

The pieces fit. *Don't open your door to strangers,* the police had advised Hannah. She hadn't allowed a stranger in. Nor had Henrietta or the other victims.

They had opened their doors to someone they knew. Home again, Henrietta removed her cloak in a daze. Should she notify the police? Before making an accusation she should confirm her suspicions.

She would start by calling on the Allingtons, Fanny's neighbors, at the first respectable hour.

Henrietta and Celia spent the afternoon in the back parlor, now rearranged as a classroom. Celia organized the bookshelves while Henrietta reviewed her plan. Willie would come tonight, for she'd given Molly a reward to ensure his presence. It would be less awkward than confronting him before his family. She was glad Garrison had returned from his fundraising trip to the Berkshires in time to help.

At six-thirty her driver delivered seven children including Willie. As Celia escorted them upstairs Henrietta made sure a guest positioned in the kitchen hallway managed to get a good look.

"Is this the boy you saw loitering in Sentry Hill Place the afternoon of the murder?" Henrietta asked.

The face of the McLarens' landlady darkened. Mrs. Baker's look of recognition on seeing the angled cap and confident stride was instantaneous.

"That's the one!" she exclaimed. "I'd know that face anywhere. Arrogant, he was."

"And still is. You've been a great help, Mrs. Baker." Now that Henrietta had the information she needed she couldn't resist. "To me as well as Mrs. McLaren."

"What do you mean?"

"Who else could have told her about my inquiries?"

The landlady flinched before her face softened. "You understand how it is. With no one to turn to, she confided in me."

Though Mrs. Baker had aided a fugitive she had also identified Willie as having been in Sentry Hill Place. They made an untrustworthy trio. Why had Willie lied? Perhaps he was so used to being sought by the police for various petty crimes he didn't want to implicate himself in a murder in which he had no part.

Arranging to have the landlady taken home, Henrietta prepared for the next confrontation.

She held Willie's hand as her carriage made its way toward the waterfront. In her other hand was Fudge's leash. She saw no point in depriving Willie of one small comfort. He asked few questions as they rode. Even when their conveyance pulled up before the School of Industry he remained silent.

As she led him inside she was relieved the evening gloom softened the facade of the three-story brick building. Watching suspiciously from under his cap, Willie gaped at the adults assembled before him in Garrison Morse's office.

A policeman waited, his gaze as intimidating as his uniform. Williston Brayman Atwood sat, cane in hand, his face so severe Henrietta suspected he was prepared to apply the cane to Willie's backside. Garrison stood behind the policeman.

The tension snapped when Fudge's leash slipped from Henrietta's hand. Before she could stop him the pug attached himself to Garrison's trouser leg. She rushed forward, grabbing him by the collar and prying him off. Knowing how Garrison disliked dogs, she apologized profusely.

With Fudge securely in her arms, she closed the door so they could proceed. Officer Roberts assumed an imposing stance before Willie. Henrietta knew nothing but intimidation would succeed.

"Have a seat, young man," the officer instructed.

The boy sat cagily in a stiff-backed chair, his legs rigid.

"Why's there a fox here?" he blustered.

"Officer Roberts wants to ask you about the thefts in my neighborhood." Henrietta sat next to Willie.

"I got things to do." Willie started to rise. From behind his chair Garrison placed his hands on his shoulders and pushed him gently back down.

"You'll mind your manners, boy," Atwood commanded, "and do as you're told."

The policeman crossed his arms, studying him shrewdly. "We have a warrant for your arrest, young man."

Willie shrank back in the chair. "I ain't done nothing. I work every day. Ask my boss."

"Mr. Penrose hasn't seen you for so long," Henrietta said, "he assumed you'd taken another job. Your family says you bring home money. Where does it come from, Willie?"

For once Willie was silent.

"No sense in lying now, son," the officer said patiently. "We know you've been stealing."

"I ain't no thief!" Willie shouted.

"I don't think you committed the thefts, but you provided the means," said Henrietta. "Why was my home robbed after you came collecting money for your grandmother who wasn't sick at all?"

"I didn't filch no money," Willie said. "You gave it to me."

So much for gratitude. "While you've chosen to miss the point, I found traces of wax in the locks of four houses that were robbed. Mr. Penrose says you're too preoccupied with wax to do your job."

Willie shrugged. "I always keep a bit of wax in my pocket."

"More than a bit," Garrison said with a trace of humor. "Enough to have taken up the chandlery business from what I hear."

Atwood's mustache twitched with disapproval. "Boldness won't serve you well here, boy. Tell the truth."

"You bought a fair quantity, according to the owner of the general store near Penrose's factory," Henrietta prompted.

"Empty your pockets, son," the policeman commanded.

"I didn't pilfer nothing." Willie was defiant, but his boldness had peaked.

"You haven't said where the money came from," Officer Roberts said.

"I'll show Penrose." Willie's anger was subdued as he rifled through the pockets of new pants. "I'm going to war first chance I get."

"You'll be in jail first, son," Garrison said quietly. "If war comes it'll be over before you're out."

Willie stared at him. Here was a new threat. He turned his pockets inside out. A ball of string, some coins, and a glob of wax tumbled onto the table.

"Let's try an experiment." From her reticule Henrietta removed the key to the lock she had replaced. She pressed it into the wax, making a perfect match. The officer looked at Willie.

"You earn money as a thief's assistant," he accused. "The burglar hired you to make wax impressions of keys. He'd make a duplicate, return at night, and rob the houses. You got in by raising sympathy for your supposedly sick grandmother. Mrs. Cobb's key hung by the door. It was easy for you to distract the new maid long enough to make an impression."

Anger stirred within Henrietta for having felt sympathy for Willie. Rather than shame there was reckless pride in his efforts. His smug countenance and stubborn silence were as clear as a confession.

"You're as clever as the Artful Dodger," Garrison said grimly. "Mr. Dickens should put you in a book."

"Mr. Morse's pupils here at the School of Industry show more promise," the policeman warned. "Boys like you, Willie, aren't fit for reform school."

"There's no glory in jail, son." Garrison had been kinder than anyone, Henrietta thought. "You don't want to end up here. We'll take care of you if you cooperate."

Henrietta checked her impulse to comfort Willie. Doing so would defeat the purpose of the confrontation. Most boys at the School of Industry weren't much older than Willie, convicted by the courts for petty crimes or vagrancy, some turned over by their parents for disobedience. Their conduct had consigned them to this place, a mere step above prison, where flogging was still done.

Willie's confidence began to crumble. His face drooped at the idea of experiencing the excitement of war from a jail cell. Henrietta took his hand in hers, surprised how sweaty it was.

"You've disappointed me, Willie," she confided. "I worried about you when you were the threat all along. Someday you'll see how you've let your family down. There's no pride in that."

Willie looked directly into her eyes, his own uneasy. Her words had hit their mark.

"I have one question," she continued. "I can understand why you obtained impressions of keys to the homes of wealthier families. Why Mrs. Burns? She had no money."

"I dunno names, just addresses." When she gave Willie the address he shrugged. "My boss don't rob stable yards."

The policeman studied Willie. "You haven't given us his name. You'd better if you don't want to go to jail."

"Don't force me to tell your mother," Henrietta remonstrated.

Willie hesitated only a moment. "Sweeney made me do it," he blurted. "He's the one who showed me how. I did good work for him."

Henrietta should have assumed it involved Sweeney, who functioned best by placing the risk on others. Having Willie obtain impressions of keys made it simple for him to enter homes undisturbed.

"I've no doubt your work was precise," Officer Roberts said. "The police are even better acquainted with Mr. Sweeney than with you. When did he hire you to do his dirty work?"

"Two months ago. He said if I got him keys to the swells' houses he'd pay me more than Penrose did. He said nobody'd look twice at a tyke like me."

Atwood sat still with silent outrage. At Officer Roberts's request Garrison summoned a guard. They watched as Willie was escorted out to be taken to the station house.

"Reprehensible. An old thief for such a young boy." Atwood's stern features turned melancholy. "That boy has a sad future."

Willie's fate emphasized the importance of education to working children so perfectly that Henrietta hoped the incident would make him reverse his decision to withhold school funding. Garrison turned to her after Atwood left, his eyes bright.

"Impressive work, Etta. I'm glad I returned in time to help stage this confrontation." He frowned. "How did you know Willie assisted with the thefts?"

"Penrose said Willie wasted time playing with wax. My lock felt waxy like Mrs. Burns's did. When I told the police my suspicions they told me New York is plagued by assistant thieves. Sweeney's connection with Willie explains how he recognized Celia that night at the docks. He had been watching our house. Exploiting children in such an immoral way is despicable." The idea infuriated her. "Who would suspect a child?"

"No doubt Boston has enough dishonest locksmiths willing to make keys from wax impressions without questioning the reason."

"The only thing worse than preying on the trust and kindness of decent citizens is corrupting the young to do it. It never occurred to me to question Willie when he asked for money until I called at his house and discovered his grandmother wasn't ill."

"I almost feel ashamed reassuring him things will work out," Garrison admitted. "I've spoken with him about reform school. Willie's learned a multitude of bad habits at a very young age."

"Maybe as a Compass Club member you can raise support for child labor reform. This incident strengthens the argument for our night school."

"Parents don't realize education will help their children earn more. Eventually these youth will tire of the work and pass their days in grog shops." Garrison paused. "And in time, theft."

Henrietta grimaced. "Children need better options than turning to theft to help support their families."

"This might not even make the papers. Tomorrow the public will turn its attention to the visit from the prince and more attractive diversions." Garrison gave her a look of empathy. "It's a good thing you made the connection when you did. You probably saved many Bostonians a small fortune."

While Henrietta had arranged to meet Freddy outside the Music Hall Thursday afternoon, she realized the futility of the plan when she saw the crowd jamming the entrance. Thousands had been released from work to attend the concert, the most notable feature of the Prince of Wales's visit. Cora had been part of the large committee needed to train twelve hundred public schoolchildren to sing in key.

With dismay Henrietta realized Freddy might be at the theater's other entrance. It would be impossible to penetrate the crowd before the orchestra started to play. She would have to meet him at their seats. Turning back to the throng flooding into Music Hall, she was startled when someone brushed against her.

She turned to see Sweeney beside her.

"Good afternoon, Mrs. Cobb," he said in an undertone. "I have news regarding our mutual acquaintance."

Thirteen

Henrietta was too stunned to reply. With most of the police force assigned to protect the prince, Sweeney was supposed to be arrested after the festivities. Rather than skip town as she feared, he had the nerve to appear at the Music Festival.

"Information about Mrs. McLaren?" she asked.

"You'll need to pay more than goods and services to hear what I know about Mrs. Burns's murder. It's one of your toffs that did it." Sweeney's eyes glistened with greed as if debating the price she might pay to learn what he knew. They had stepped away from the crowd, but the excited chatter made conversation difficult. "Will you be at the ball tonight?"

"Yes, I have tickets." The thrill of seeing the Prince of Wales faded in contrast to finding a thief in the midst of the policemen surrounding Music Hall.

"We'll meet while the others are inside." He looked at her intently. "I need money."

To get out of town, no doubt. She could see the police on the periphery of the alley. Undoubtedly Sweeney would rather share his information with her than with them.

"Five hundred in gold," he intoned. "Meet me at eleven thirty. Mason Street, the stage entrance."

He vanished in the crowd like an ordinary citizen rather than a criminal sought for robbery. Henrietta considered his words. While the others are inside, he had said. At that hour Mason Street would be packed with stable hands and waiting carriages. Who did he want to avoid? The people who would be inside were those attending the ball, most of high character and reputation.

One of their toffs, he had said, an acquaintance. Was it possible someone she knew had killed Hannah? The idea sickened her. Hannah's death had to be related to her friendship with Myrth.

At least they would meet in a public place. If she needed help someone at the ball might step outside for air. What good was Sweeney's word without proof? Whatever information he had must be significant.

Possibilities filled her mind as the crowd swept her indoors and she took her seat beside Celia. Freddy had already arrived.

"Where were you?" she said. "I waited in Music Hall Place."

"We agreed Hamilton Place was more convenient," he retorted.

"It was worth waiting at the wrong door. I met someone the police have been seeking." Henrietta told them of her encounter. "If Sweeney does know who killed Hannah he probably knows more about Myrth. He spends time at the livery."

Freddy absorbed the news in silence. Finally he spoke, venom in his voice. "He should be thrashed, making us pay for information. It's extortion."

"I have only silver at home and no time before tonight to make the exchange at the bank."

"It's all in confidence," Celia countered. "He wouldn't go to the police."

"Sweeney survives by putting a price on whatever he can," Henrietta said. "His information might be worth the cost to us."

Freddy sighed resignedly. "We have no choice but to consent to his demands. I'll add half the silver to your collection tonight. I'm as anxious as you to learn who killed Mrs. Burns."

Further conversation was cut short by a hush signaling the start of the concert. Anxious from her encounter, all Henrietta could do at present was turn her attention to the platform where Boston's schoolchildren assembled. The floor was so crowded with officials there was barely room for the future King Edward VII.

She was pleased to see Mr. Emerson and Dr. Holmes on stage. Voices filled with anticipation echoed from galleries hung with blue and crimson, adorned with the arms of England and America. Flags filled the upper cornice while shields lined the walls.

It was after five when the Prince of Wales and his suite entered Music Hall accompanied by Mayor Lincoln and Governor Banks. Sporting a cane, wearing a black coat, gray trousers, and lavender gloves, the youthful Edward flashed a smile as men cheered and ladies waved handkerchiefs. The children began with a rendition of "God Save the Queen" with stanzas written for the occasion by Dr. Holmes. Nothing of this magnitude, Henrietta reflected, had occurred in Boston within memory.

As strains from Mendelssohn, Mozart, and Beethoven filled the hall Henrietta sat back to enjoy the music. The evening ahead was beyond her control. Sweeney had the upper hand, at least for the moment.

Several hours later in the privacy of her study, Henrietta withdrew the required silver from her desk and tucked it into her reticule. She took only a minute to slip into a dress of burgundy brocade figured in gold, selecting a garnet necklace as the only accent.

After her maid dressed her hair with gold netting she located Celia in her room. Having taken obvious pains with her appearance, Celia blushed with embarrassment.

"You look exquisite, my dear," Henrietta marveled. "It suits you perfectly."

Celia's outfit had been designed by a dressmaker Henrietta reserved for special occasions. She had spared no expense for the joy of seeing the excitement on Celia's face. The ivory silk dress featured a swag of deep green leaves and ivory roses across the bodice. It was complemented by a small headpiece of ivy and white lilies. To complete the effect Henrietta offered her a diamond choker and earrings from her own jewelry box. The result was stunning. Celia smiled as Henrietta stared with admiration.

"I feel rather like a princess," Celia confided, then grew serious. "But I won't focus on the trivial with all you're facing. Shall I come along when you face Sweeney?"

"It's best if I see him alone," Henrietta said. "If I'm gone for long you might step out for air."

"If you're not there I'll know something has happened." Anxiety clouded Celia's eyes.

Henrietta smiled with a confidence she didn't feel. "I'll have to react to the moment and hope my judgment is sound."

Their discussion ended with Mrs. Biddle's arrival. "Madam, you'd best come," she advised. "Flash has escaped and is gnawing at the drawing room drapes. The rascal keeps eluding me, and I haven't a peanut to lure him back."

"I'll show you where I keep some for next time."

Stepping into the corridor, Henrietta reflected how easily her squirrel had escaped from the cage she had secured this morning. If a contained creature could escape his captors, how would the police locate and capture an elusive killer?

As conveyances drew up before the Boston Theatre Henrietta found the noise unimaginable even for Washington Street. Amid the joyous clamor were the high-pitched voices of young ladies like her nieces who had talked of nothing but the ball for weeks. *Alec, who would be in his early thirties now had he lived, would have delighted in this evening,* she thought wistfully.

"Women outnumber gentlemen nearly two to one," Celia observed as they alighted from their barouche.

"We needn't have brought cloaks," Henrietta complained. "In this crush of people it's as warm outdoors as it will be in."

Their steps slowed by those ahead of them, they eventually reached the foyer, where Henrietta realized her comment about the heat was hardly exaggerated. On their way to the ballroom they met Fanny and Admiral Browning.

"Three ladies have already fainted," Fan said gaily. "Too much excitement, I fear."

Henrietta suspected the kind of excitement awaiting her was different from that of most people here, but if Fan knew the danger she faced she might interfere with her plans. As if reading her mind Fan grew more serious.

"You've had your share of excitement lately," Fan confided. "You're certainly heading toward the truth where Mrs. McLaren is concerned, but this isn't the place for such talk. We're here to welcome the prince to Boston."

Henrietta was glad Fan had redirected the conversation. Thrusting her worries from her mind, she smiled and waved to acquaintances. The dowagers and debutantes of Boston society filled the hall, many with eminent husbands at their sides. Dressed in finery fit for royalty, the ladies of means looked altogether different than when dressed for charity work, clothed so as not to make the poor feel inferior.

"Why is it called the Renfrew Ball again?" Browning asked, showing more interest in the sherry in his hand.

"The prince is traveling disguised as Baron Renfrew, hence the name," Fanny explained. "His disguise is a great success."

British and American flags greeted them in the ballroom, the festooned galleries filled with those anxious for a glimpse of Britain's future king. Urns of oversized palms divided nooks for private conversation. Henrietta and Celia squeezed through the crinolines, seizing the chance to sit when a trio of women vacated their alcove. Henrietta saw Garrison across the room, with Edith the essence of refinement in green moire. Not long afterward Freddy and Cora appeared with their daughters. Cora's manner seemed markedly improved as she waved to Henrietta.

"Corinthia's positively glowing," Henrietta whispered to Celia, noting how the floral-patterned maize brocade flattered her. "She looks as happy as Felicity and Prudence. This afternoon's performance must have been well received."

"Professor Newell seems in unusually high spirits," Celia noted.

Henrietta wasn't convinced the success of the Music Festival alone accounted for the buoyancy in Cora's spirits. As she made her way across the room Cora spoke frequently to Freddy, pausing to accept accolades on the concert. Her daughters looked feminine in contrasting shades of pink silk, Felicity's with a lace overdress, Prudence's trimmed with magenta ribbons.

"Did you bring the money?" Freddy asked when they were alone. "I feel like a criminal merely asking. Here's my share."

"Thank you." Henrietta slipped the silver into her bag. "I know the feeling, but I'm prepared."

"There will only be grooms and cab drivers outside at eleven thirty." Freddy's face was full of concern. "I'd feel better if you'd let me escort you."

"Sweeney has no reason to trust anyone at this point. I'll make the transaction and learn what I can." Henrietta glanced at the ballroom. "Cora's enjoying herself."

"It feels a bit like accompanying a stranger." Freddy smiled tentatively. "She's decided a slap against me is a slap against herself. She's been rather defiant with others of late, to my benefit. I can only speculate what's created such loyalty."

"Be grateful," she advised. "She must feel a great weight was lifted with the success of today's concert."

In this elegant setting it was hard to imagine Freddy and Corinthia as suspects despite the evidence that pointed to them. Henrietta watched Cora chatting with members of the Music Festival committee, hardly noticing Sam Ingraham walking past. If they'd had questionable dealings neither showed any trace of it.

Could Annie Jackson have mistaken the identity of the visitor at Ingraham Piano? Looking discreetly but critically at her sister-in-law's size, she thought not. As Corinthia left her group Henrietta approached her swiftly.

"This is the first chance I've had to congratulate you on today's splendid concert," she began. "It was truly memorable."

"Let's hope the prince feels the same," Corinthia beamed.

"I wanted to thank you for attempting to help Freddy with your visit to Ingraham Piano," Henrietta ventured.

Cora looked at her quizzically. "That had nothing to do with him. It concerned the rental of pianos for concert practice."

"That's certainly a valid reason," Henrietta said awkwardly.

Cora's reply seemed cool and a touch evasive. Had Henrietta imagined deception on her part? Cora must worry with Myrth still in hiding. The return of the Brownings ended her reverie.

"Good to see Cora and Freddy looking so jovial," Admiral Browning said as Cora turned to a group of friends. "Never mind, in a few weeks Freddy will be at the ballot box casting his vote for Mr. Lincoln along with every other man of sense in Boston."

The highlight of the evening was the announcement of the Prince of Wales's arrival. His appearance was elegant and his manner unassuming as he promised to dance with numerous partners during the evening, making Prudence swoon with anticipation. The waltzing began with the first dance going to the governor's wife. Within moments the ballroom was in full merriment.

Henrietta had tucked her father's pocket watch in her reticule beside the silver. Consulting it now, she saw she had two hours to go. She chatted with friends to pass the time, realizing the topic had shifted while her mind wandered. Some time later Edgar and Lavinia Brattleby joined Henrietta and Celia. In pale lavender Lavinia appeared as graceful and inconspicuous as possible despite her height.

"Apparently the prince managed to travel without fuss," said Edgar. "His train journey was so smooth he was able to consume a lunch of ham and woodcock with the car in motion."

"I wonder what sort of man he is," Celia mused.

"Supposedly a well-mannered fellow," Edgar said. "Genial disposition, unpretentious for a lad of nineteen. Seems more American than British."

"I find the British to be very warm," Henrietta said, "when they're addressed on subjects such as dogs and literature."

"In other words," Lavinia smiled, "when one has something in common with them as you do, Etta."

The waltz ended and the dancers parted, exchanging a bow and curtsey. To their astonishment Edward looked in their direction, pausing before he bowed to Celia.

"Could it be Baron Renfrew fancies Mrs. Chase?" said Edgar.

Color flooded Celia's face. "I barely acknowledged him. I don't imagine he was looking at me."

"He wasn't looking at me, my dear," Henrietta said, amused. "You present a far more charming figure, I assure you."

Sam and Bertha Ingraham strolled by, Sam gazing in one direction, Bertha in the other, wearing an unflattering eggplant shade. Henrietta felt sympathy for Sam despite the likelihood of his guilt. He displayed none of the enthusiasm of other revelers, his stride slow and deliberate, his face serious.

Henrietta reflected on the duality of their natures as Sam paused to address Charles Sumner, the former senator. She watched as he and Bertha meandered toward a large fern where they stopped to converse privately. Since they hadn't seen her she moved closer so she could listen, focusing her gaze elsewhere.

"Can't this war be forgotten for one night?" Bertha complained.

"We must prepare for a halt in business," Sam argued. "You heard Sumner. If we go to war, the country could go either toward slavery or freedom. The only sure thing is it won't be divided. Half its men can't be free while half are slaves."

"It will never be worth the cost of our young men." Bertha wrinkled her long face in disgust. "We're just fortunate McLaren is gone. Let's talk of other things."

Henrietta moved away as Sam changed the subject. It would have been easy for Bertha to plot Angus's death. Yet the lack of guile in her words made her sound more like a woman who had her sons' welfare at heart than a murderess. Henrietta walked back to Celia convinced Bertha lacked the subtlety required of a killer.

She had no sooner returned than her group was approached by a distinguished, well-dressed Englishman.

"Good evening, madam," he said, bowing graciously to all and turning to Celia. "My name is Englehart. I am private secretary to the Prince of Wales. His Royal Highness has requested the honor of a dance with you in a later set."

Amazement crossed Celia's face before she could respond.

"How nice," she stammered. "Thank you so kindly."

She gave a flustered reply as he requested her name. After he had departed Lavinia gave a little gasp of laughter.

"What a tremendous honor, Celia," she said.

"And a surprise," Celia replied in disbelief.

Henrietta smiled triumphantly. "Didn't I say you'd be as lovely as anyone here? Clearly the prince thinks so."

Conversation of a social nature helped pass the minutes. She discovered ordinary pleasantries lessened her anxieties. How much easier it would have been had Sweeney given her just enough time to collect the necessary funds and return to make the transaction.

She asked a gentleman the time to be sure her father's watch was accurate and was disappointed to find them in agreement. It was over an hour before the meeting would take place. She was startled when Celia clutched at her sleeve, her face ashen.

"This way, quickly. Those people mustn't see me." Panic rose in Celia's voice. "They'll tell my husband I'm here."

While Celia had acknowledged the existence of a husband, encountering anyone from her past was the last thing Henrietta expected tonight. She followed Celia's gaze to the opposite side of the room.

"You have nothing to fear. You reside with me now. Is it that woman in blue?" Henrietta studied a couple who were deep in conversation. "You'll be called to dance with the prince shortly. How well did they know you?"

Calmer now, Celia studied the couple. "We didn't dine with the Addisons that often."

"I know we can rectify this. For now keep your back to them, and stay out of sight."

They slipped into an alcove where Celia averted her face.

"If only I could assume another identity," she said quietly.

"It's not as if you've never acted before." Henrietta's reassurance sparked a look of wry humor from Celia as a group of acquaintances approached. "My meeting is at hand. Will you be comfortable with Edith's education committee until I return?"

"I'll try to blend in like a lifelong Bostonian. If you don't return within the hour I'll come looking for you." Celia's voice wavered with concern. "Be careful. I'll miss you."

"Let's hope no one else does," Henrietta concurred.

It was nearing half past eleven when Henrietta took her place by the stage entrance. Ostlers milled restlessly about in the quiet of Mason Street, for few revelers had left the ball early. The stables would remain open all night with the waltzing promising to go on for hours. Feeling conspicuous with her bag full of silver, she took refuge in the shadows, knowing Sweeney would find her.

Two minutes passed. Her edginess increased. She had hoped he wouldn't keep her waiting. To calm her nerves she thought about Celia. Perhaps there was a way she could assume another identity. A solution presented itself suddenly, so clear it almost made the wait worthwhile. She wished she had thought of it sooner to put Celia's mind at ease.

Ten minutes passed with no sign of Sweeney. Her nervousness turned to annoyance at having to linger outdoors on this brisk October night. It wasn't likely she had missed him. She questioned a cab driver at a nearby stand who confirmed no one had come.

Her resentment ebbed to disappointment, the moments enlivened only by an occasional whinny or the clattering of hoofbeats. It was unlikely Sweeney changed his mind. He had made the exchange seem urgent. Perhaps he'd procured money from another victim and left town to avoid arrest.

In the distance the Park Street Church chimes struck midnight. Time for supper to be served at the ball. Henrietta's absence would be noticed if she lingered much longer.

With deep foreboding she left a message with a stable hand in case Sweeney appeared. Then she returned inside the theater.

Fourteen

In a daze Henrietta followed the crowd advancing toward the supper table. She enjoyed being indoors amid violin strains, laughter, and warmth. She must let Celia know she was safe and make sure she had avoided the Addisons. She met Garrison as she reached the door to the Melodeon where dinner would be served.

"Have you seen Celia?" she asked.

"She was with your nieces. They're probably at supper by now." He looked at her cloak. "Were you outdoors?"

"I planned to meet someone."

"Odd time for an appointment."

"Someone promised me information but never came. I'm not sure how to proceed."

Garrison frowned. "Information that might help Freddy?"

"That's why it's so urgent."

"You don't look well. Let's sit where we can talk."

Allowing others to go ahead, Henrietta accepted Garrison's offer of a seat, grateful to be with someone she could trust.

"You needn't feel you must confide in us, but know that Edith and I are here to help." Garrison's face reflected sympathy. "Don't jeopardize yourself just to rescue Freddy from straits of his own making."

His kindness failed to relieve her worry. "I might take you up on that offer later."

Henrietta gave her cloak to a servant and stepped back in line. She spotted pink dresses and assumed Celia was adequately concealed amid potted ferns. By the time she reached them her nieces were already engaged, allowing her to speak privately with Celia.

"Sweeney didn't come," she announced. "I don't know what to do except continue watching for him."

Celia set aside her plate, dumbfounded. "I never considered that possibility."

"At least I had time outside to find a solution to your problem. You already have a new identity. Now you'll have a fiancé as well. There's the person I need to speak with." Henrietta's gaze settled on her target. "I'll return before the Addisons do. They're in the ballroom."

"That's a relief. I have yet to dance with the prince."

Henrietta joined a small gathering of her salon members, taking Edgar Brattleby aside discreetly.

"You must try this Roman punch." He lifted his cup with enthusiasm. "In keeping with your salon theme."

"In keeping with the theme of dangerous women," she said, "I've a favor to ask, if the salon hasn't frightened you away from marriage."

"Marriage is a rather large favor," Edgar said dryly.

"This one only lasts the evening and will enhance your acting skills."

"Very well." He gave her a grudging glance. "If you'll sit through the entire performance this time."

"Edgar will be your fiancé," Henrietta told Celia, pleased with her own ingenuity. "While you dance with the prince Lavinia and I will congratulate him on your engagement and keep the Addisons preoccupied."

Celia looked uneasy. "You're sure it will work?"

"The suspicions of others carry no weight against a Bostonian. Edgar and Lavinia are entirely trustworthy."

"I hope you're right. You must eat, Etta," Celia urged. "The variety of food is unimaginable."

"I'll invite Lavinia to join us so you won't be alone."

Attention to detail had gone into preparing the lavish table laid with linen, china, and silver. At its head were stewed oysters and pates followed by croquettes and sweetbreads. As far as the eye could see there was food: smelts, soups, and cheeses. Next came chicken zephyre, platters of turkey, and fish. As dishes were depleted more appeared--mutton, duck, woodcock, quail. Anyone with room for dessert could sample puddings, ice cream, and all manner of fruits and sweets. Henrietta fortified herself before another attempt to locate Sweeney.

At the end of the supper line she felt the insistent prodding of an elbow in her ribs. She was startled to find Jasper Penrose, so elegantly dressed she might not have recognized him.

"It's not every day we hobnob with royalty," he winked.

Henrietta hoped the prince would be spared meeting Penrose, his presence incongruous with the evening's refinement. "I didn't realize you would be here."

"Mr. Ingraham paid for the missus and me." He indicated a woman with unkempt hair stuffed into a garish red crinoline with a waist that had inadequate space for the amount of food she was consuming. "I'm coming up in the world, Mrs. Cobb."

She couldn't help but smile as he edged toward her confidentially.

"'Member what I said about the bosses and the chief? Don't say I told you, but look yonder."

Henrietta watched Sam talking with his brother and the police chief. A new possibility struck her. Had Myrth feared Sam? She had been reluctant to approach the police. The men were friendly enough that the chief might overlook any rumors.

Excusing herself from Penrose, Henrietta returned to Celia and Lavinia to eat in haste before retrieving her cloak. Outdoors once again, she inquired at Nims's Stable for Sweeney, but the stable hand reported no sign of him.

She knew with ominous certainty something was wrong. After fifteen minutes in the cold she returned to the ballroom. If Sweeney didn't come she would seek him out.

She searched the crowd for Freddy or Admiral Browning without success. Who else could she call upon? Williston Atwood might help. She spotted him deep in conversation with a group of abolitionists. *Too deep,* she decided, *to be interrupted.*

Returning to her companion, she observed the movements of the Addisons, tensing as she spotted Sam and the police chief in a corner. He was the last person who could know about her scheduled rendezvous. They mustn't arrest Sweeney until after the exchange.

At one o'clock Celia's name was announced. Edward, future king of England, turned to claim her as his partner.

"You will shine," Henrietta whispered.

"My dance skills are weak," Celia said in sudden panic.

As Celia took her place in the center of the ballroom Henrietta and Lavinia moved to a gallery where Edgar conversed with the Addisons.

"We've looked everywhere for you, Edgar," Lavinia exclaimed.

"Lavinia, I'd like you to meet Walter Addison and his wife from Baltimore." Edgar made introductions.

"No doubt you've been congratulating Edgar on his good fortune," Lavinia said. "My brother is engaged to be married to the woman on the dance floor. That is, if the Prince of Wales doesn't make her an offer."

Mrs. Addison's eyes bulged in her pale face, her gaze glued to the ballroom floor. "Walter, isn't that—it can't be!"

The group turned toward the waltzing couple.

"It is," Edgar said cheerfully, "My fiancée."

"What did you say her name was?" Mrs. Addison asked sharply.

"Chase. Miss Chase. Have you heard of her?" Edgar asked.

"She reminds me of someone I knew in Baltimore."

"I believe she's visited," Edgar said, at ease with his performance, "although she's spent more time traveling to Britain and the Continent. It wouldn't surprise me if the prince finds they have much in common."

Celia managed to maintain her part of the charade, smiling in the arms of the prince, the eyes of the crowd upon her.

Mrs. Addison's disbelief turned to doubt. "The resemblance is remarkable. Have you known her long?"

"We were both born and raised in Boston. We've no plans to leave. Why go elsewhere when everything one might desire is here?"

Before Edgar could elaborate on Boston's cultural assets the waltz ended and Henrietta led him away from the couple.

"Your masquerade was remarkable," she said amid applause. "You might be better onstage than off."

"That depends whether I've convinced Mrs. Addison."

Henrietta glanced back to see the woman glancing toward the prince.

"She probably can't believe her eyes, but I think she believed you," she told Edgar.

Edgar straightened his jacket and looked about. "While my luck holds perhaps I'll find myself a real prospect."

"I have nieces you might try."

Relieved to be on the sidelines, Celia beamed nonetheless. Henrietta hoped the incident would prompt a full account from her companion later. She felt her ingenious solution had earned her an explanation.

"None of the prince's other partners talked with him nearly as long," Lavinia said with admiration. "Don't keep us in suspense. What did you say to each other?"

A trace of humor filled Celia's eyes. "I happen to have seen some watercolors his mother did of the Highlands at Balmoral. Having done some sketching myself, I found quite a bit to say."

"Now that your dilemma is resolved," Henrietta said privately to Celia, "I must find someone to help me find Sweeney before the police do."

She looked about critically, seeing no sign of Freddy or Fan's husband and unable to locate Atwood in the crowd. It was half past one. Garrison Morse waited to one side while Edith chatted with friends. Henrietta approached him quietly.

"Garrison, I'd like to accept your offer of help. I need to call on Mr. Sweeney at Humphrey Place." He appeared so startled she continued. "I know it's late, but he promised to meet me hours ago. I can't imagine what's kept him."

"Must you call tonight?" he asked, incredulous.

"If I wait until morning he might leave town."

Garrison interrupted Edith briefly to tell her his plans. As Henrietta updated Celia they were forced to yield to the prince and his entourage. Edward caught Celia's eye while passing and bowed to her. She curtsied in return.

"I should like to see your watercolors one day," he said in a respectful tone.

"I'd be most honored." As the entourage moved on Celia laughed with embarrassment.

"Your adaptability amazes me," Henrietta admitted. "You're equally at ease with royalty as with women of the street. Perhaps you should take up acting."

They turned abruptly to see the daunting figure of Mrs. Addison. Once again the woman raised her monocle to Celia, looking her up and down.

"You're thinner than I remember," she began, "but you are indeed Mrs. Roger Hartwick from Baltimore. Miss Chase, my eye."

Celia remained silent but stood her ground.

"I thought it strange the way you disappeared one night without a trace. No one knew what happened." She glanced past Celia toward Edgar. "Now I understand. Do you deny it?"

"Hello, Lydia," Celia said. "I don't deny my former identity."

Her lips thinned. "Of course I must inform Roger of your deception."

Defiance lit Celia's eyes. "Tell him," she said with sarcasm. "Please give him my regards. I haven't the vaguest notion when I'll see him again. I hope never."

Celia turned and walked away. Suitably trounced, Lydia Addison swept from the room with her husband.

Henrietta hurried after Celia, unable to contain her sense of triumph. "How wonderful that you asserted yourself."

Celia's eyes flashed. "I'll pay for it. Lydia will return to Baltimore and tell Roger where to find me. I might live to regret this."

"Your regret ended tonight," Henrietta said firmly. "Your life is your own."

Celia smiled, still shaken by the encounter.

"Time's running short," Henrietta said hurriedly, "and other lives are at stake. I'll return when I can."

"It's you I worry about," Celia said. "You're in more danger than I."

They clasped hands briefly before Henrietta rejoined Garrison, filled with foreboding as they retrieved their wraps and stepped into the night. Garrison hired a carriage since they had sent theirs home.

"Please don't think I'm foolish," she apologized. "I can't help but fear the worst. We were so close to learning the truth."

From the window she saw a steady drizzle had begun. The opulence of the Melodeon vanished as they turned onto Bedford Street, where the comfortable ride over cobblestone was replaced by rough unpaved roads. Through raindrops Henrietta saw schooners anchored offshore, lanterns swinging in the rigging, casting a futile glow into an impenetrable darkness.

Their driver left them on Broad Street without an attempt to maneuver the narrow entrance to Humphrey Place's tiny courtyard.

"If you don't mind," the cabby said, "I'll ask you to pay your fare now, and I'll be on my way."

"How are we to summon you afterward?" Garrison snapped. "You're to wait for us here. I'll pay you upon our return."

They walked silently through the passage into the yard. Henrietta regretted bringing anyone here at this hour, but the urgency of her mission dispelled any guilt. Nearby amid laughter a woman screamed playfully, making Henrietta blush despite her six decades. As they approached the rickety steps known as Jacob's Ladder she hoped the darkness hid her fear.

"Would you rather wait in the carriage?" Garrison asked.

"No, I must see Sweeney tonight," she insisted.

He eyed the steps. "You should go first. If you stumble I can block your fall. At least there's a railing."

There was little railing to cling to, she realized as she mounted the staircase. Every other step was missing a sizable piece of wood, leaving gaping holes. The waste in the drain alongside must be unbearable in July, she thought. She concentrated on each step, dreading what she would find at the top. She trembled as she reached the landing.

"Didn't Officer Roberts say Sweeney lived at Number Twenty?"

Henrietta glanced at the doors. The first two weren't numbered.

"Here's Number Twenty."

Garrison knocked on the door, its peeling paint throwing jagged shadows in the moonlight. The apartment was silent. Henrietta prayed they weren't interrupting a romantic tryst. Judging from the outbursts of the woman below, any behavior was acceptable here.

"Open up, Sweeney," he called. "It's Morse and Mrs. Cobb."

Garrison tried the latch. The door gave easily. Henrietta followed him inside to find the flat in darkness but for the faint glow of an oil lamp from an inner room.

"Mr. Sweeney," she called, "I have what you requested."

She stepped forward in the lamp's glow. A thin trail of red branched across the floor.

"Wait here," Garrison ordered, entering the next room.

Mesmerized by the sight, she couldn't stop herself. Stepping into the doorway, she saw Sweeney. The Irishman lay on his side, one arm thrown across the broken rungs of an overturned chair, his pose ghastly, unnatural. Blood streamed from a wound in his chest where he'd been stabbed, making rivulets across his shirt onto the floor.

Garrison knelt by him, then stood up.

"It's fortunate I had the cabby wait," he said quietly. "He can summon the police."

Henrietta wondered if the department could spare a patrolman with so many assigned to guard the prince. While the wait seemed interminable, two patrolmen came within minutes. One searched the apartment while the other interrogated them. The parlor was shabby but preferable to the grisly sight in the bedroom.

"Working by candlelight ain't easy," one officer said. "What can poor folk do? Probably could only afford one lamp."

The other glanced at the victim before leaving the bedroom. "He could afford better. He liked the rough element."

Sweeney offended many, Henrietta mused, one of whom wanted him dead. Had someone wanted the proof from Hannah's badly enough to steal it? It stung to think Sweeney was murdered before they could meet. Proof of Myrth's guilt died with him. Neither Harkness nor Nicholas would admit the truth although both knew. Sweeney's reputation made it doubtful the police would take his word.

Yet he had a key to Hannah's. If he'd stolen Myrth's documents they might still be here. The room had few hiding places. Had he attempted to blackmail someone who retaliated with murder? Had it been Myrth?

"Pat?" A young woman appeared in the doorway, staring with mild surprise. "Pat got himself pinched again?"

"You his sweetheart, miss?" one policeman asked.

"Not bloody likely," she retorted. "Pat's got too many for my liking. Name's Nell Flynn. He going to jail again?"

"Worse. He's headed for the morgue."

In disbelief Nell followed the light into the bedroom. Henrietta accompanied a patrolman to the doorway. The method of murder was more dramatic than Hannah's. Nell Flynn studied Sweeney stretched out on the floor.

"Pat, what've you done?"

She knelt beside him, taking his head in her lap. Before anyone could stop her she grabbed the edge of the bedspread, brushing the blood from his wound.

"Here, you're to leave him alone," the policeman ordered.

"Not like this," she returned.

Another female voice was heard. Henrietta was started to see Willie's older sister Eileen push her way in. Her features harder than Molly's, Eileen stopped when she saw Sweeney.

"Wot's happened?" she demanded.

"Someone's gone and done Pat in," replied Nell.

Eileen knelt by Sweeney's side, taking his hand.

"He promised we was to be married!" she wailed. "Now what do I do? No love and no money."

"Let's go, love," Nell said. "Nothin' we can do for him now. Best we take care of you."

As Nell led Eileen from the room Henrietta suspected she would miss the money more than the man. The family never knew how to keep it once they earned it. Sweeney's overblown talk must have seemed an appealing solution.

Henrietta glanced about the room. Clothes hung from bureau drawers. Was robbery the motive? She took a final glance at Sweeney. As unsavory as he was he had helped her, even if it was for a price.

"Don't worry, ma'am," a patrolman reassured her. "When we catch the ruffian that did this he won't harm anyone again."

He had mistaken her stiffness for fear. She expressed her gratitude, returning her attention to the body. The officer had increased the brightness of the lamp. Now, with the blood wiped away by Nell, she noticed the wound.

At first glance she thought Sweeney was stabbed with a knife. On closer inspection she realized the incision in his chest was made with a thin blade. The wound was cleaner and more efficient than that of a traditional sword.

What type of instrument made such a fine thrust? A military weapon? Certainly no kitchen knife.

She was startled out of her reverie by the return of the police with Garrison. In the time she had been here the officer had questioned witnesses outside.

"Found a fellow who claims he saw a gentleman after dark," he said. "Thinks it was around nine, but he's too drunk to say with any accuracy."

Henrietta stiffened. It was just about nine when she noticed her brother missing from the ballroom of the Boston Theatre. Where was Freddy at that hour?

The police suspected him of one murder. Was it possible he was guilty of a second?

Fifteen

Instead of going to bed after the ball Henrietta and Celia retreated to the library. It was hard to imagine it was five-thirty. Neither had slept. By three o'clock there had been room to waltz comfortably in the auditorium, and the dancing lasted until four-thirty. In all, Celia reported, the prince had danced seventeen times. But her account of the night's activities, she was quick to add, dulled in comparison to Henrietta's.

While Celia hadn't removed her crinoline Henrietta changed into nightclothes while the tea was steeping. She tried to erase the murder from her mind but found it impossible. Freddy had as much reason to be guilty of Sweeney's murder as Angus's. He hated the Irishman for intending Myrth harm and trying to extort money.

"It's hard to believe Sweeney's gone." Celia gave Henrietta a look of gratitude mixed with embarrassment. "I can't thank you enough for your help. My past is the last thing that should have intruded tonight."

"Don't you think it's time you told me, Celia dear?" Henrietta ventured gently. They were on their second cup of tea before Celia managed to raise the issue.

"I've wanted to tell you, but what would you have thought if I told you earlier I abandoned my children?"

"I would assume you had good reason."

When no judgment descended Celia took a deep breath and continued. "My children are in Baltimore with their father."

"Then they aren't abandoned. I'm sure they're well cared for."

"I left them in the best circumstances I could arrange."

Celia removed a gold locket from her neck and opened it with trembling fingers. Inside Henrietta found photographs of a boy and girl.

"The boy looks just like you," Henrietta murmured, "and the girl has a charm all her own. They're lovely, Celia."

She gave the locket back. Celia replaced it around her neck, holding it as if she couldn't bear to let go.

"I hardly know where to begin." Celia stood up and paced, bumping a crystal lamp that tinkled with her unsteadiness. "On a business trip my father met a man he felt would make me a suitable husband. I left Portland to marry."

Her tone turned resentful.

"I might as well have been sold to Roger for what little love he felt. Once we returned from our wedding trip he expected subservience. The first time I expressed an idea that differed from his he beat me. The second time it was three years before I spoke my mind again."

She laughed as if trying to shake off the memory. Henrietta listened without interrupting.

"My parents advised me to make the best of it. I had two sisters for whom they had to find husbands. I couldn't believe a man seemingly so polite could be so brutal. When Roger drank he became a different person, someone I barely recognized."

Celia's expression ranged from loathing to sarcasm as she returned to her chair. After a moment she managed to compose herself.

"Roger had other women from the start. He spent his nights drinking and gambling. I endured it in silence. In public he made ours seem the perfect union." A bitter smile twisted her mouth. "I stayed for the children. There were few options. When I realized my son might grow up like his father I knew I had to leave. After marriage Roger controlled my money. He doled it out sparingly, but I saved it over time to escape. I'd tell him we needed a new tablecloth. I kept a worn linen cloth for proof."

"A trick worth sharing with others in your situation."

"Trickery was the way to deal with Roger. He credited me with so little intelligence it was easy to play the part." Celia's eyes hardened at the memory. "Had he behaved as a husband should I might have remained as meek as when we met, but I couldn't live under his tyranny. I got off the train in Boston, knowing he'd look for me in Maine."

"Who cares for the children?"

"Emily and Benjamin." Celia was silent for a long moment. "The housekeeper and their nanny treat them as their own. I couldn't have left otherwise. Roger values sons. Ben will receive the best money can buy. He'll leave Emily to the care of her nanny, Louisa, who'll raise her as I directed. We planned to reunite in time. I hope they remember me when we meet again."

"They will," Henrietta assured her. "You didn't consider bringing them?"

"You probably know the laws better than I." Celia pulled her emotions under control with difficulty. "They're Roger's property. He would sooner kill me than let me have them. I waited until they were old enough to remember me. I told them I'd see them again, though I have no idea where or when, or under what circumstances."

Exhausted, Celia fell back in her seat. As the gaslight caught her profile Henrietta saw her anguish in eyes rimmed with red, made more painful by tears that would remain unshed. She had seen many women in similar situations that hadn't ended as well.

"So Roger has no idea where you are."

"Nor will he offer any reward for my return." Celia smiled wryly. "He can hardly send a slave hunter to find me."

"But you've effectively prevented him from marrying again," Henrietta noted.

"I'm not familiar enough with the laws to know what happens next," Celia admitted. "Perhaps he'll try to have me declared dead so he can remarry."

"You've probably made him want to avoid marriage for a very long time." Henrietta smiled with irony. "We share a bond, Celia. We've both lost sons, mine through death in war, yours through separation in marriage. But you have hope. Once you're more settled we'll turn our efforts to getting Emily and Benjamin out of Roger's clutches."

She turned away so she wouldn't have to see the unbearable hope she knew would fill Celia's face. Before she encouraged her further she wanted to consult her solicitor on the chances of success in such a venture.

"In the meantime I need to keep Freddy out of Myrth's clutches and away from the police—and choose a reading for the next salon."

"With the presidential election less than a month away slavery is on everyone's mind. *Uncle Tom's Cabin* might make for a lively discussion."

"You've been most helpful filling in my lack of imagination these days, which reminds me that I must write Nicholas Trindell to see if Hannah left a diary. Perhaps we can bring her murderer to justice. You might wish to notify your parents, Celia, of your whereabouts. Your accent always did remind me of Maine."

Celia's eyes were bright. Henrietta suspected her mind had reverted to the possibility of seeing not only her children again but her parents as well.

"There is no way I can ever repay you," she said.

Henrietta smiled, fighting off her sudden weariness. "First thing tomorrow we'll commence your immediate employment as my companion. You need work, and I require assistance with projects. It seems a suitable match, wouldn't you agree?" She took a last sip of tea. "Certainly better than the match your father made for you."

The next afternoon, refreshed by sleep, Henrietta returned to the correspondence on her desk. She was relieved to find Flash in his cage where he belonged. If only all of life were so tidy.

On the blotter lay a fleck of jimsonweed Freddy had missed, too small to convince the police Hannah was poisoned. Abruptly she realized Myrth inadvertently gave her a valuable clue. Knowing the killer's identity was reason enough for him to want her dead. Why lie about being the target when she already had the perfect excuse? Myrth hadn't had time to think up a lie.

A prickling along her spine convinced Henrietta Myrth had told the truth. Who killed Hannah? Did Sweeney know she had something of value? While Sam had reason to want Angus dead, many felt the same. No one individual had motive to want all three dead.

On the surface Freddy seemed passionless. How much better she'd come to know him. It might be the only good that came of it. Her ruminations were cut short by the arrival of Mrs. Biddle with a letter from Mr. Thoreau.

Concord, Massachusetts
October 14, 1860

My dear Mrs. Cobb,
The content of your was letter was, as always, startling. I hope you were not suggesting I sample the enclosed leaves. I'd fully expect any unfortunate tempted by them to meet with dire results.

The wet leaves are jimsonweed as you suspected. Herbal tea brewed from its leaves is fatal. The dry leaves are harmless chamomile. It appears poisoning has indeed occurred.

Headache, delirium, and convulsions appear within hours and can result in coma and death. The poison lies in the roots and seeds, with the juices and leaves especially deadly. The fruit appears this time of year. The seeds cause burning thirst, hot and feverish skin, and pupils so dilated that light is painful, symptoms suggesting your experience.

Having lectured from Bangor to Philadelphia on the subject of abolitionism, I have the deepest respect for anyone abiding by such principles. Whether your brother killed Mr. McLaren is for the law to decide.

*My opinion is that all men should be able to trust their
wives more than their enemies.*
    *I find your friend's behavior most suspicious and
wonder why anyone would want something so deadly.*

Yours in health,
Henry David Thoreau

Disregarding his opinion of Freddy, she read the final
paragraph again. Why indeed? Thoreau's warning added
credence to her suspicions, except Myrth had trusted
Hannah with her biggest secret. Had Myrth come to see
Hannah as a threat? Someone had either succeeded in
disguising Hannah's murder or knew Myrth well enough
to make her appear guilty.

Thoreau's letter confirmed that Henrietta had felt the
effects of jimsonweed from touching the plant. With the
fruit being in season it was easy for someone to travel to
Lenox and return to Boston in time to make a tea from
freshly picked jimsonweed with enough seeds and leaves
to kill.

Henrietta set off early the next day for the women's
shelter. With Celia's future assured she no longer felt
guilty calling simply to drop off blankets. She would check
on Freddy later. She pictured Corinthia basking in the
festival's success with Freddy sharing in the glory.

She wasn't likely to reach their home before the start of
today's military display in honor of the prince's visit. The
companies would assemble in State Street and wind back
to the Common, joining with others at Beacon. On her
return up Boylston she heard the parade before it

appeared, the airs of fifes and drums followed by clapping and shouts of jubilation.

On Tremont Street she stopped among the thousands gathered to observe the troops representing New England's independent citizen soldiery. Men dressed in full regalia rode proudly on horseback, the cold air giving life to their step. To her right a young woman waved a handkerchief with abandon as the Lynn Light Infantry passed. The Roxbury City Guard went by in such high spirits Henrietta wondered how their optimism could be warranted.

Most felt the potential election of Mr. Lincoln made civil war a certainty. As she watched the units parade before the crowd her wistfulness deepened to melancholy. The display seemed almost a premonition of what awaited many young men here who might suffer Alec's fate. She hoped Neville would delay his return from Europe.

A flash of sunlight split the clouds, hitting the edge of a sword carried by the regiment before her. The weapons carried by these men were too thick to have killed Sweeney. These swords were too honorable for the vulgar nocturnal killing of a man in cold blood, even one wanted by the police.

Between military units she spotted a gentleman across the street whom she recognized as Freddy's friend from the Compass Club. The walking stick he carried caught the sun's glare. It was a sword stick like the one her brother owned, offering discreet protection for men walking at night who risked being accosted. Freddy claimed the sword's narrow blade concealed within his walking stick gave him a feeling of security after staying late at the laboratory.

Sweeney's wound flashed through her mind in horrifying detail. It was more like the cut a sword stick might make than the thicker blade of a regular sword. No gentleman needed to defend himself in Sweeney's apartment, for no one of their class had reason to visit.

Then she remembered the witness who claimed he had seen a gentleman nearby. She had been unable to locate Freddy around midnight. *Fanny's husband and Corinthia's father,* she reflected, *were missing as well. All were fashionable gentlemen who carried sword sticks.*

It sickened Henrietta to realize no common thief had killed Sweeney, but one of her own class. If the police investigated every Bostonian who owned such an accessory the murderer would have plenty of time to escape. Why investigate further when they suspected Freddy? If he'd killed McLaren, he wasn't above killing Sweeney.

Her talk with her brother seemed more urgent now. She hastened toward Pemberton Square away from the rousing songs of revolution, her mind squarely in the present.

When Henrietta reached Freddy's home her nieces met her in the foyer in a state of panic.

"Father's gone," Prudence sobbed.

"The police arrested him." Felicity's voice was fearful.

"Arrested!" Henrietta echoed.

"On charges of murder," Prudence finished.

Henrietta hoped it was only one. "Mr. McLaren's?"

"Yes," Felicity said in despair. "I thought they had dismissed the idea of his guilt."

"I'd hoped so also. When did this happen?"

"Early this morning." Prudence's voice quavered. "Mother went to the Station House with Father."

Their reunion happened just in time. Freddy would need their support. After gathering her nieces in an embrace, Henrietta left them with words of reassurance to go to their father's aid, hoping the help he needed wouldn't come too late.

"I'll show you to the Tombs, ma'am," offered the policeman in Station House Number Three on Joy Street. Taking up an enormous key ring, he stopped short on seeing Henrietta's expression. "Sorry, ma'am. Not very euphemistic, but not bad as these places go."

It might as well be a tomb, she thought. As they descended into the cellar they passed tiny cells filled with vagrants and drunkards before reaching the end of the corridor.

"You can visit as long as you like," the jailer said. "Shall I return in fifteen minutes?"

"Perhaps longer. Thank you."

He paused at the final cell to unlock the door, allowing her to enter before locking it again. Freddy sat on a narrow bunk. At her arrival his head snapped up. They fumbled for each other's hand in the dim light.

"Etta! Who would have thought I'd end up here, except you, in the cellar of a watch-house." He smiled wearily.

"It's dreadful," she said feelingly.

"They've already given me bread and coffee. Lunch is bread and cheese. A vagrant might rather live here than on the street."

Relieved he had maintained his sense of humor, Henrietta studied their surroundings. The cell was small, with a bunk for sleeping, a pail to relieve oneself, and a tin cup. Even with her charity work this was her first time in a cell. It had no windows and no hope. Her legs felt unsteady, but there were no seats for guests.

"Oh, Freddy." Her voice sounded hollow even to herself.

"Welcome to my lodgings." Laying his hand on her arm as if he feared she might cry, he eased her down on the bunk next to him. "Don't look so forlorn. My stay won't last long."

"I thought Corinthia was here with you."

"She's gone to see Stafford to arrange for my release." He looked serene in spite of his Spartan surroundings. "Cora's a formidable enemy but a better ally."

"On what grounds did they arrest you?"

"For murdering McLaren. The public feels someone needs to be arrested. The police claim to have evidence, though it's circumstantial."

"The footprint in the parlor matches that of thousands of men."

"I had motive, means, and opportunity. I was arrested for having contact with Myrth. They think I'm protecting her. They hope I'll reveal her whereabouts." His smile was bleak. "I would if I could. I met her after we were to meet at Hannah's grave. She denied having anything to do with her death. I wondered if was protecting the killer."

She studied his face. Perhaps Myrth hadn't told him of their encounter, fearing Henrietta might mention Nicholas. "What makes you think that?"

"Myrth was different, downcast, her spirit almost gone. Said she no longer had proof of the killer's identity and regretted much of what she'd done. I doubt I'll see her again." The bitterness in Freddy's tone startled her. "I tried to make her see the gravity of my situation. I asked if there was someone she loved more than me. She admitted there was."

She had, of course, meant Nicholas. Henrietta closed her eyes briefly.

"There's something I must tell you, Freddy. I wanted to raise the matter sooner, but I'm not terribly tactful and couldn't find the words. Myrth kept a secret from you and the rest of the world." She spoke gently. "Myrth has a son. A grown son."

"A son!" His face filled with shock.

"The young man walking with Hannah when we first met, the actor you saw in *Florine*. Nicholas Trindell is Myrth's son."

Freddy's face was white with recognition. "How do you know?"

"On my visit to Myrth's I saw Nicholas was mentioned in Angus's will. Then I saw his picture at Hannah's. I remembered seeing a picture of him at Myrth's. It all fit. After the play I confronted him."

"You what?" Freddy stared at her in disbelief.

"He admitted Hannah raised him, that Myrth was his mother. That he hated Angus." She stopped, emotionally drained. "I know this comes as a shock. She feared she would lose you."

"Why didn't she tell me?" His face was a mixture of distress and resentment. He gestured helplessly, beginning to pace. "I don't know what to say. You've spoken with her?"

"Yes. I'm sorry. I met Myrth at the cemetery," she admitted. "She was delayed. I went to meet you but found her instead. I never thought she would come."

"Why the devil didn't she tell me?" He ran his fingers through his white hair. "When she admitted there was someone else I assumed it was a lover from long ago. I never guessed she had a son. I need to be alone, Etta. I need to think."

Although she shared his distress she doubted he knew the depth of her concern. He must resent being deceived, having suspected her of being in love with a killer.

Henrietta was grateful for Corinthia's support. Despite their differences Cora was devoted to him and would help any way she could. Cora blamed their failed communication on Freddy's refusal to confide in her. His disillusionment with Myrth might reunite them. There was pain etched in his face.

"I'm sorry, Freddy. For once I take no satisfaction in having been correct."

His face was a ghastly gray. "At this point we must take stock of the damage and remedy it."

"Did Myrth say anything significant?"

"She said there are letters with someone she trusts that explain everything."

"She gave the letters to Hannah. Unless they were stolen they're either with Nicholas or still in Hannah's apartment. I'll look into it at once."

"Thank you. I'm not accustomed to feeling helpless. I dislike it immensely."

Henrietta calculated the number of policemen she knew at other station houses. She frequently consulted the police in assisting the city's poor, but the homeless immigrants and paupers who filled the jails on winter nights didn't live in Beacon Hill. Here in her own neighborhood she knew none of the police.

"Cora's with Mr. Stafford now," she said, "and no one's more influential than her father."

"He isn't convinced I didn't kill McLaren." He smiled wanly. "And he doesn't appreciate the scandal."

A thought occurred to her. "How did the police know you had contact with Myrth? Did you tell anyone?"

"Only Holmes, but he's too much of a gentleman to disclose details. Have you discussed it?"

"I told Fanny, and I did tell Edgar and Lavinia. They're trusted friends, not gossips intent on mischief."

"Women are too efficient at communicating their thoughts," he muttered wearily.

"I wonder how the police knew you saw Myrth. Could she have reported you anonymously?"

"Anything's possible. She's protecting herself. If she did kill Angus I find it impossible to believe." Beneath his white hair and side-whiskers Freddy looked sad and infinitely older.

"If she was lying she was very convincing," Henrietta admitted. "I'll focus on helping you and cancel my next salon."

"Not on my account. Holding it will serve as a forum for ideas that could produce something of value."

"It might at that. *Uncle Tom's Cabin* will take people's minds off the present. I hope the police don't suspect you of Sweeney's death as well."

Henrietta looked expectantly at Freddy. He stared back.

"Have you any doubt?"

"You were unaccountable for part of the ball, but so were many others," she said. "Thousands were in the theater."

"The police already asked. I spent my time at the ball with Cora. The locals saw someone near Humphrey Place around half-past eight, but no one could describe him. All drinking heavily, I expect."

Her mind reeled. "I suspected Sweeney was murdered with a sword stick. He must have been killed earlier that evening."

Freddy looked at her with admiration. "You haven't failed to notice a thing."

"That's not quite true. As the eldest I failed to preserve our family's honor. I failed to notice our family bonds were deteriorating, and I still don't know what motivates Myrth. But I have letters from Mr. Thoreau, and you have jimsonweed."

"I'll gladly return it to you," he said dryly.

"I'll give them to Mr. Stafford. There's still a murderer out there, perhaps more than one."

"Not that I wish to protect Myrth more than she deserves, but if she left the jimsonweed behind, what did she use to poison Hannah?"

"Maybe she had more. Who else would have some? Myrth is the only one with a possible motive for all three murders."

The sound of the jailer's keys indicated their discussion was at its end. Henrietta rose to leave, the realization of the work ahead weighing on her.

"Perhaps now that you've been arrested Myrth will show her true colors." She smiled briefly. "It's not a moment too soon for her to come forward if she cares enough to do so."

Sixteen

Returning home, Henrietta found she had received a letter from a longtime friend. After some words of consolation regarding her difficulties, Louisa May Alcott's note consisted mostly of her anticipation of changes the coming election would bring. "Don't you wish we were men?" she wrote.

"At the moment," Henrietta told Celia, "I wish I had the opportunities afforded men. Louisa doesn't even know Freddy's been jailed."

Skimming the details of life in Concord that closed Louisa's letter, Henrietta would concentrate next on preparing the information she had promised Mr. Stafford. Celia perused Louisa's note as Henrietta gathered Thoreau's letters.

"The last line is promising." Celia's voice was hopeful. "Miss Alcott says Mr. Thoreau will be in Boston next Saturday during your salon in his usual lodgings at the Parker House."

"While Hannah protected Myrth," Henrietta mused, encouraged at the prospect of speaking with Thoreau directly, "I wonder if Myrth poisoned her, or, if not, why someone else did. Hannah represented a threat to someone." She paused. "How friendly would Ozymandias be to me given the opportunity to follow his instincts? That reminds me, I'd better feed him."

"I wonder how the police knew your brother had seen Mrs. McLaren," Celia pondered, "when few people knew."

Freddy had been rather quick to assign blame, Henrietta reflected as she went downstairs to the alligator. She had only told those who might be of help, knowing Edgar and Lavinia had her family's interests at heart.

Another memory flooded back, hazy but with growing clarity. In her efforts to expose the truth she had confided in one other person, someone who had known both. Sam Ingraham, a close friend of the police chief.

Henrietta was forced to wait until the factory opened on Monday before she could confront Sam. She called on Edgar and Lavinia beforehand to ascertain they hadn't shared her confidence. Their reassurances only added to her trepidation and deepened her suspicions about the upcoming meeting.

She arrived at the factory with a resentment that grew on her way to Sam's office. At one time she had hoped his connections might help Freddy. Now she believed he had exposed information she shared privately.

He greeted her with the aloof politeness he reserved for business callers. Briefly she told him Freddy had been jailed.

"I know you're friendly with the police chief," she began. "I hoped you might intervene on Freddy's behalf for his release."

Sam's mouth tightened. "Frankly, I think it an imposition. I'd rather not take advantage of our friendship that way."

Yet he willingly took advantage of the friendship to protect his business by silencing inquiries into McLaren's death. She repressed her indignation as he continued.

"Dan's trying to pacify city residents, convince them everything's being done to see justice met. I doubt you appreciate the extent of his responsibilities."

"I doubt you appreciate the extent of the danger Freddy faces," she retorted. "You think he's guilty. Why else would you reveal he's been in contact with Myrth?"

Startled, Sam took a moment to regain his composure. She gave him no chance to defend himself.

"It was information I shared with you in confidence that led to his arrest," she said coldly. "The police believe he's working with Myrth."

"They're as curious as you to know where Myrth is." Sam spread his hands, the gesture patronizing while he attempted to console her. "Freddy isn't the first to find himself in a relationship with a younger woman. Such dalliances are common with men of a certain age."

Or of a certain type, she mused. *He probably wouldn't object to having a dalliance with Myrth himself as a respite from Bertha.* The years between them seemed long suddenly.

"I'm sure you know Willie McCurdy's charged with assisting at burglary."

"Penrose had to replace him. What's he doing now?"

"He's in jail. He's had too many immoral influences. I hope incarceration will turn him around." She paused, gathering strength. "For a long time, Sam, I've wished I might count you among those who work for child labor reform."

Henrietta waited for an answer. His silence was an admission of his ethical failings. Four decades ago their relationship was one of promise, with hopes of civic and cultural contributions. Now the gulf between them could not be bridged.

"Can't you see the harm in instilling the desire for money at a young age? His family's finances are not Willie's concern."

"It's financial need that brings these children to work." Sam's voice hardened. "It's admirable that Willie wanted to help his mother. I understand she has little money."

"She spends it on gin. If she pocketed what she earned the children could attend school as they should." Her cheeks burned. "All Willie knows is work. What kind of future do you think he has?"

Sam shrugged. "There are Horatio Algers to be made in this city yet and opportunities for those who apply themselves."

His voice was tinged with impatience, his placid expression gone. They might have been strangers, she reflected. While Sam saw the financial rewards jobs afforded children, she saw the dangerous machinery that blinded them and tore off limbs.

"These children are doomed to lives of poverty," she said. "Working from a young age doesn't improve their chances in life. It decreases them. It's a cycle of failure."

His mouth remained set. Though her point was valid Henrietta had lost the argument. Sam would never relent, for now that old wounds were reopened it was a matter of pride.

"The way I see it, Sam, you're responsible for Willie and Freddy being in jail."

"I offer children the chance to escape from lives of crime and idleness, not pursue it as Willie has." Sam's tone was crisp. "I'm sorry to have to tell you, Etta, but I'm moving Penrose's factory to larger quarters for expansion."

She told herself her night school would counteract his efforts. "Where you'll hire more children."

"Many work side by side with their parents. They're paid for their work."

"They're paid poorly and get injured often. You see one side of it, Sam. I see the other."

"There's a cost to advancement. I wish you could see that."

Henrietta considered how much he had compromised to advance his interests. He hadn't been the only one to pay those costs. If her mother could see him, she thought, she'd congratulate herself on her accurate judgment in discouraging the match. Henrietta added silent thanks to her mother's. Gathering her cloak, she rose to leave.

"I'm afraid I understand better than you, Sam."

A week and then another passed with Freddy in jail. Discussions produced no solution other than to leave the matter in Stafford's hands.

Taking Freddy's advice, Henrietta scribbled an invitation to Thoreau the day before her salon and left it at the Parker House. An hour before the salon was to start she'd had no reply, nor did she expect one. Ellen Emerson, the daughter of Thoreau's neighbor and friend Ralph Waldo Emerson, once warned her that he rejected invitations more often than he accepted them. Henrietta wasn't disappointed by his silence. The value of his letters was enough.

"A rainy afternoon is ideal for literary talk," Fanny said when the Brownings arrived early.

"That or a cozy doze by the fire," Browning said cheerfully.

"Please don't fall asleep yet," Henrietta begged. "It would reflect badly on me to have a retired military hero sleep through a debate on an issue that might spark a war."

Edgar and Lavinia Brattleby arrived next, followed by Edith and Garrison Morse. Felicity and Prudence came last, their spirits as downcast as the weather. Henrietta was disappointed by Bertha's absence. She would have liked hearing Bertha's views on *Uncle Tom's Cabin* and her sentiments regarding the election of Mr. Lincoln the previous Tuesday.

"Weather's not fit for a duck." Edgar brushed raindrops from his sleeve as he took his seat. "Hope it's not an omen of what we can expect from our new president."

"Surely Mr. Lincoln will stop these rebel threats," Garrison replied. "He'll be a man of action, decisive and firm. I hear Holmes plans to contact him directly, if necessary, to ensure Freddy's release."

"Father's already spent three weeks in jail," Felicity murmured, "but at least Mother remains optimistic."

"I brought hope with me today," Lavinia announced. "Reading Mrs. Stowe's book again, I felt downhearted until I realized our country just took the first step toward ending slavery."

The group launched into a discussion of *Uncle Tom's Cabin* without preamble.

"It's dreadful to have one's home threatened as Augustine St. Clare's was," Lavinia continued. "I thought of Professor Newell when I read about Uncle Tom's troubles. They're both good men trapped in circumstances not of their own making."

Freddy's problems, Henrietta acknowledged, were indeed his own fault. There was an awkward pause at the inconsistency of Lavinia's well-intended remark until Edgar resumed.

"The evidence is circumstantial," he insisted. "The arrest was made merely to calm the public."

"Once war is declared," Browning added, "sympathy for McLaren will fade, support will replace distrust, and Freddy will be released. It was the Scots, remember, who took up a penny emancipation fund for the slaves when they first read *Uncle Tom's Cabin*."

"Kindness has a power all its own," Fan agreed. "Look at the Quakers willing to risk their lives to help George and Eliza escape. The abolitionists are the same, looking for justice while following their principles."

Henrietta smiled. Fan would be at home in the Quaker settlement. Her work with the Ladies for Liberty reflected as much compassion as the actions of Rachel Halliday helping the runaways. She thought of the scene in which George and Eliza were reunited as Freddy and Cora were now.

"Men live or die by their principles," Edith agreed. "Apathy breeds rebellion, so people have to act. Augustine St. Clare's careless attitude toward social evils caused his downfall."

"Although he's likable," Celia countered, "I had the sense that while he defended his actions he knew they were immoral."

As did Sam, thought Henrietta. Like St. Clare, Sam would maintain his indifference until social change reached a point where he couldn't ignore it. It was mere luck no children had been injured in his factory.

"It takes someone with more integrity than St. Clare to rescue those in need," Edith maintained. "Luckily our Northern men will arrive in time to help the Southern slaves."

"It reminds me of George Shelby, going south to help Uncle Tom but arriving too late." Henrietta sensed Williston Atwood and Garrison Morse were cut from that same substantial fabric.

"Miss Ophelia was also a rescuer." Prudence smiled, a rare sight these days. "Of all the characters she seemed the most familiar. She could be anyone from our city."

"She reminds me of Edith and Etta organizing a school to teach working children," said Garrison.

Ophelia, like Edith, was committed to teaching. Visiting the South, Ophelia was motivated by ignorance and poverty to teach the unruly Topsy and reorganize the kitchen staff. Henrietta could picture Edith leading a similar life.

"It's hard to imagine a faith as strong as Tom's," Lavinia admitted. "None of us have endured such trials."

"Remaining positive through hardship is the mark of faith," Edgar said. "You see his strength in the early cabin scenes."

"You also see that faith in the Quaker settlement," Edith agreed. "We've all known places like that."

Tom's home offered shelter and comfort. Was Harkness's Livery like that for Hannah, living upstairs while the boy she raised as her nephew worked in the stable as a youth? Even Myrth felt safe there. One of many Bostonians who sheltered slaves through the Underground Railroad, Harkness had a brusque temperament that was offset by his nobility. Henrietta wished Freddy could find such a safe escape.

Hannah and Myrth were like Cassy and Emmeline, friends and confidantes, one a mother who'd raised her child, the other a daughter separated from hers. How similar the circumstances were to those of Myrth, having to relinquish her son. Where was Myrth now? Recalling Eliza's flight across the ice on the Ohio River, Henrietta pictured her escaping into Cambridge across the Charles.

"Even at the hands of Simon Legree Tom never loses heart," Felicity continued. "If he could maintain hope through that ordeal, I suppose we'll survive having Father in jail. I can't think of anyone worse than Legree."

"Jasper Penrose comes close," Henrietta said. "He'll continue to hire young children to work on machinery far beyond their capabilities until the law forces him to stop."

"Despite Eva's sweet nature," Prudence said, "I find it hard to imagine any child her age could be so wise."

Could not wisdom be paired with youth? In childhood, mused Henrietta, *wisdom sometimes appears as insight.* Eva called to mind Molly McCurdy. Although Molly was older and without the advantage of class, her faith in the future was a light in a hopeless existence. The slaves on Augustine St. Clare's estate lived in luxury compared to those in Boston's slums.

"Mrs. Stowe's book doesn't take the step we did," Garrison noted. "She looks at the realities of slave life without the threat of war--or the promise of it, depending on one's outlook."

"When I planned this salon slavery felt very far from our society," Henrietta said. "It doesn't now."

"The South can't possibly win," Edith said. "The war will last a matter of months, after which life will resume. Now that the die is cast we must see it through."

"With John Andrew as our new governor abolitionism will rule," Lavinia added. "We all know which way the wind will blow."

Silence descended on the group. Henrietta considered the parallels between Mrs. Stowe's characters and her acquaintances. One parallel had not been made, for the identity of one person was unknown. Somewhere in town might still be an anonymous counterpart for the slave catchers of *Uncle Tom's Cabin*. For that, justice had never been served.

"I think it's time we adjourn for tea," she said, "and stewed oysters are just the thing for today."

Henrietta was glad her salon ran shorter than usual, for it gave her time to locate Mr. Thoreau. Though he hadn't answered her invitation, she planned to make an effort to visit him at the Parker House. If he wasn't there she would try Harvard.

With little time to spare she called for her carriage. Learning he'd left the Parker House, she directed her driver across the West Boston Bridge to Cambridge. She passed few students crossing the rain-soaked green toward the Natural Sciences wing. If Thoreau were here he'd be in Professor Louis Agassiz's office.

A man of rare insight, he had a broad knowledge and understanding of the natural world as well as human nature. Thoreau understood the nature of jimsonweed better than the police. She had a feeling he could shed light on the mystery as no one else could.

Destiny favored her. Even with his head bowed as he walked across campus, there was no mistaking the hooked nose, black hair, and lanky frame. She quickened her step lest he turn off the path before she did.

As he raised his head she saw his serious blue eyes and grave aspect. Even with his short stature he was considerably taller than she. He studied her as she approached, his recognition apparent.

"Mr. Thoreau," she began.

"Mrs. Cobb," he returned.

"You do remember. If I might have a minute of your time, though the day is dreary." Her concern was foolish. He was far more comfortable in the wet than she. She rushed on. "I thank you for your letters. I'm no closer to locating the woman I seek, but a more urgent matter is that my brother is in jail, and it falls to me to discover and expose the truth."

The frown over his beak-like nose did little to improve his countenance. "Do you know the truth?"

"I know he didn't kill anyone. I know far less about the woman in question."

"To find the truth, Mrs. Cobb," he said tightly, "I measure people by their values. I examine the life. To know her, study her. You know she keeps poisonous plants. One doesn't find them growing on Cornhill."

Thoreau's piercing gaze did not waver. "Look to see who had access to jimsonweed, Mrs. Cobb. There's your criminal."

She was stunned by the simplicity and inherent truth of his advice. Others might have had access to Myrth's flat as they did Hannah's. Perhaps the letters Myrth left Hannah contained jimsonweed. A gust of wind brought a shower of raindrops down on their heads from the trees above.

"Surely, Mrs. Cobb, just as I do, you have more pressing matters to attend to than to remain in this downpour. Is there anything more?"

"You've been most helpful, Mr. Thoreau, more than you know." Excitement shot through her at the idea he had given her. "Please give my regards to Mr. Emerson."

Seventeen

As the raindrops subsided, leaving a quiet dullness in their wake, Henrietta prepared greens for her parrot while mulling over Thoreau's words. She considered her reaction to jimsonweed. Her experience had been less intense at Myrth's flat than at Hannah's, where it was overwhelming.

Had Myrth's lost its potency? Captain Kidd seized a leaf with his beak as she stroked his feathers. If only she could reach out so easily and snatch the proof she needed. What did Myrth's letters contain that was so vital?

Most Bostonian gentlemen owned sword sticks. Whoever had jimsonweed was cleverer. Thoreau raised a critical point. Myrth probably had the plant for years. Mrs. Baker had access to Myrth's belongings. Yet anyone could find jimsonweed in the Berkshires, a convenient day's journey.

Any clue to Myrth's past must be in the letters. The killer had time to explore after Hannah's death. If she knew her life was in danger, she probably gave the letters to someone for safekeeping.

Did victims always know they were in danger? Henrietta studied Ozymandias resting in his tank, unusually quiet. His history proved him capable of viciousness. Who else preyed on his victims with such precision, perhaps in the guise of a gentleman with a walking stick?

Nicholas had had time to consider her request to view any correspondence Hannah left. Though he might not welcome her, he should be her next call. Henrietta watched Kidd use his talons to shred another leaf, devouring it with enthusiasm, and wished she could dissect this muddle so easily.

Leaving Celia to prepare lessons, she set off for the theater, her spirits lifting at the prospect.

At the Boston Museum Henrietta sat in a quiet chamber while an understudy went to find Nicholas. While waiting she overheard the director giving notes to a male baritone rehearsing a monologue. Nicholas arrived with the lead actress from Edgar's play. She lingered by the door, curious to see who the caller was.

"You were marvelous as Florine," Henrietta told her, recognizing her as the woman who had flirted with him opening night.

"We're starting rehearsal on our next production, Mrs. Cobb, so get on with it." Nicholas's posture was tense. "What is it you want?"

"You must have received my note regarding your aunt. I intend to find out who murdered her and why."

"Murder seems to be going around," Nicholas retorted.

Being reminded of Freddy's tenuous position made Henrietta less confident Nicholas was McLaren's killer, but it was Hannah's killer that concerned her now.

"Your mother entrusted your aunt with letters that might have cost her her life," she said softly. "I'd like to read them."

Nicholas's eyes narrowed. "I have no letters. Adam Harkness might have what you want. My aunt gave him a package."

She caught her breath. The letters hadn't been stolen from Sweeney's, because he never took them. She couldn't believe her luck.

"Thank you. I'm truly sorry. I wish you consolation in memories."

Henrietta turned to the actress in the doorway and wished her success in her new show. While she appreciated Nicholas's cooperation she wasn't sure the liveryman would be as cooperative.

The stable yard was more subdued than usual. She mounted the narrow staircase, startled to see the framed sketches of Myrth in the passageway had been damaged. One was askew while the other had broken glass. She heard her heels grind on the shards littering the steps.

She found the office door wide open. Adam Harkness appeared distracted, the fingers of his large hands splayed on the desktop. His expression changed minutely as their eyes met.

"Good afternoon, Mr. Harkness," she began. "I hope I've not called at an inopportune time."

"I've no idea what to expect from one moment to the next," he snapped. "Make yourself comfortable, but make it brief."

She stepped into the office and took the seat he indicated. The sketches of Myrth behind his desk were also broken, with fragments of glass scattered on the floor. Such destruction was intentional. Someone filled with hostility had been here recently.

"I've come for Mrs. Burns's letters," she began. "Nicholas Trindell gave me permission to read them."

His surprise was quickly replaced by resolve. "They aren't here. I put them in a bank vault."

"That was wise, but you can trust me. If you doubt my word Mr. Trindell will verify it. Perhaps I can view them tomorrow."

"I've a busy day ahead. I'll get them as soon as I can."

His stubbornness made her determined to obtain the letters. Seeing a familiar envelope among his correspondence, she assumed he'd entrusted the letters to a bank with whom he dealt. "I'm acquainted with the president of Atlantic Mortgage and Trust. I'm sure the staff will release them to me."

Harkness opened a ledger on his desk. "They can only be released to me, and as I said I have a full day tomorrow."

No matter what solution she proposed, he would find an excuse. "I know Nicholas took Mrs. Burns's dog. What about her canary?"

"I imagine his life goes on as usual."

"It won't unless someone feeds him," she pointed out.

Harkness looked at her. "You offering to take him?"

While she would have preferred the letters, she accepted the bird. Harkness went to retrieve it. In his absence she studied the broken picture frame, wondering who felt such fury.

He returned in a moment, the cage covered by a cloth. "So he won't catch a draft," he said gruffly.

Surprised by his concern, she took the cage. "It's a shame Myrth's picture was damaged. You must watch that glass."

Henrietta waited to see if he'd deny the identity of the subject after Hannah had confirmed it. She hoped the name would startle him into revealing the truth. Instead he stared at her and sat down.

"It's nothing that can't be fixed," he said simply.

Who had smashed the pictures? Nicholas was the only other acquaintance of Myrth's that Henrietta knew. "Perhaps a more secure hanging would prevent further accidents," she suggested.

"I think a good hanging is exactly what we need."

Harkness ignored her as he returned to his ledger. Stung by the reference to Freddy's plight, she took a deep breath.

"My brother doesn't deserve to hang. Though the police say Mrs. Burns died of a heart attack, I believe she was murdered. I'm investigating her death in addition to Angus McLaren's. I must have those letters."

He watched her as she spoke, his brow furrowing. "What makes you think she was murdered?"

"I'm convinced she was poisoned." If he ever decided to be forthcoming she would give him more details. "Did she have any complaints the night she died?"

"I told you, I didn't see her that evening."

The jimsonweed acted quickly, she surmised, *perhaps taking effect after Hannah went to bed. If Harkness called on her he would have realized how sick she was.*

"Did she have any visitors?"

"Can't say. Once I go home the residents are accountable to themselves. The tenant on the other side works as a groom here days. Says he sleeps so soundly he wouldn't have heard her even if she cried out. It's a shame. A bad end for a good lady."

Henrietta smiled thinly. "I don't think we've heard the end of it, Mr. Harkness. Thank you for your help."

"Enjoy the bird. I hope for your sake it ain't your brother that's hung," she heard him say as she started down the hall.

At home Henrietta was disappointed to learn Celia had gone to purchase books for the night school. Disheartened by developments, she wanted to talk. If Harkness had read Myrth's letters before putting them in the bank, he might have realized the need to contact the police.

She put the canary in her study, hoping his singing would lift her spirits. At least the liveryman possessed a trace of mercy. Why had Myrth's drawings made him uneasy? The only reason Harkness couldn't produce the letters was if he didn't have them.

A thought gripped her. *Could Myrth have taken them?* Perhaps in a fit of emotion she'd smashed her own pictures. She must be distraught with fear that she would lose Freddy or that the police would suspect Nicholas of murder. If she had managed to retrieve the proof, she must be preparing to come out of hiding.

Henrietta rose to her feet, some protective instinct coming into play. Myrth wouldn't have remained in hiding this long if she didn't fear for her life. The fact that she'd been running made Henrietta realize where she must be hiding. A memory flooded back, faint but powerful. It was the last place one would expect to find her, just as Celia said.

It was embarrassingly clear, so easy to see in retrospect. The many times Henrietta visited the

McCurdys, and it never dawned on her. Molly's grandmother, so feeble no one listened.

"Mirthless," she'd said. "You made a joke."

Half Moon Place hadn't been mirthless. That was where Myrth McLaren had been hiding.

And the joke, Henrietta thought, *is on me.*

Beside her Fudge startled her with a bark and a wag of his tail, as if he understood the demands on her time but wasn't willing to sacrifice his needs. Absently she rubbed his fur.

Dear Fudge, so unlike Hannah's little Gyp who welcomed everyone. She scratched his ears, the short hairs reminding her of two incidents. Dogs were creatures of routine. Only when they received new stimuli did their behavior change along with their reactions to strangers--or friends.

She was so disillusioned by Willie's guilt she had overlooked the idea that someone in her circle might not be trustworthy. She remembered how Fudge had clutched Garrison Morse's leg during the confrontation with Willie as if he'd never let go. He had found the scent of a female. With dawning horror she suspected the trouser leg would be covered with scruffy hairs from Hannah's dog.

Where had Garrison been twenty years before, when abolitionists were so horrified by the anonymous Northerner who'd helped return runaway slaves to their owners? Whoever it was would want to keep it secret. He might even kill for it.

A suffocating fear filled her. Perhaps the puzzle piece she needed had been at her feet all along in the guise of a dog who waited patiently for attention.

She had to talk to Garrison so he could deny the vision taking shape in her mind, but she had one other stop to make. She scribbled Celia a brief note before leaving for the McCurdy home.

The wheels of her carriage had never turned so leisurely as her barouche lumbered down Batterymarch Street toward Broad. She stared out the window, knowing where Myrth had hidden herself. No wonder the prostitutes remembered seeing her in the vicinity of Fort Hill.

Rather than wait for her driver she jumped from the carriage when it stopped. She slowed her pace only as she approached the steps to the cellar apartment, wondering what she would say if she found Myrth.

The household was in the midst of preparing supper. Molly and Eileen cut wilted vegetables at the small table, their grandmother snoring while Mrs. McCurdy sewed in the corner. Stout, toothless but for a few ragged dental remains, Biddy McCurdy looked up with hazy blue eyes in her red complexion.

Henrietta greeted them perfunctorily. "I'm looking for Myrth McLaren," she announced. "I know she stayed here." She glanced at the slumbering, elderly woman in bed and back at Biddy. "Your mother knows who she is."

Some silent parental warning kept the girls from replying, but recognition swept their faces.

"It's a matter of life or death," Henrietta insisted. "Mrs. McLaren is in grave danger. It's imperative I find her at once."

"She ain't here." Biddy McCurdy joined her daughters at the table. "It's all right, girls. I know I told you not to say anything, but we can trust Mrs. Cobb."

Henrietta studied the woman, assessing her to be less inebriated than usual. She couldn't recall a time when she'd seen Biddy completely sober. "Was she staying here?"

"You mean Mrs. O'Rourke? That's the name she goes by."

Henrietta was crestfallen. Why hadn't she thought to ask about her on previous visits?

"Charming lady," Biddy said. "She'd bring the children trinkets and sit with us over dinner."

"If only I'd known she was here," Henrietta lamented.

"I don't think anyone besides Sally Kelly and meself and the children knew. Secretive, she was. Told us a man was after her." She lowered her voice, stepping close enough for Henrietta to feel her stale breath. "Between you and me, Mrs. Cobb, I never asked questions. She was nice enough, better than most. She dressed poor, but we knew she was quality."

"How was it she came here?"

"Sweeney set 'er up. Told Mrs. Donahue she could earn an extra penny if she'd have a boarder. Ambitious, I call that. Pat Sweeney was ambitious." She looked at Henrietta knowingly. "Mrs. O'Rourke weren't here more'n two weeks before he tried making money off 'er. She said she had to find new lodgings. He planned to sell her out to the man she was running from. A bad egg, he was, but ambitious."

So Garrison Morse had been in league with Sweeney. She saw how Garrison, Myrth's former lover, had twice gained access to Hannah's flat, once to rob her, the second time to kill her. Sweeney hadn't robbed Hannah, but he knew how to duplicate keys. He made one for Garrison.

It explained why the wax on the doorknobs of wealthy homes was also on Hannah's. Sweeney, the petty thief, robbed those with money. Morse, the gentleman, robbed Hannah Burns because she had something more valuable. After watching Myrth's movements Sweeney found her a room here only to blackmail her.

Henrietta watched Eileen turn scarlet as they spoke of Sweeney. She felt sorry for Eileen and realized how quiet the room was without Willie.

"How are you managing without Willie?" she inquired gently.

"It's easier, I suppose, with one less mouth to feed." Biddy pushed a gray hair into place. Henrietta couldn't tell if she was being frank or cynical. "He wouldn't listen to me. Maybe he'll learn something where he is now. It's hard without his money, but people are looking out for us."

"He's young and has a chance to turn his life around," Henrietta said. "Thank you for telling me about Mrs. McLaren--O'Rourke, you said. How long ago was she here?"

"Little more'n a month."

She did a quick calculation. Shortly after Hannah's murder.

"Fancy you askin' today of all days," Biddy marveled. "We didn't see Mrs. O'Rourke again until this afternoon."

Henrietta's heart leaped. "Do you know where she's gone?"

"She left two hours ago. Told us she couldn't stay for supper because she might visit her boy's father. Said it'd been too long since they'd spoke. I never knew she had a son."

Realization washed over Henrietta. She had suspected Garrison of murder but never fatherhood. Biddy McCurdy had given her the motive for murder, but it was Myrth's actions that concerned her. What might Myrth do in her distraught state? If she'd visited Garrison it might already be too late.

Biddy screwed up her face. "Why would a fine lady who's on the run be wanting to visit people from her past?"

"I have some idea," Henrietta said. "Thanks to you, I know where to find her. If you see Mrs. O'Rourke within the hour tell her I'm acquainted with the father of her son, and that's where she'll find me."

Henrietta retraced her steps by carriage. Had she known where Myrth was headed she could have gone directly to Garrison's home on Chestnut Street around the corner from her own.

She sat back in frustration. Who knew what Garrison or Myrth might do if either was threatened? She knew how her alligator would respond.

As she rode Henrietta reviewed coincidences she had missed. The Lenox connection. Thoreau's suggestion. Garrison had returned from his fundraising mission to the Berkshires with newly harvested jimsonweed in time to murder Hannah and attend the ball. She had thought pressed flowers implicated Myrth in the death of her friend. With a pang of guilt she realized she'd unintentionally given Garrison a clue at her salon by revealing that Myrth possessed jimsonweed, implying she was a murderess. She gave him the clue he needed to turn any small tide of sympathy in Myrth's favor against her.

Her salon participants had decreed poison a woman's weapon. It was an ideal device for framing the innocent. The jimsonweed killer wasn't a woman but a clever man, one who fathered Myrth's son twenty years ago. Who knew her history. Who made it appear she committed two murders.

Perhaps he'd written the coveted letters and wanted to destroy all evidence against himself. Henrietta remembered the torn corner of an envelope on Myrth's floor. The letters she struggled to retrieve before Angus's murder were her proof. Myrth knew Garrison was desperate enough to kill for them, first Hannah and then herself. If he could find her.

Henrietta felt sick. The truth had been staring her in the face for months. The lies weren't spread by Myrth but by a man protecting his past. She could hardly wait to confront Garrison, furious he deceived her and took advantage of Freddy.

When the carriage drew up at the Morse residence and the front door was opened, she demanded to see him at once. The astounded maid stammered she might find him in his study. Henrietta hurried down the hallway, entering the room without knocking.

Replacing a volume on a shelf, Garrison turned nonchalantly at her entrance. She looked about the room, surprised Myrth wasn't there. Had she already come and gone? Henrietta closed the door behind her.

"What's this about, Etta?" Garrison studied her face.

"Has Mrs. McLaren arrived yet?"

"I wasn't expecting her," he said calmly. "Frankly, I'm surprised you're not with Edith at tonight's committee meeting."

In her excitement the meeting had slipped her mind. She felt uneasy knowing Edith wasn't home.

"Who cleans your fireplace grate, Garrison?"

He stared at her. "The servants do the menial work."

"How do you account for the coal dust on your Compass Club ring? I'm sure if the police were to examine it under Freddy's microscope they'd find traces of anthracite and some gold chips missing. The design is distinctive. A compass pointing north to represent the Union. It would be easy to damage such an intricate pattern."

Garrison had turned white. "I don't know what you're talking about."

"It's clear from your expression you do," she went on. "Myrth told me she was the target of Angus's murderer. You went to their home looking for her, found Angus instead, and fought with him. Later, when you realized you'd lost a piece of the ring that could be identified as yours, you had to sneak back to retrieve it before the fireplace ashes were removed. You could be incriminated on that alone, but there's more."

She continued boldly, mindful of his look of loathing.

"It was you who broke into Hannah's and killed her. You tried to make it look as if Myrth did it," she accused. "You were lucky. Gyp's so friendly she didn't bother you. Fudge couldn't leave you alone. That surprised me since he dislikes you as much as you dislike him. Now I understand."

Garrison was silent, staring at her intently.

"It wasn't until I remembered him grasping the cuff of your trousers the night we confronted Willie that I realized he smelled Gyp. He'd met her, knew her scent. I'm sure the police will find terrier hairs on your pants that will prove you were in Hannah's apartment."

"I can explain." Garrison spoke slowly, struggling to remain calm.

"No one will believe you happened to pet Gyp on the street. It's too bad you never developed a fondness for dogs."

Henrietta paused in her wrath. Morse remained where he stood, watching her with bright eyes.

"No wonder you didn't get along with Angus," she pursued. "It's a good thing Edith mentioned you knew him. Once you were both in abolitionist circles your paths might have crossed. You had to avoid associating with Myrth."

Morse began to tremble, his face filled with desperation. He had fallen victim to a past he'd sought to destroy. Now defeat was at hand.

Before he could speak Henrietta prepared to deliver her strongest blow.

"I'm more perceptive than you thought, Garrison. Everyone will see the irony, the mockery even, in your being elected to the Compass Club when you're the traitor they've sought for the last twenty years."

Eighteen

Garrison stood speechless as Henrietta savored her triumph. She had believed Nicholas's illegitimate birth was the proof Myrth planned to use against him. She never suspected until today that he was the partner of the slave catcher Orson who besieged Boston two decades ago. It was unthinkable that Garrison had helped return to their masters fugitive slaves unlucky enough to get caught.

"You murdered Angus," she accused. "After you surprised Myrth at home that afternoon she was reduced to running for her life."

"I was protecting my reputation," Garrison said with cold intensity. "I had friends in the South, plantation owners. It seemed sensible at the time. I was paid well for it."

"Paid for your treachery," she said.

He looked at her with hatred. "My future was uncertain. I didn't know how long I'd remain in Boston."

"Long enough to father Myrth's child. You were never a real father. The word doesn't begin to describe you."

Shock swept over his face as he realized she knew the truth.

"You sent her letters. That's what she fought to save. That's why you ransacked Hannah's flat. I always suspected it wasn't Sweeney but someone more devious, more desperate."

Garrison laughed shortly, relaxing his stance a bit. "It was me. I admit it, though it's damned unsatisfying to be caught this way. A rather undignified, pitiful way to go."

"You murdered Hannah by switching jimsonweed for chamomile. You followed Myrth to her hiding place at Hannah's before Sweeney took her to Half Moon Place. She had to leave there because she was running from you." Her suspicions made her cringe with regret. "And I wondered if Myrth killed Hannah. You used jimsonweed to frame her. I gave you the perfect scapegoat. I told you Myrth had poisonous flowers."

Her own candor surprised her yet made her want to press on.

Garrison raised an eyebrow. "Your accuracy in figuring this out is impressive."

"You killed Sweeney because you feared he would expose you. He made you a key to Hannah's. After her murder he knew you were up to no good. Sweeney earned his living by blackmail. He failed with Myrth and then with you."

She continued, knowing she'd placed herself in jeopardy. She was alone with a murderer who had a great deal at stake. Yet here in his study, with servants at home, surely nothing could happen.

"How ironic, Garrison, that you'd been to Humphrey Place the night I discovered Sweeney's body. You went there hours earlier to kill him." The terrible memory washed over her as she stared at Sweeney's murderer. "You had the murder weapon in your hand when you talked to the police."

Instantly she regretted mentioning the murder weapon. Garrison's walking stick rested in a stand by the door. She noticed it when she entered the room. It would be easy for him to withdraw the sword now. He could kill her quickly and quietly, with no one the wiser.

"There are probably still traces of blood on the sword stick," she challenged. "Is that why you didn't leave it in the umbrella stand downstairs where it belongs?"

She couldn't control her recklessness.

"Why did you do it?" she demanded. "Three deaths, all from an evil you committed twenty years ago. It's not as if you were obeying the law by turning in runaway slaves. You didn't have to do it."

Standing in the center of the room, Garrison relaxed a bit more, the tension leaving his limbs.

"I regretted it later," he admitted, "but at the time I was desperate for money. Myrth had no business keeping those letters. She had no right."

Henrietta feared the resentment in his expression that mirrored his words. He studied her intently.

"It's amazing you've done all this for a woman you hardly know," he said casually. He took a single step but stopped when she backed away. "Especially when she left Freddy hanging, perhaps literally. Your compassion is commendable. Too bad it won't do you any good."

His gaze was riveted on her face. Her throat felt dry.

"You can't kill me now, Garrison. I came to protect Myrth because she was coming here. She might still come."

Garrison laughed, pausing to cross one ankle over the other. "Why would she do that, Etta, if the truth is as you describe it? I'll bet she's a hundred miles away by now. She probably caught the first train out after Freddy was jailed."

His fingers rested lightly on a tabletop, his ankles still crossed. Not an easy position from which to run. He reminded her of a crouching animal waiting for the right moment to spring.

"Myrth plans to confront you tonight. She'll be here. Or one of your servants might walk in and find me." Grasping at the slightest hope, she heard herself growing hysterical. "What will you do, Garrison? There's no bust handy as there was at Myrth's."

Their eyes locked. She must have lost her mind to speak so. She took a step back.

"It was easy to kill Hannah and Sweeney," she went on. "It will be harder to get rid of a body here at home. I suppose you could feed me to the fire. I wouldn't put it past you."

"Or I could put your body in that closet while I make up my mind what to do with you," he said very softly.

Henrietta felt lightheaded. She had few alternatives. He knew it as well as she did. If she were going to scream for help, she'd have to do it soon.

"You've hanged yourself, haven't you, Garrison?" She laughed, unable to stop talking. She could be as sarcastic as he was. "Do you think you can wait for the ashes to cool like you did with Angus and then clean up? Not all messes can be swept away."

It is I who've gotten myself into a mess, she thought with numb concentration, *with no one to help.* Her voice had vanished with her physical strength.

Any chance of escape had disappeared as well. The hall beyond the closed door was as silent as a tomb. Garrison eyed her like a snake preparing to bear down on its prey.

Henrietta turned to run as he lunged for her, grabbing her arms and covering her mouth. Instinct replaced hope. She reacted involuntarily by attempting to kick him, but she hit the wall with her foot. Thrashing about disoriented her as he dragged her from the door, her only means of escape.

He stopped in the middle of the room, realizing at the same moment she did that he'd left the sword stick by the door. *It's useless at close range,* she thought with a spurt of hope. *He'll have to let me go if he plans to use it. He can't hold me down and stab me simultaneously.*

The possibility gave her strength. Even with her mouth covered she could emit guttural grunts. He pressed harder, preventing her from biting. Another faint hope was extinguished. She felt determination in his muscles.

She saw a glint of steel in his hand as Morse grabbed a letter opener from his desk and raised his hand. Neville's face flashed through her mind, and Alec's. Soon she would join him.

Her hopes were just about exhausted when the door was thrown open. Lieutenant Tripp, four uniformed policemen, and Celia rushed into the room. Garrison dropped her to the floor, still clutching the letter opener.

Celia ran to her and knelt down, helping her to her feet. Henrietta watched as the policemen grasped Garrison's hands and pinned them behind his back where they handcuffed him.

"She had no right to do this," he echoed bitterly as a policeman took hold of each arm. "No right at all."

Consumed by the past as he was, Henrietta assumed Garrison referred to Myrth. She recoiled as a policeman picked up the letter opener from the floor and returned it to the desk. *Myrth had no rights,* Henrietta reflected. She understood why Myrth risked recognition at the theater. Having been denied his other accomplishments, she was not about to miss her son in his first dramatic success.

After ascertaining she wasn't injured Celia released a deep sigh, as visibly shaken as Henrietta.

"Thank goodness you left a note telling me where you'd gone," she exclaimed. "How could you come here alone?"

"I'd think twice before doing it again," Henrietta admitted, watching as Garrison was led away.

"Sad case, this one. So young."

The jailer shook his head as he led Henrietta through the labyrinthine cellar of the Sargent's Wharf Station House. This was the second jail she'd visited this month. There would be no third to Garrison Morse.

Willie was another matter. It had been nearly a month since the nine-year-old was jailed. The guard who accompanied her past cells inhabited by immigrants and drunken sailors was an elderly man who had seen his share of criminals.

"Orphan train's what he needs," he went on.

"His mother would never consent to it." Biddy hadn't shown much remorse either. "I doubt he'll go anywhere as forgiving as the School of Industry."

Henrietta knew other situations could be worse. She wished she could change her mind and turn back before she saw him, but who else would make the effort? She felt numb.

"If only the lad would repent." The guard's face was grim. "The authorities say he's only good for the House of Reformation."

Her heart sank. Willie would become a delinquent considered beyond rescue. Consigned to the facility on Deer Island, out of sight of society, children who were seen as hopeless could be forgotten. It was easier to incarcerate, she reflected bitterly, than to educate. Willie's destiny had been determined by economy rather than compassion.

It had taken her the entire morning to reinforce her resolve to visit. Now she hardened her emotions as she spotted the boy leaning against the wall in the last cell, silent and dispassionate. He stared indifferently as the guard opened the door and allowed her to enter the cramped cell.

"Hello, Willie," she said inadequately.

He seemed younger suddenly, too innocent to be exposed to the thieves in the surrounding cells. Expecting him to imitate the behavior of the others, she spoke first.

"Words can't express my sorrow." She wished she could say he didn't deserve his fate, but she had always been honest with him. "Your mother looks forward to your coming home eventually."

Willie's face was bland. She sat on the bed to bring herself to his level. He remained by the wall.

"Can you see the damage you've done?" she said gently. "Why did you lie about seeing Mr. Morse near Mr. McLaren's home the day he was killed?"

His eyes were frank, their expression unchanging. "He asked me not to tell."

"It involved a murder investigation that was more important than any promise. Why didn't you tell me?"

"Mr. Morse gave me five dollars to say nothin.'"

Knowing part of the truth, Willie chose loyalty to someone dishonest. His explanation deepened Henrietta's remorse. She had failed to penetrate his morality.

"What about the meeting at the School of Industry? You never said anything even when you were arrested."

"Mr. Morse said he'd protect me. Figured I'd do the same for him rather than get him in trouble."

Henrietta's wrath rose as she remembered how supportive Garrison was. "Has he ever visited you in jail?"

Willie shrugged. "No."

"He can't visit because he's in jail, Willie, just like you," she informed him. "Mr. Morse is the killer the police have sought the past two months."

"I didn't know nothin' about that, honest."

Silent now, Willie appeared awed rather than dismayed, looking younger in the new shirt and trousers bought with money he'd earned either from Sweeney or Morse. The old cap remained. He still had the fascination with new ideas she had observed, but it was tinged with an indifference that frightened her.

Perhaps the city is correct, she thought, *in assigning him to the House of Reformation. He's been corrupted by temptations that sealed his fate.*

"I'm going, Willie," she said abruptly, her tone sharper than she intended. "I have a night school meeting to attend. It's time I focus my efforts on those who want help."

No longer wishing to remain, she rose to summon the guard. As she waited at the gate she saw Willie's confusion and thought she detected a cloudiness in his eyes. As quickly as it had come it vanished, replaced by the arrogance that had overtaken his innocence.

"Me mum's still got me brothers to help," he said sullenly. "I'm glad I got out. I got bigger things waiting."

Henrietta had a better sense of what awaited him than Willie did. From the next cell someone called him by name. She looked, hoping he would cry before his attention was diverted, but his hard exterior was not about to break even in jail. Perhaps especially there.

For now Biddy McCurdy would have to get by with less income and, in her words, Henrietta remembered, one less mouth to feed.

Freddy and Corinthia gathered their families and a few close friends the week before Thanksgiving to celebrate. Their home was ablaze with laughter and light until well after midnight. Cora played the piano, accompanied by her daughters on violin and harp, the memory of the past two months forgotten amid the merriment.

Fanny took advantage of a lull to sit with Henrietta.

"You arrived late," she observed.

Henrietta smiled, amused. "Annie Jackson visited me today. She'd been fired from her job at Ingraham Piano. The women's shelter needed a bookkeeper, and Annie has experience in that area. It was a good match."

"You've altered so many lives you need your own company." Fan's eyes twinkled. "Did you hear? Mr. Atwood plans to buy and renovate Penrose's factory as a school."

Henrietta turned as their sister-in-law joined them.

"It's true," Cora said with an ironic smile. "Father offered more than the place is worth so the Ingrahams couldn't refuse. The location is ideal for a school for working children."

"And it will give Penrose some competition. Thank you, Cora," Henrietta said sincerely. "It's more than I ever imagined."

"I didn't call on Sam Ingraham to rent a piano for the Music Festival as I told you," Cora added. "I went to ask if they would donate a piano to the school. Children need music as well as academics. Sam's given us an upright piano."

"It must be guilt that prompted such generosity," Henrietta told Celia in private. "I'm glad he still has a sense of charity."

Henrietta watched her brother with grudging admiration, grateful he had a loyal wife on whom he could depend whose priorities matched his own. He might have shattered her faith and threatened their future, but she would continue to fulfill her marital commitments. Cora's life was built on family, Henrietta thought. Her home was the center of the hub, the rest spokes that radiated outward. Without that foundation the circle would crumble. Cora was smart enough to recognize the differences, and Freddy knew it.

Henrietta pointed out Oliver Wendell Holmes and his wife to Celia as the couple chatted with Freddy and Corinthia.

"Dr. Holmes is pleased with how it's turned out," she observed. "That means Freddy's tenure will go on, although it's tragic for many others." She sobered at the memory. "Angus and Hannah are dead, and Sweeney as well, and Edith will be widowed again."

"So Garrison will hang," Celia concluded.

"Hypocrite that he is, it's no less than he deserves. He spent the last fifteen years working in juvenile reform," she said bitterly. "Sweeney worked for him long ago. He learned from Garrison how to use children to his advantage. Morals mean little to those who are desperate."

"I hope Garrison feels some degree of guilt," Celia said. "I suppose he confessed so people will understand his motive."

"If they do they won't forgive him. His behavior isn't justifiable." Henrietta sighed. "Yours might not be acceptable in Baltimore, but you're among friends here where you'll be respected for your decision and subsequent actions."

"I'll need more than respect if Roger comes looking for me." Anxiety clouded Celia's features.

"You're not a fugitive slave," Henrietta reminded her. "You have rights of your own. We'll face it no matter what."

Before leaving Henrietta seized the chance to see Freddy alone.

"There's one final step in all this." She spoke gently.

"I'm well aware," he said in a tone of deep gloom.

"You must face Myrth and renounce her." Henrietta tried to sound casual. "It isn't worth risking the harmony here tonight."

She was convinced Freddy would choose the woman who represented everything solid in his life. Cora was tied inseparably to his research. Happiest in the academic circle he'd entered with her father's help, Freddy had repaid the debt through marriage. Myrth was a mere temptress, the role she played best.

"Perhaps we can arrange a meeting at your house," Freddy suggested.

Nineteen

"Mrs. McLaren is here to see you, madam," Mrs. Biddle announced two days later. "I've made her comfortable in the receiving room."

Henrietta descended the staircase slowly, as she had on Myrth's first visit. Myrth had arrived twenty minutes early, the subtle scent of day-old flowers announcing her arrival.

How odd their adventure would end in the same room where it began. The fragile, metallic trill of the harpsichord drifted into the foyer, filling Henrietta with a mixture of affection and pain. The last time she had heard the instrument played with such skill it was through her mother's interpretive fingers.

Myrth stopped when Henrietta entered the room. She rose at once, stepping gracefully into the center of the room, the gesture welcoming scrutiny. The time for scrutiny was over, Henrietta acknowledged. She knew Myrth as well as she cared to.

While she was thin and pale, Myrth was still as beautiful as in the Godiva, although the portrait couldn't capture her vivacity. Her hair was redder, her eyes larger and more hazel. Henrietta saw what Freddy had in her.

"Hello, Henrietta," she said warmly. "It's good of you to see me. I owe you an apology."

"And an explanation." She refused to be taken in as her brother had been. As Myrth glanced uneasily at the alligator on the side table, Henrietta knew which was more dangerous.

"I wanted to speak with you before Freddy arrived," Myrth said.

Myrth began to pace slowly. Henrietta took a seat.

"I find it regrettable you don't regard my brother's safety as you do your own," Henrietta said evenly. "Your disappearance left him the main suspect."

Myrth flushed. "I can see how you believed I killed Angus. I felt I had to go into hiding."

"From my perspective you were more concerned with revenge than with seeing Freddy released," Henrietta accused. "He was let out of jail with apologies, but that is little comfort."

"It was our meetings that sustained me," Myrth said demurely. "Once Freddy was jailed my world shattered."

"Your world shattered long ago. What happened with Freddy hardly compared to what took place twenty years ago."

Myrth colored slightly. "I'm glad Mr. Morse will receive the punishment he deserves. I'd like to visit him in jail. Perhaps you might come with me."

"I've visited enough jails," she said coldly. "You should have gone there with proof of Garrison's guilt rather than let Freddy suffer. I secured his release by nearly getting myself killed. I went to Garrison's expecting to save your life, not to risk mine."

"I wanted to confront him. I was waiting--"

"For the right moment? If only you were as concerned with justice as with drama," Henrietta said, unable to hide her sarcasm.

"I knew the moment would come. That was why I kept his correspondence with Orson as proof."

"You kept those letters for spite. I understand your fear of the police. You appeared guilty even to me, but you let Freddy's life hang in the balance. He was willing to sacrifice his for yours."

Bitterly she reflected how alike Myrth and Nicholas were. Their circumstances determined their actions as well as their morals. Most of the time, both were desperate.

"Celia said you would hide where we'd be least likely to find you, among the poor, the Irish, the anti-abolitionists. You have a fine sense of irony." Henrietta gestured to a chair in frustration. "Sit down. I'd like to hear how this came about."

Myrth sat opposite Henrietta, keeping her distance.

"I met Garrison many years ago when he came to Lenox on business. He was the most charming man I'd ever met, but he wasn't upper class, and my parents didn't approve. When he invited me to return to Boston with him, I seized the chance." Myrth smiled self-consciously. "Changing my name from Myrtle to Myrth and taking up the stage was the most exciting thing that had ever happened to me."

"That must have been about the time you posed for the Godiva portrait."

"I never was a success at acting. Nor did we marry as I'd expected." Myrth hesitated. "When I found I was with child I returned home. My parents rejected me. Garrison wrote to say he couldn't provide for me. He aspired to a better life."

Her expression hardened as she spoke. Henrietta envisioned her as a young woman turning to her

Karen Frisch

aristocratic family for support and finding none. Instead of a promise for the future she received a rejection from the man she loved. What was it the prostitutes had said? *A pretty face didn't do a girl no good if she couldn't find an honest man.*

"Talk about a sense of irony," Myrth continued with sarcasm. "Garrison certainly had that. He picked jimsonweed flowers when he was in Lenox and enclosed them in his letters from Boston, saying their beauty reminded him of me, that the plant was beautiful but deadly, just as love could be. He berated me for sharing my secret with Hannah. When I left him I took the letters from Orson regarding deliveries of slaves. Garrison wanted them back. We fell out of touch, and I kept them."

"And lives were lost protecting them."

"He didn't care who got hurt," Myrth continued, "as long as his Southern friends were pleased."

"He hasn't changed. He felt no remorse for Hannah either."

"That's my only regret." There was a catch in Myrth's voice. "Hannah ran a rooming house when we first moved to Boston. Garrison and I were among those she took in after her husband died. When I realized I had no future in Lenox, I left for good and went back to Hannah." Taking a deep breath, she smiled. "One year later Garrison had left Boston to make his fortune at the factories in Lowell, I was married to Angus, and Hannah had a nephew. I paid her to care for Nicholas with the understanding that we would remain close. She was a good soul. No one else would have done that for me."

"She even let him keep your last name. Mr. Harkness protected you also."

"He suspected Garrison was a slave trader but couldn't prove it. But I could." Myrth looked away. "For a time I was happy with Angus, but it wasn't the life I was used to. He was coarse, brutal at times."

"He must have known the truth about Nicholas."

"Angus would have thrown me out in the street if he'd known. I didn't tell him I was pregnant when we married." She laughed harshly at the memory. "There were whispers as soon as Nicholas was born. Angus confronted me for the truth and made me give up my son. I don't know what I would have done without Hannah."

How ironic, Henrietta mused, *that Myrth married to give her child a father, yet he grew up without one.* For two decades she had regretted her decision. It was a complete miscarriage of justice.

"I didn't belong in either class, but marriage gave me respectability," Myrth resumed, fire in her eyes. "Garrison and I both had to marry someone else to find that. I lost everything because of him."

"When did you meet again?"

"I saw him at an abolitionist rally I attended with Angus last year. I couldn't bear his success. By then he'd married into money, just as he believed he'd marry into mine until my parents disowned me." Myrth laughed coldly. "It was lucky for him his wife's parents never had a chance to warn her against him as mine did. She might have had the sense to listen when I didn't."

Henrietta thought defensively of Edith, soon to be a widow. She felt acute sympathy for her friend, within a fortnight subjected to stunning revelations and years of pain ahead.

"When Garrison appeared with his fortune the injustice was more than I could bear." Myrth's face darkened. "I had to watch him live the life I lost after he ruined me."

"You switched places in society." While Myrth fell from grace Garrison rose, inheriting respectability through marriage. Henrietta remembered Edith's happiness at their wedding. She wondered how her friend would cope now. Myrth's tone grew strained, more impassioned.

"He threatened to ruin me as he'd done before," she said with a sob, "this time in the eyes of my husband, my son, and later Freddy. I watched him succeed while I was cut off from my family and the life I'd known." This time Henrietta had no reason to doubt the earnestness of her tears. "The hypocrisy of his election to the Compass Club after dealing in the slave trade was the final blow. I kept the letters out of spite. It was the only way I could threaten his security."

Having married into wealth, Henrietta knew, Garrison wanted to remain there. Politically he was obligated to side with the abolitionists. A hopeless situation forged in despair. She almost felt sorry for Myrth until she remembered Freddy.

"I wasn't about to let him ruin me a second time. If my life was to be destroyed, his had to be also." Myrth took a deep breath. "He was so insistent on retrieving the letters I finally asked him to call on me at home. On a whim I asked Freddy to be present. I planned to tell him the truth because I trusted him."

"Did you think Freddy had less at stake than your husband?" Henrietta asked skeptically.

"As much as I cared for Freddy, I could see how fragile our relationship was. He wasn't quite ready to tell his wife."

Nor would he ever be. That, Henrietta mused, *was something Myrth never understood.* The tenderness on Myrth's face was replaced with sorrow.

"Angus came home unexpectedly early that afternoon. If he hadn't he'd still be alive, and I'd be dead." She wiped away a tear before resuming. "He overheard me tell Mrs. Baker I expected a caller at three. He suspected I was having an affair. When Garrison arrived Angus thought he was my lover. His assumption came nineteen years too late."

"And of course Freddy was tardy," Henrietta said quietly.

"By then I'd left. While Garrison and Angus fought I took the letters and ran."

"Dropping jimsonweed petals along the way," Henrietta said. "Angus was dead when Freddy arrived, just in time to face the consequences."

"I went to Hannah's, but I knew it was only a matter of time before Garrison looked for me there."

"You couldn't go to the police because you appeared guilty, yet you were safe while you had the proof to incriminate him."

Myrth's eyes were bleary. "From Hannah's I went to Half Moon Place where Patrick Sweeney found shelter for me. Once he turned against me I was on my own."

"Eventually you must have returned to Mr. Harkness for the letters."

"Hannah was wise, leaving them with him." She shook her head. "My last visit was particularly unhappy."

Henrietta remembered the smashed picture frames. Undoubtedly by then Myrth blamed all her troubles on her past. "How did Garrison know Sweeney?"

"Sweeney worked for Garrison as a boy."

So the cycle continued, Henrietta thought, putting the final connection in place. *Sweeney had poisoned the minds of young boys as Garrison did. No wonder Sweeney obeyed his command to let Celia go at the waterfront. Garrison had been his teacher.*

Beyond the closed doors she heard Freddy arrive in the foyer. Myrth's demeanor changed instantly. The alarm that flooded her features initially was replaced by a grace and composure. The world, Henrietta decided scathingly, had definitely underestimated her acting ability.

Within moments Freddy was standing before them, still in his overcoat, hat in hand. He studied Myrth with a troubled expression, saying nothing. Henrietta could only guess at the tangled emotions tearing at both of them.

"Freddy," Myrth said with affection, rising.

He made no move to approach her. "You look well, Myrth."

"I am." She gave a little trill of laughter. "I'm staying with my son and his wife. I have a new granddaughter. Hannah Trindell has a promising future ahead."

Henrietta hoped she would take after her namesake rather than her grandmother. Myrth's gaze was calm but beseeching. Her tears had vanished quickly, Henrietta observed, rising to leave.

"Please don't go on our account," Freddy urged at once.

She resumed her seat, wishing she were invisible. Having endured the confession to Cora, she'd endure this one. Perhaps Freddy feared Myrth's powers of seduction. He fell all too easily under her spell once. Henrietta would ensure it didn't happen again. Sensing the tension, her parrot squawked from his perch as if instructing them to move matters along.

"A lot's happened, Myrth." Freddy's voice was hoarse.

Her eyes searched his face. "Let's not talk about the past. It's the future that matters, isn't it?"

"That's what we need to discuss."

They stood opposite each other like figures on a chess board, eyes locked. Freddy seemed to grow taller before Henrietta's eyes, his position magnified in the silence, while Myrth shrank visibly. They were on opposing sides now, and only one would win.

"I see," Myrth said mechanically. "It's society's fault, not yours. That's how I shall remember this, without regrets."

Henrietta suspected their earlier conversation had prepared her for disappointment. It was difficult for Freddy to let go without blaming himself. Henrietta sensed Myrth was conscious of the triangle they formed and wondered if Myrth saw her as a ghostly reminder of Corinthia.

Myrth resumed with as much cheer as if a friend had just conveyed pleasant news.

"I hope our paths cross again." With a half-smile she continued to study Freddy's expression. "But I doubt they will. Well, I'm off to the theater," she added brightly, adjusting the clasp of her cloak. "I met a charming actor about my own age while visiting Nicholas. Perhaps he'll come tonight."

There was no vindictiveness in her tone, only hope and private reassurance, but her words were brittle, full of the forced optimism that becomes habit after years of struggle. With a final expression of good wishes Myrth departed without a backward glance, her head high. She'd walked out of Freddy's life the way she lived her own, with confrontation and drama. At a loss for words, Freddy gestured as she swept from the room. *At this moment,* Henrietta thought, *silence is golden.*

"There is no stopping destiny," she consoled him after the door closed. "There was bad blood between her and Garrison from the start. When they met again there was just too much hatred."

"Perhaps I might have prevented it," Freddy faltered.

"Myrth brought about her own downfall. Nothing anyone could have done would have helped. Others tried before you."

"I sacrificed a great deal for her," he offered in explanation. "I'm not sure she ever felt the same."

"We can't know. I doubt you really loved her even though you think you did."

"I didn't know the cost would be so painful," he admitted huskily.

"She genuinely believed you would leave Cora." Henrietta paused. "Perhaps from her ill treatment at Garrison's hands she'd come to think of desertion as a justifiable option. You knew it wasn't."

Myrth had either been apart from refined company long enough to have forgotten the power of class difference, Henrietta told herself, *or else she'd lived without hope for so long she had seized the chance to experience it again.* She wanted to tell Myrth there were those in the upper class whose respect transcended social boundaries, but it was generally the poor they chose to forgive for their transgressions rather than the rich.

She tried to think well of the woman to whom Freddy had given his heart. If her own choices had been different fate might have cast Henrietta in the same role. She thought briefly of Sam and realized she and Myrth were not as dissimilar as she once thought.

Henrietta smiled. "Just think, she has what she wanted all along—freedom, a future, and life without Angus. You gave her that. All in all I think she did quite well."

Deciding routine was needed, she rose to ring for tea, hot and slightly bittersweet.

"Myrth did say it's the future that counts. Let's forget the past." She smiled at her brother. "Or at least parts of it. Wouldn't you agree?"

"It's debatable," he finished.

Meet Author Karen Frisch

Karen Frisch has written and illustrated stories since she was seven. Her fascination with genealogy began when her grandmother gave her a family photograph taken in Scotland in 1903.

For 15 years she hosted Rhode Island's cable TV show "Pet Talk," educating the public about pet care through interviews with veterinarians and other animal enthusiasts. She lives with her husband and two daughters adopted from China. She loves hearing from readers and can be reached through her website at http://karenfrisch.webs.com.

Breinigsville, PA USA
24 May 2010
238558BV00001B/1/P